LOVE HURTS

Also available from Headline Liaison

Killing Me Softly by Laura Aspen
Wilful Ways by Lacey Carlyle
Voluptuous Voyage by Lacey Carlyle
Dark Deception by Lacey Carlyle
Magnolia Moon by Lacey Carlyle
Sensual Storm by Lacey Carlyle
The Journal by James Allen
Love Letters by James Allen
A Private Affair by Carol Anderson
Autumn Dancing by Adam Chandler
Portrait in Blue by Lucinda Chester
Vermilion Gates by Lucinda Chester
The Paradise Garden by Aurelia Clifford
The Golden Cage by Aurelia Clifford
Green Silk by Cathryn Cooper
Sleepless Nights by Tom Crewe and Amber Wells
Hearts on Fire by Tom Crewe and Amber Wells
Seven Days by J J Duke
Dangerous Desires by J J Duke
A Scent of Danger by Sarah Hope-Walker

Love Hurts

Laura Aspen

Liaison

First published in 1997 by
HEADLINE BOOK PUBLISHING

A HEADLINE LIAISON paperback

10 9 8 7 6 5 4 3 2 1

ISBN 0 7472 5588 1

Typeset by Avon Dataset Ltd, Bidford-on-Avon, Warks

Printed and bound in Great Britain by
Mackays of Chatham PLC, Chatham, Kent

HEADLINE BOOK PUBLISHING
A division of Hodder Headline PLC
338 Euston Road
London NW1 3BH

Love Hurts

Chapter 1

Mary had a terrible hangover after the hen night. Why, oh, why, she asked herself reaching for the aspirin, had she accepted the invitation?

But it was too late for regrets. Too late to scold herself for drinking too much with the other girls in the Kingfisher's Arms. Too late to feel sorry for the fact that, along with seven other young women all suitably tanked-up, she'd finished the evening at *Movers and Shakers*, the new nightclub that specialised in exotic dancing of a kind that Mary had only read about in the Sunday papers.

Crawling out of bed, she'd gone to the bathroom for some water and had caught sight of herself in the mirror. She looked terrible. Her pale blue eyes were bleary and her hair, normally a mass of soft blonde curls which framed a pretty, delicately featured face, was lank and tangled. She should have trusted her own judgement, she thought as she turned on the tap.

Despite her initial reluctance she'd gone along with what the girls in the accounts department had planned in the way of entertainment, feeling it would be churlish to turn her nose up. 'An all male revue,' they'd told her. 'Go on,' they'd said conspiratorially, 'you'll love it.'

And who was she to refuse? They were a good crowd and she liked them. And, after all, it was Jinny who was getting married. Jinny was entitled to decide what she wanted to do for the evening and she'd said it would be a laugh.

But for Mary it had been more than a laugh. Sitting at a table at the edge of the dance floor, she'd surveyed the people around her. They were at least ninety per cent female with just a sprinkling of men, all talking loudly as they drank and laughed and moved to the rhythm of the music. The waiters ran around carrying trays, weaving in and out of the tables with expert ease.

Sipping her Pina Colada she'd realised that, much to her surprise, she was really enjoying herself. 'You okay?' Jinny had mouthed to her across the table and Mary had nodded, smiling. The air was heavy with anticipation, the atmosphere charged with excitement. The club was crowded. Tense, animated women with their eyes shining and their lips parted were yelling their approval at the glamorous drag-queen compère.

Then the dancers had appeared in their lycra and leather as a spotlight lit up the back of the stage. A great chorus of hooting and cheering went up from the women, all but drowning out the heavy beat of the music to which the men began to dance, gyrating their bodies and thrusting their hips, teasing an audience hungry for sensation.

Mary had watched the dance troupe with fascination, their taut, oiled torsos exciting her more than she'd cared to admit. Then they'd moved among the crowd, the women leaning forward to stroke their smooth skin and, swept along by the mood, attempting to touch the heavy bulges that nestled between their thighs.

Mary's eyes had explored each of the men in turn, comparing their broad chests, prominent thigh muscles and tight little bums. There was a particular boy who'd caught her fancy. A boy with a smile which spread right up to his dark, twinkling eyes. She'd imagined being pinned under the weight of him, held firm and unable to move as she felt his thick cock drive between her legs. The prick of a stranger deep inside her. What would it be like? she wondered.

The air in the club smelled of sex and abandonment and Mary had succumbed to its heady persuasion. When the dark-eyed boy had caught her eye and saw her look down, she felt he'd guessed what was going through her mind.

To a chorus of catcalls and cheers, he'd come across to her table, standing close and smiling as he moved his pelvis in time to the music. The shape of his '*lurve* muscle', as it had said on the posters, was clearly visible inside the skimpy pouch he was bursting out of. She could feel the heat from his skin as he stood close to her, taking her hand and placing it against a stomach that was rock hard, the muscles moving beneath her fingers like a rippling tide. The music had thumped in her ears, urging her on as he guided her hand over his belly and down towards the leather pouch which strained against its contents, the smooth leather which she longed to pull aside, her senses on fire at the thought of what lay beneath.

The other girls were watching her closely, laughing and whistling. She felt herself blush. But they didn't matter.

She'd wanted to slide her fingers inside the pouch like a child reaching into a lucky dip. She'd wanted to take his cock in her hand, to feel its warmth and firmness. She'd wanted to stroke the boy's iron-hard erection, to caress the smooth, stretched skin of his penis. She'd wanted . . . oh, everything. But she'd taken her hand away.

Somehow, the boy had understood and holding her fingers gently again within his own, he had guided her hand further up his body, placing it over his heart and smiling at her.

She'd fingered his chest. She could smell a faint whiff of sweat and the intoxicating scent of his manhood as he leant towards her and touched her hair. He'd held her head, bringing her face to within inches of his pouch, whispering softly into her ear, making her blush even more.

As he held her face close to his prick he'd taken her hands in his once again, moving them around his body till she was stroking his small, hard buttocks, naked beneath her touch except for a fine covering of downy hair. The heat from his body seemed to envelop her. She felt her pulses race and, much to her embarrassment, a sudden rush of moistness between her legs, cascading like a waterfall, softening the innermost lips of her vulva which throbbed uncontrollably.

Then he'd lifted her face and kissed her as the crowd around her hooted their approval. She'd been oblivious to them all, conscious only of the gentle probing of his tongue and the softness of his lips against her own.

She'd wished they'd all melt away. That there'd be nobody

here but her and this dark-haired Adonis, and that he'd kiss her like this all night.

She didn't want to know anything about him. Not his name nor where he came from, how or why he had become a dancer, nothing. She didn't even want to hear his voice. All she wanted was to reach up and stroke his warm, golden skin. To peel away the pouch which held such fascination. To see him naked and to touch him.

In her imagination, she'd brought her face down to take the thick knob of his prick between her lips, anointing its quivering, eager tip with a kiss. She'd felt it move and swell inside her mouth as she explored its every undulation with her tongue. Sucking softly, it had grown hard within her embrace, slicked with her saliva as it sprang and shuddered into life.

Mary was shaken by her reaction to this boy. Why had he disturbed her so? Was she so in need of attention that she'd flirt with a stripper? By now, the boy was back in line, dancing his routine. She'd caught his eye. He'd winked at her. Despite herself, she'd smiled. She was taking this too seriously, she'd decided. It was only a bit of fun.

Mary had had another drink. The girls from the office teased her mercilessly. What would Paul say, they'd asked, if he knew what she'd been up to?

Mary went along with them, pretending to be alarmed, swearing them to secrecy. But what *would* Paul say?

Paul would know that Mary would never be unfaithful. He'd know that she'd always take care of business when he was away and be there when he got back.

Mary was as sure of herself as Paul was, but something about the evening had disturbed her. She'd got drunk. She'd danced too much. But what did it matter? It was a one-off. It wouldn't happen again.

And anyway, after all these years, Paul was still the sexiest man Mary had ever seen. Dark eyes and lashes which almost brushed his high cheekbones, thick black hair and a sensuous mouth out of which came a voice that was a deep and melodious drawl, lazy almost, full of the self-assurance that comes of knowing that the world will wait to do your bidding.

Confident and relaxed, when he walked into a room Paul filled it with his presence. And when he came near her and touched her, running his lips across her neck, Mary wanted no one else on earth.

So why, when the dark-eyed dancer had probed her mouth with the tip of his tongue, had Mary simply parted her lips and relaxed? The question had gone over and over again in her mind.

Admittedly, these days Paul spent much of his time travelling. Their life together was often 'on hold', sometimes for weeks at a time. But that should make it better, shouldn't it? Absence making the heart grow fonder and all that?

And she had a lot to be happy about, she never ceased to remind herself. A beautiful home in one of Manchester's smarter suburbs, a responsible job running Paul's business and, most of all, Paul. She wasn't some passing fancy but a permanent fixture in Paul's life. They were together – as they had been for over seven years.

So why had she acted so stupidly? Why had she let the boy kiss her? Mary had ignored the question and had had another drink. And then another.

Sometimes it was just too hard to cope when Paul was away. At the office, she came in contact with many men and naturally, some of them chatted her up. Fully aware of the fact that she was Paul's girlfriend, they still asked her out. But she always refused.

And yes, she supposed she must be pretty, she'd been told so often enough. Men looked at her as she walked by in the street. 'Hi, blondie,' they'd whisper, or they'd simply stare, running their eyes over her figure, looking her up and down and smiling appreciatively. She caught them staring at her in restaurants when she was having lunch with friends. But she was Paul's. Paul's alone . . . as she had been since she was old enough to be loved.

Okay, if she was honest, she was a little frustrated. Maybe, more than a little. But that was no reason why she should have acted so daft! She'd felt instantly embarrassed after the boy dancer had kissed her. Embarrassed to have been kissed by a stranger in front of the girls from the department. After all she was their boss – in practice if not in theory. Paul left it all to her when he was away. She'd covered up her embarrassment. Brazened it out. But she was confused. Confused and a bit shaken.

They'd teased her again, on and on all evening, pleased to have the chance to address her for once on completely equal terms – as a woman, and not as deputy to the man who paid their wages. The women had all made lewd remarks, attempting to leave Mary in no doubt that their husbands and boyfriends would cope admirably with the consequences of their sexual arousal. They'd looked at her questioningly, willing her to join in the conversation, knowing that she would not. Knowing that Mary was the soul of discretion. 'Too dependable sometimes, for her own good,' they'd muttered to each other.

But even if she had been one to bare her soul, what was there to tell? Nothing that Mary would have been willing to talk about. Returning home she'd found it impossible to sleep. Stroking herself between her legs she'd thought about the boy dancer and imagined herself touching his leather pouch, moving her fingers across its smooth, warm surface. She closed her eyes and saw herself back at the club. She was on her knees on the stage on front of him, exploring his posing pouch with her fingertips.

She could feel the lumps and bumps and the thick rod within, surrounded by two heavy balls which slid out of her grasp as she stroked them.

With her eyes closed, she could almost smell the leather. Mary had slipped her fingers deeper between her pussy lips and had begun to stroke the hardening tip of her clitoris. In her mind's eye, she could see the boy smiling at her as she eased the leather pouch down over his cock, dragging it over his thighs and releasing a thickening member which unfurled from its confinement, fat and blooming like an exotic flower after rain. Then, in her imagination, the boy had reached down and opened the buttons of her shirt, fumbling inside till he cupped the soft globes of her breasts in his hands and his long fingers found her nipples. He began to roll them between his fingertips. One minute he stroked, the next he squeezed, sending spasms of pleasure throbbing between her legs, fuelling a hunger that only his beautiful cock could satisfy. Mary saw herself stand up as the boy reached for her hand. He led her out of the hot spotlight and now he was guiding her backstage and into the darkness, pushing her roughly against the nearest wall.

He pulled her skirt up and her panties down, holding his cock in his hand and searching her little furry mound for its dark and secret entrance. And then he'd told her what he was going to do to her and Mary had got wetter still. 'Beautiful girl,' he'd murmured. 'Beautiful wet pussy.'

Spreading her legs, she guided him into her slippery opening, catching her breath as he thrust his cock up inside her. He crammed her against the wall, reaching for her nipples with his mouth. As he pumped inside he sucked and licked, his tongue keeping time with the thrusts of his cock, the friction from his fat prick and the pressure of his lips sending waves of deep and thrilling pleasure coursing through the softness of her. She could feel his penis stretching her deep inside, feeding the ravenous hunger which each plunge of his manhood strove to satisfy. The delicious pull of his cock against her throbbing clitoris was exciting her to the point of no return. But it wasn't his prick. It was her own fingers. He wasn't here. Not really. She was alone and the man who should have been here to satisfy her, the only man she'd ever allowed to make her fantasies a reality, was hundreds of miles away down south, taking care of business.

She knew she shouldn't feel so restless. She should be proud. After all, the hard work she and Paul had done together had paid off handsomely. And so much of it was due to her efforts. Mary had been in at the start, right at the beginning, helping Paul to build his business empire, encouraging him when things got rough, urging him to keep trying when it all seemed hopeless. And it had worked. It was all a success.

But now she was on her own so often that all she had to distract her was work and more work. 'All the responsibility and none of the power,' as a disgruntled employee had pointed out to her one day with a sneer.

The girl had been wrong, of course, but somehow Mary had been unable to forget her remark. If only Paul took her away with him sometimes. Just occasionally. Just for a treat. But he never did.

She knew he had a flat of some sort in London – though he'd said it was merely a bedsit. He hadn't even bothered to install a phone line.

'Ring me on the mobile,' he'd say. But nine times out of ten it was switched off and she had to wait till he phoned her.

He'd seemed reluctant when she'd mentioned coming to London. 'Mary, it's like this,' he'd said, 'I'm busy all day and at night I just go back to the room and sleep. You'd be bored, and I'd have no time to entertain you. Best not . . .'

Of course, she'd had her suspicions. Wondered about other women. Unable to resist the temptation, she'd gone through a phase of rifling through his pockets but had found nothing. Little notes to himself, that was all. 'Ring the depot,' 'Ring Alex,' notes to call his accountant or one of a dozen other colleagues. But all men's names. No, 'Send flowers to Caroline,' or anything like that. He was working. She had to believe him.

Again, she'd closed her eyes and seen herself with the boy dancer's cock in her mouth. She was on her knees, stroking his buttocks and he was pressing her face into his groin. Back and forth back and forth . . . she sucked him in long, slow, rhythmic glides, feeling the veins on the surface of his penis stand out as her lips slid along its length and it grew, ever harder, beneath her soft embrace. Holding his prick at the base, she began to nuzzle its very tip, her little butterfly kisses and gentle sucks causing a slippery film to escape which she spread with her mouth in soft, circular movements around the knob, causing him to shudder beneath her touch. He was delicious. And now he was thrusting deep in the back of her throat and she knew he was about to come. She could feel the tension in every thrust, the little shivers as his cock grew harder still and his climax built and . . .

Mary had opened her eyes again. This was crazy. She'd got up, made some tea, read a little. Then she'd tried to sleep again. I must, she'd thought. I must.

[illegible]

[illegible] 2

[illegible]

[illegible] and [illegible] all dress in the [illegible], and she [illegible].

Before [illegible] she had [illegible] what it [illegible].

As [illegible] carried her along the Knightsbridge pavement [illegible] as a cloud, she thought back to [illegible] but in [illegible] like you had a [illegible] time. But all that was over. We never [illegible]

Chapter 2

Alex had spent the morning behaving like a first-class, cut-glass bitch. And now it was nearly lunchtime. The pavements were covered in pink and white springtime blossom from nearby fruit trees and she smiled to herself as she drifted along, burdened with nothing but the weight of her Prada handbag stuffed with credit cards and cash.

In the last three hours she'd bought nothing, but she was well pleased with her shopping trip. She'd started off looking at jewellery in Butler & Wilson and the designer collections in Harvey Nichols, then she'd 'done' the whole of Knightsbridge and Kensington, luxuriating in the feeling of power she wielded over the sales assistants in every glossy boutique where she'd deigned to set foot.

They knew, and she knew they knew, that when Alex was in the mood she could spend a fortune. But today she'd simply enjoyed treating them like a cat with a succession of mesmerised mice, forcing them to fawn and simper while she talked to them in her friendly, almost intimate way, pretending to be tempted to buy, raising their hopes only to dash them with a shrug and a sigh.

She saw from their expressions how much she was loathed. Behind their smiling mouths it was all there, in the eyes, and she revelled in the fact.

Before Paul came into her life, she too had been a minion. She knew what it meant to put all your effort into your job, only to end up reviled.

As her Manolo Blahnik shoes carried her along the Knightsbridge pavements as if on a cloud, she thought back to how it felt to live on a pittance, but to need to dress like you had a fortune. But all that was over. No more. She had

Paul. And now she was leading the life she was made for. She was born to look good and to get what she wanted through sex and scheming. Nothing more, nothing less.

Paul had saved her. It was Paul who had shown her the way out of her career as a trainee hotel receptionist. It was Paul who had taken her away from all the bitching and a manageress for whom she could do nothing right because Alex was too pretty for a fading forty-five-year-old alcoholic to cope with. Alex, with her long Titian hair and hypnotic green eyes, gold in the middle like some strange gemstone. Alex with her eyelashes like a soft curtain hiding a mystery, her full and rounded breasts, her legs that went on to eternity.

Yes, Alex was far too pretty and she'd paid for it. All her hopes of having a 'real' career had come to nothing. She'd always wanted to work in the hotel business, but all she'd known were miserable days of being picked on and belittled. Then Paul came along and she'd seen her chance and taken it.

To Alex, the whole idea of political correctness and female equality in the workplace was a joke. The general manager of the hotel had said he was sorry to see her go, that she had 'management potential'. Alex had smiled at him, knowing that all he wanted was to get inside her knickers. As a parting gift she'd left the bitch of a hotel manageress a bottle of meths, wrapped in silver paper, and a note telling her not to drink it all at once. And then she'd quit her job, moving into Paul's Thameside apartment before he'd had the chance to change his mind.

That was a year and a half ago and in all that time, things had only got better. So why did she need to torture sales girls with all the relish of a sadistic ten-year-old pulling the wings off flies?

Alex decided not to think about it. It was time for lunch and then some more shopping, perhaps. Maybe she'd buy Paul that wonderful black cashmere jacket she'd seen in Simpson of Piccadilly. As rich and black as his hair, it would suit him perfectly. Yes. She might just do that.

* * *

Mary bit into her tuna salad sandwich and surveyed the mountain of paperwork on her desk. Despite the fact that they were fully computerised, the paperwork still seemed to go on forever. She had decided that when Paul came home, she'd have to talk to him. It was no use hiding how she felt. She'd summon up all her courage and tell him how miserable she was. How tired she'd become.

No doubt he'd smile and tell her to take a few hours off, go to the cinema. He'd tease her and make her laugh. Make her feel silly for whingeing on at him. Paul had a way of bulldozing through other people's emotions. In part, it was the very quality that had helped to make him successful. But no matter how much he dismissed her, she knew she didn't want to go on like this.

They'd had dreams, back in the old days. Dreams of what they'd do when they'd made some money. But now they'd made it, the dreams seemed to have died. Mary threw the rest of her lunch away. She seemed to have lost her appetite.

In the cold and sober light of day, she knew that she'd really wanted to make love to the boy dancer she'd seen at *Movers and Shakers*. Even in the mundane surroundings of the office, the thought of him turned her on. It hadn't been a sudden impulse in the heat of the moment. She'd wanted to make love to someone with whom she could simply 'let go'. Someone she didn't care about. A no-holds-barred, no-strings-attached romp.

When she made love to Paul it was always with the knowledge that soon he would be leaving her again. Whether he was at home for two days or two weeks, the moment always came. Suitcase in the back of his sleek, black Jag. Breakfast. Then gone. Mary would load the dishwasher and then prepare herself for work, fighting the familiar ennui that always threatened to engulf her. She planned what she'd do next time he was home. She'd cook him a wonderful dinner and then she'd try and tell him how she felt.

She wouldn't, of course, mention that she'd wanted to make love to a male stripper. But somehow she'd show him how frustrated she was. How tired of waiting just for them to be together. She'd tell him she wanted them to take a holiday, like normal people did. Get away from it all, just the two of them. It was something they'd never done, not in all the years they'd been together. Long weekends in country house hotels were the extent of their breaks from routine. No doubt, Paul would make her feel guilty for even wishing to change their lives because that was Paul's way. He'd imply that they'd be neglecting the business if they went away. But, for once, she'd have to stand up to him if she could find the words to do so. Mary needed . . . so much more. The boy dancer had shown her that.

Paul knew perfectly well he shouldn't touch the girl. He'd made it a rule never to mess around with secretaries, but she was so pretty he'd known he wanted to fuck her from the moment he'd seen her in reception, one of the many 'temps' he hired as and when business got busy.

And now she was sitting on a bar stool in an afternoon drinking club, giggling and holding out her glass at regular intervals to be refilled.

Paul looked around. He shouldn't have allowed himself to be brought to this tatty place. He shouldn't have taken the girl along to a business lunch, either. After all, she was only seventeen. She'd told him so. But he'd taken her and now here they were.

Full of good food and too much wine, Paul and his business associate had left the restaurant at three o'clock, strolling comfortably along Old Compton Street in the direction of the Vegas Club. The girl had trotted along beside Paul, trying to control her hiccups.

Stepping out of the glare of a glorious spring afternoon they had descended some steps into semi-darkness, the faint smell of floral disinfectant mixed with the musky odour of cigars and booze assailing Paul's nostrils as his eyes adjusted to the gloom.

Within seconds, the girl was comfortably ensconced at the bar. Her long legs were crossed and her pert little arse perched precariously on a red velvet bar-stool. She'd looked at Paul and smiled from behind heavily mascara'd lashes, tossing her long blonde hair over her shoulders.

Going on to the club hadn't been Paul's idea. It was the other man who belonged to the sleazy drinking club and he who'd suggested they move on somewhere after lunch to 'relax'.

The club was no more than a pickup joint. Paul looked on in amusement as a tall, heavy-breasted girl sidled up to his business associate and began to talk to him, touching his arm, gazing up into his eyes, whispering something in his ear that made him throw back his head and roar with laughter.

Paul moved across to his secretary. He could see she was a little unsteady. He topped up her glass.

For a moment, Paul and the girl looked at each other. 'What's your name?' Paul said. 'I can never remember.' The girl giggled. 'Suzie,' she said. 'I'm the one who makes your coffee just the way you like it.'

'I'm sure you do everything just the way I like it,' Paul replied and smiled his lazy smile.

Paul bought her another drink. She was easy to talk to, if a little slurred. And when he suggested they go into a private room to 'unwind' some more, she didn't object.

One of the club hostesses carried an ice bucket and a bottle of Taittinger champagne, placing them on a table in a small, dark room at the back of the club. Paul noticed that the hostess had placed a packet of condoms on the tray. He handed her a fiver. 'Have a good time,' she said, and left. There was a red velvet chaise longue. A table. A lock on the door. Nothing more.

Paul and the girl stood opposite each other in silence. He could hear her breathing. A moment of delicious anticipation. Then Paul raised his hand and traced the contours of her breasts with his fingertips. He felt her nipples respond to his touch and caught a whiff of her perfume as he moved closer. Paul slid his hand under her skirt and up her leg. She was wearing stockings. The girl went to pull her skirt down, but Paul placed his hand over her own to stop her. He felt his prick give a jolt inside his boxer shorts and then he was down on his knees, dragging her skirt up around her waist and burying his face between her thighs. The crotch of her panties was wet as he pulled them to one side and snapped the flimsy wisp of lace that held them together.

He opened her legs and, drinking in the smell of her warm pussy, Paul's tongue probed between the wet lips of her slippery vagina, lost among the folds of flesh which rippled beneath his touch.

Her legs were trembling and, glancing up at her for a moment he looked into her eyes. 'I'm not sure,' she whispered softly.

'Don't worry,' Paul replied. 'You'll be all right.' Making a mental note to get rid of her from his employ as tactfully as possible, he stood up and led her to the chaise longue. He sat the girl down, put his hands on her shoulders and pushed her on her back. He knelt beside her once more and opened her legs, spreading the lips of her labia between his fingers and lowering his head to seek out the firm little bud of her clitoris which he grasped between his lips and began, once again, to massage with his tongue. He paused and looked up. Her eyes were closed and she was breathing deeply.

'Ready for action,' thought Paul. He looked down at the soft, puckered folds of her womanhood which lay open to him like a glistening fig. This time he pushed his tongue deep inside her vulva and she moaned as his licks turned to nips and sucks.

Unzipping his fly, Paul released his cock, pulling it out of the front of his trousers and fingering its smooth surface. Leaning over the girl he began to rub her nipples through the flimsy, cheap material of her blouse. She was enjoying this, he felt sure. But she was drunk. She was no more than a kid. He knew he should feel guilty, but he pushed any reservations to the back of his mind. He paused and looked at her, her blonde hair spread out behind her like a halo in the gloom. He couldn't stop now. And besides, Paul Mason always got what he was after.

Holding his penis in his right hand, he opened the condom packet and rolled the rubber over his straining prick. Then he held her on her back and pinning her legs wide apart, he drove into her with one huge thrust. The girl gasped as Paul began to pump, her body crushed against the chaise longue as her tits bounced inside their cotton blouse.

He could feel his excitement mount as the girl's pussy gripped him tightly, her body squeezing his cock, massaging him to the point of no return. The tip of his prick drove hard against the mouth of her womb as he gave a deep shudder, groaning as he buried his face in the scented curtain of her hair.

She was a brilliant fuck. It had been a good day. The deal with his lunchtime companion had gone well, he'd be going home soon and Alex would be waiting for him. At last, pulling his fast-shrinking cock out of the girl's body, he looked down at her.

'You okay?' he grunted. She nodded, silent in the semi-darkness. 'Will I see you again? Like this, I mean?' she said. He stroked her hair and kissed her, muttering empty words of endearment. He'd put her in a cab and send her some flowers. That would do. And when he phoned the temp agency and told them he no longer needed her services, he'd give her enough money to bring a smile to her eyes. What did he have to feel guilty about?

Paul left the club by six o'clock, the blonde-haired girl hanging on his arm. By now she was very drunk and, hailing a cab, Paul gave the driver twenty-five pounds and told him to look after her. Paul recalled her telling him earlier that she lived somewhere in East London. She'd be all right. He turned his back and crossed the road.

He'd go for a swim at the Bond Street Club of which he was a member. He liked belonging to a smart London club, enjoyed taking Alex there to dine, showing her off. But first, he must phone Mary and tell her he'd be back on Tuesday. Wednesday at the latest.

She'd be pleased about the deal that he'd fixed up that day – he was to provide a fleet of chauffeur-driven cars to a major City-based insurance company – a contract he'd been angling for for months. Along with his three London minicab businesses, his Manchester-based car hire firm and the countrywide haulage business he ran, Paul was doing very well indeed.

Mary was still in the office, as Paul knew she would be. She'd probably be there till seven o'clock. First in, last out as usual.

She told him she'd been out with Jinny and the other girls to a hen night, though she was vague about the details. 'Go home, Mary,' he said. 'You work too hard.' She'd sounded tired. But yes, she was delighted about the deal. Couldn't be better.

Alex lay in bed with her eyes tightly shut, listening to the boats on the river. By now, she knew all the different sounds of the river traffic – the tugs, the police barges and then the pleasure boats, their disco music drifting towards her, followed by the gentle lapping of the water when it got late and the river again fell silent.

Paul would be home soon. She felt an ache in the pit of her stomach at the thought of him and, reaching between her thighs, her fingertips found the fleshy tip of her clitoris, poking its small, wet head out of the red hair that formed a neat, dense triangle at the top of her long legs.

She heard Paul's key in the door and with a mew of pleasure, got out of bed and moved across the room, opening the door to see him coming towards her, pulling his tie from around his neck and throwing his briefcase onto the leather settee which stood in the hall leading to their bedroom.

'Hard day, baby,' he said, wrapping her sleep-warmed body against his chest as Alex nuzzled into his neck, pressing her nipples against him and softly biting his earlobe. Her fingers moved down to the front of his trousers to find the bulge that she knew would be waiting for her.

'Hey,' he said, 'slow down . . . let me get a drink . . . take my shoes off.' Alex's reply was to reach for his hand, guiding his fingers across the silk of her nightgown to the front of her belly and down, pushing his fingers against the little forest that lay beneath the silk, rubbing his hand against the front of her mons, coaxing him to explore further.

Paul reached down and pulled up the hem of Alex's flimsy silk robe. She felt his fingers move between her legs, sliding into her chasm as his body tensed against her own. He squeezed her tightly to him, supporting her weight and Alex lifted her legs around his waist, clinging to him as he finger fucked her deeply and roughly, carrying her towards the bed and lowering her onto her back.

Alex smiled up at him, licking her lips, reaching up to grapple with the zip of his fly which strained over the bulge beneath.

Alex loved Paul's cock. Relished the evenings when he would return to her, preoccupied with his business concerns, and she would fumble around inside his trousers to release the 'real' Paul, the Paul who sprang thick and erect from the confinement of his beautifully cut business suits, the Paul who was ready to fuck her senseless. As he would tonight. As he did every night when he was at home. Paul's fingers were deep inside her, stretching the walls of her vagina as she guided his zip over his engorged prick and lifted it out of his pants, a thick rod of angry red flesh with a huge, bulbous tip, the foreskin stretched to breaking point as the blood pulsed through it. Alex lay back on the bed and looked at the man whose body was straddling her own. Paul was still wearing his suit. His cock poked out of the front of his trousers in stark contrast to its impeccably tailored surroundings.

Alex stared up at the mirror on the ceiling above them to see herself, legs wide apart, Paul's fingers working away inside her. She lifted her hips off the bed to take each thrust, willing him to go deeper. Two fingers inside her then three, then four, but still she couldn't get enough and she longed for more. The sight of them reflected in the mirror turned her on and she performed for the mirror as if it were a camera.

'Fuck me, Paul,' she pleaded, 'please . . .' but though his prick was hard as a battering ram, still he did not enter her. Alex clenched her thighs around Paul's hand as she felt the first hot wave of orgasm send its darts of pleasure zig-zagging through her clitoris. She pressed her pubic bone hard against Paul's fingers, driving herself against him in rhythmic thrusts.

It was good, oh yes . . . but she hadn't wanted this. She'd wanted him to fuck her, but now it was too late to turn back the tide. She felt Paul's nails bite into her buttocks as he lifted her arse higher off the bed, pushing his fingers further into her as his mouth reached for her nipples, slicking them with saliva as he lapped and sucked at each hard, fleshy protuberance in turn.

'Come on, baby,' he urged her, 'c'mon . . . that's right, let go . . .' He looked at her closely as she moaned beneath his expert manipulation. Alex pressed down on his hand as his fingers flicked and twisted deep inside her and she drove her clitoris against his knuckles, bathing his hand in her slippery juices as her whole body shuddered.

She pushed herself against him harder, faster, straining and panting as she climaxed. She felt her clitoris throbbing like the beating of her heart as the spasms quickened and her female essences poured into the softness of her tender pleasure zone.

But it was a shallow affair this masturbation. Nothing compared with the feeling of Paul inside her, riding her to the point of no return. Then her orgasm would go on for ever, starting deep inside, teased and stroked into being by each stretching thrust of his miraculous prick as it slid backwards and forwards in the wet warmth of her velvet passage.

Her body would tighten around him as the sweat trickled between her breasts, his fingers all the while pinching and squeezing her tender nipples. She liked pain. She liked pain and hard fucking and she liked taking risks – fucking in doorways and in the backs of cars. Anywhere where they might get caught or spied on, or even arrested added to Alex's enjoyment. But they hadn't done anything like that for a long while. Maybe, thought Alex, it's time that we did . . .

But tonight all she'd wanted was for him to slip his penis out of his trousers and straight up inside. No preamble. No foreplay. She'd wanted to feel the zip of his fly rubbing against her pussy lips as he fucked her. She liked that kind of pain. The kind that made her gasp and cry out. Paul would grab hold of her hair then, twisting it around his fingers as his mouth covered her own and he bruised her lips, driving his tongue to the back of her throat as he pumped harder still. Why hadn't he fucked her? Maybe he really was tired tonight. As Paul's hand slid from between her legs, Alex closed her eyes and sighed. When she awoke some time later it was to see a trail of his clothes leading to the bathroom. She could hear the shower running.

Chapter 3

Paul's riverside apartment was part of a complex built in the late nineteen eighties, a 'yuppie' flat, Alex had thought to herself the first time he'd taken her there.

The floors were bare wood, stained and polished, there were huge glass windows and a balcony from which, had Alex felt so inclined, she could have jumped straight into the Thames below.

Often, at night when Paul was away on one of his interminable business trips, she'd stand on the balcony, staring out across the river, gazing for hours at the boats which passed her by. Sometimes, on hot summer evenings, she'd wave to the pleasure cruisers and the people on board would occasionally wave back, smiling and shouting to her, their voices carried away on the night breezes.

Alex hated it when she couldn't hear what they were saying. 'What?' she'd yell back, moving to the front of the balcony and leaning over. But then she'd remind herself that people who lived in apartments like these didn't go yelling at strangers. She'd check herself. Pull back. Go inside and switch on the TV.

In true late eighties style the apartments had a complex security and surveillance system, an underground car park, all the stuff that made the residents feel important and protected but to Alex, seemed little more than an affectation. Though she loved the river, she hated the phoney exclusivity of the complex, especially when she'd first moved in. And that was when she'd met Gina.

Gina was married to Marcos and they lived one floor below Alex and Paul. She and Alex had got chatting in the underground car park one day and had become firm friends.

A mass of blonde highlights and giggles, Gina called her husband Marcos 'a big fat Greek'. She made no bones about her attitude to the portly, middle-aged man to whom she'd pledged her troth. She'd married him for his money and was determined to enjoy it.

Paul hated Gina, telling Alex she was a silly tart. But when they met, Gina would simply smile sweetly at him, her eyes betraying nothing.

Alex would always be eternally grateful to Gina. Without her, she wouldn't have known how to adjust to her new life. For though it was what she'd longed for, living with Paul wasn't quite what she'd anticipated.

When she'd first moved into Paul's apartment Alex had been unable to settle. When he left for work in the mornings she'd wander from room to room, convincing herself that if only she closed her eyes and opened them again, she'd be back in her cramped little bedroom at the hotel. She could still picture herself there, waiting to go on night shift, applying her make-up in the tarnished mirror over the washbasin that stood in the corner.

Alex would lay in Paul's beautiful marble bath for hours, drinking in the scents of soap and bubbles. Floating in her pool of comfort and warmth, she'd watch the sunlight which poured in from the huge balconied windows as it played on the droplets of water which quivered against her skin.

Then, wrapped in a soft white bathrobe, she'd pad silently across the flat and into the master bedroom, opening Paul's wardrobe to stare at his clothes in wonder. Row upon row of perfect suits, shirts from Turnbull & Asser and any number of pairs of shoes, from Gucci loafers to the finest Church's brogues, polished till they gleamed.

At first, she'd been reluctant to use the gold credit card that Paul had given her. She'd restricted her purchases to minor items of underwear and extravagant food, visiting Fortnum & Mason and Harrods for delicious canapés and champagne, ready-prepared salads and cold salmon and beef, welcoming Paul home with wonderful meals, the preparation of which was not of her doing. Most of the time, though, she'd simply spend waiting for him to arrive. She'd polish her nails, read magazines . . . and wait.

It was Gina who had broken the spell. Knocking on Alex's door one morning she had found Alex still in her bathrobe, cleaning out the fridge, a sight upon which Gina had gazed sorrowfully.

Flopping uninvited onto the cream leather sofa in the living room and gazing idly out across the river, Gina had given Alex a lecture of the perils of, as she put it, playing the *hausfrau*.

Alex had defended herself, telling Gina that she liked to keep the flat looking good. She insisted that she liked to be there when Paul got home and to have a meal on the table. He was away from home far more than she'd expected, so when he *was* around it was cause for celebration. She *liked* to look after him, she told Gina. What was wrong with that?

'He fancies you because you like a good time,' Gina had volunteered. 'He fancies you because you appreciate the good things in life and he can give them to you. If you don't get out there and spend his money and enjoy it, you'll be breaking your part of the contract. Even worse, he'll get bored.'

Alex had been amazed by Gina's breathtaking cheek. She hardly knew the woman. Much to Alex's horror, Gina had then taken a bottle of blood red nail polish from her bag and had begun to touch up her nails, the polish-laden brush hovering precariously over Paul's carefully-chosen Italian leather suite.

'Look,' Gina had continued as, much to Alex's relief she had screwed the top back on the polish bottle and put it away, 'he can get anyone to clean the fridge.'

Despite her discomfort, Alex had had no choice but to see the sense of what her new and pushy neighbour had pointed out.

She'd got dressed, and with Gina beside her had set out on her voyage of discovery, learning what it really felt like to live as the girlfriend of a rich man.

It didn't take long to begin to enjoy the deferential attitudes of doormen and waiters, hairdressers and bank managers. It didn't take long to get used to the unrivalled pleasure of never, ever having to travel anywhere except by taxi.

Under Gina's tutelage, Alex had bought dozens of new outfits, luxuriating in the pleasure of buying colours she'd never have dreamt of in fabrics that didn't need to be washed – because now she could afford any amount of dry cleaning.

Buying shoes that matched only one outfit in her wardrobe was a singular pleasure for a woman used to choosing pairs in neutral colours because they had to 'go with everything'. Alex began ordering fresh flowers for the flat, trying out the most fashionable florists in London to see which she preferred. She began to have a weekly massage, manicure and pedicure. In a matter of weeks, her life had changed completely. There'd be no going back. It was impossible.

At first, Paul had baulked at the size of Alex's credit card bills. But, as instructed by Gina, she'd stuck to her guns, insisting that every item was strictly necessary. Paul had looked at her strangely for a moment and then he'd smiled. 'Gina's right,' Alex had thought. And carried on spending.

Though Gina had at first pretended that she was doing Alex a favour, her woman-of-the-world demeanour and attitude was just a façade.

Lonely and unhappy holed up in Marcos's flat, she was thrilled to have someone to spend her days with, someone to fill in the long and idle hours. Most of the time Marcos was out haranguing his employees, making money and stuffing himself with Greek food in the company of his odious friends, often returning late at night, drunk and reeking of garlic.

Gina had been a waitress in one of his restaurants when they met. From the very first, the portly widower had taken a shine to her and within weeks, had made her his own.

Immediately, it became apparent that Marcos had a little difficulty with, as Gina put it, 'getting it up'. Too many years of alcohol abuse had taken their toll and all Gina's best efforts at arousal were needed to enable Marcos to achieve an erection. He loved it when he did, though. His joy was unbounded and after a successful fuck, he'd lie in Gina's arms and cry like a baby.

He liked to watch her masturbate and at first, Gina was happy to oblige. She'd recently become a keen if unaccomplished tennis player and Marcos would watch as, dressed in her tennis whites, Gina would parade around the bedroom in front of him. As Marcos fingered his flaccid cock, Gina would begin her routine. 'My panties are too tight,' she'd murmur. 'Too tight to play tennis. I want to take them off so my pussy can breathe,' and, pointing her rump in his direction, she would bend over and remove her frilly white panties. Throwing them to an eager Marcos, the pantomime would then continue.

'I feel so randy,' Gina would lisp, stroking the handle of her tennis racquet. She'd then sit on the bed and part her legs, stroking the handle of the racquet against her labia, parting her outer pussy lips and wrapping them around the racquet head, moaning as she did so and rubbing her breasts in mock enjoyment.

'This racquet head is nearly as big as my Marcos,' she'd murmur. 'Oh, if only he were here to fuck me.' By this time, Marcos's prick was usually showing some signs of life and, timing her performance to keep pace with his arousal, Gina would fake the build-up to orgasm. Sometimes the performance was real, though. As she dragged the head of the racquet across her slippery labia, the touch of the leather-clad handle against her clitoris would begin to arouse her and, if she was able to forget that Marcos was in the room, often she'd manage to bring herself off.

The routine was usually the same. When she'd played with the handle of the racquet, Marcos liked her to turn it around and hold the strings against her open pussy. Gina had a long, fat clitoris and if she squashed the racquet tightly enough against her inner lips, the tip of her clitoris could be squeezed through the strings.

Just the tiniest sliver of flesh, but oh, how he loved it! With a trembling finger, Marcos would touch Gina's clitoris as if touching a sacred object, licking his lips and stroking his little worm of a penis which by this time would begin to show some movement.

'You are too big for me. I must protect my poor little pussy,' Gina would say as Marcos snuffled against the front of the tennis racquet, drinking in the smell of her which flooded through the strings.

'Rub your tits,' he would plead and, obligingly, Gina would raise one hand to her breast and begin to tweak and massage a nipple. Holding his precariously fragile erection in his hand and stroking it lovingly, Marcos would then move up her body, taking her hand away and fixing his full and fleshy lips around the hard, pink nipple that pointed at him, as if in defiance.

She didn't mind this bit, because he would bite her quite hard and she liked it. At first he would circle her nipple with his tongue and then quite unexpectedly, his teeth would clamp around it, sending a wave of pain and pleasure through her body and straight between her legs.

Gina would begin to rub the strings of the racquet against her clitoris as Marcos bit, dragging it across her inner folds as the juices flowed from within her and the racquet became sticky with her essence.

Darting backwards and forwards between her pussy and her tits, Marcos would scrabble frantically across her body, longing to be admitted to the inner sanctum of her womanhood, though enjoying the merciless teasing which was the only thing that seemed to get him going, the only thing that seemed able to persuade his sad little cock into showing signs of arousal.

Pushing the tip of his little finger through the strings, Marcos would occasionally manage to touch wet flesh, coating his finger in Gina's juices which he would then wipe along his prick, coaxing it to grow as if it were a baby in need of nurturing.

On his knees in front of her, rubbing his cock like fury, Marcos would then lick the strings of the racquet, his tongue dragging over taut catgut and soft flesh as his right hand went into overdrive and his cock began to swell in earnest.

'Take the racquet away,' he would moan, and Gina would always refuse. 'Please,' he would beg, by now desperate to remove the obstruction to the full enjoyment of her feminine delights.

'Oh, no,' Gina would moan. 'I can't allow you near me. You're too big. Your cock is too big for little me.'

The charade would continue until Marcos felt his cock

had reached its full potential. With a cry of 'now,' he would prompt Gina to throw the racquet aside at which point his fragile erection would be poked into her.

Despite all the pelvic floor exercises that Gina did daily, despite her best efforts at squeezing him, she could barely feel the presence of Marcos inside her though, as expected, her moans of ecstasy knew no bounds.

'I can't take it!' she would pant as Marcos grunted his way towards orgasm. Eventually, with six sudden and rapid strokes inside her he would come, either crying with relief or if she were in luck, rolling off and falling asleep with a murmured 'thank you, my angel,' before turning into his pillow.

But Gina would not sleep. Bored and frustrated she would begin to fantasise – about men she had known, men she had met and all too often, Paul Mason, the man who lived one floor above. Slim and dark-haired, he had a bulge at the front of his perfectly cut trousers that not even the best tailoring in the world could fully disguise. Though they'd barely spoken before Gina had become friendly with Alex, Gina knew that he didn't like her and, in time, her lust turned to bitterness. But he was always the one she thought about as she began to masturbate, moaning out Paul's name while Marcos slept.

Jolting her body against her fingers she dreamt that it was Paul's cock sinking inside her, his mouth on her breasts and his hands in her hair. Alex was one lucky bitch, she would think to herself as Marcos began to snore.

Gina had nagged Alex for months about joining the Mottlesham Tennis Club. Frequented by stars of stage and screen, minor Royals and major crooks, the club occupied six prime acres of lush countryside on the London/Essex borders. In the summer, it played host to many of the top tennis stars who would show up to practise on its perfectly manicured courts before the Wimbledon tournament began.

In the proud tradition of celebrity groupies everywhere, the lady members of the Mottlesham would make valiant attempts to bed the top stars, their place in the club's female hierarchy dependent upon which celebrity cock they'd managed to slide inside them before the championships were over.

To her credit, Gina didn't take part in these little games. But such were their amusement value that she'd describe them in detail to Alex over their long, girlie lunches, swallowing mouthfuls of ice cold Chardonnay and pushing sushi around her plate as she elaborated on some of the more colourful details.

Alex hadn't wanted to play tennis. But it had been something to do. And she had to admit that she looked good in her little white skirts. She'd chosen them at Lillywhites, under Gina's direction. Racquets, tennis shoes, shirts, socks, sports bag, bras . . . she'd also felt it necessary to choose a whole new range of make-up and invigorating shower and body products, just to get in the mood.

The new tennis coach at the Mottlesham tennis club had arrived soon after Alex had joined. The changing rooms were abuzz with speculation about this tall, blond youth – though within a matter of weeks it had all quietened down when it became apparent to the female members of the Mottlesham that he was 'no go'.

Young, fabulously handsome in a sharp-featured kind of way and with the type of well-developed thigh muscles that fuelled a thousand female fantasies, the lady members had each booked a course of lessons with the boy. Dutifully, he had told each of them in turn that he was a student, taking a year off before university. Tactfully, he had resisted their subtle advances. He had been a junior champion, playing at Wimbledon only the year before. His name was Kurt and his father was a German diplomat. 'How interesting,' the ladies had lisped, each in turn. Kurt could see nothing interesting in his father's occupation, though of course he didn't say so. He simply nodded, politely.

Kurt had loathed his father, Herr Grünhaufer, for as long as he could remember, hating and despising the weakness and cowardice which his father disguised as a cool detachment.

But while Kurt disliked everything about his father from his coldness to his bourgeois way of life, nothing compared with the poisonous hatred he felt for his stepmother, the statuesque Frau Helena.

As a boy growing up in his father's elegant and austere mansion in Cologne, Kurt had watched his stepmother entertain a succession of lovers each young enough to be her son.

She'd sworn the young Kurt to secrecy, telling him that his father would be annoyed if he knew she had 'young friends'. Not angry with her, of course, but angry with Kurt for failing to keep her company during the long, lonely hours when Papa was away, performing his important duties on behalf of the nation.

Kurt's father was a junior diplomat in those days and had met the delightfully pretty Helena Schwartz six months after the untimely death of his wife. At first, Helena's modest demeanour had persuaded him that she would be a more than adequate stepmother for the quiet and surly fourteen-year-old boy.

Seduced by her appealing modesty, Otto Grünhaufer had begun to court Fraulein Schwartz who, once she'd got him on the hook, swiftly took him to her bed, introducing him to delights of which previously, even in his wildest dreams he'd had no experience.

For some strange reason, he found nothing odd in discovering that the habits of a whore came naturally to a woman who spoke with the voice of a nun. The moist cavern between her legs became the focus of all his desires. Within weeks of their acquaintance, he had married her.

In contrast to his father, who, for all his faults, was a highly intelligent man, Kurt's stepmama was vain and cruel and entirely oblivious to the sufferings of either her husband or her highly sensitive stepson.

Exhausted by his increasingly demanding workload, over the years Otto Grünhaufer became a less-than-enthusiastic lover, causing the insatiable Helena to taunt him mercilessly and to seek her revenge through the corruption of the young Kurt.

Bringing her boy lovers back to the house, she would force Kurt to watch while she took her pleasure.

'Look, Kurt,' she would say, undressing whichever street urchin she had lured back that particular afternoon, 'look how his cock stands firm and ready.'

'Mmm,' she would say, sniffing her latest victim's erect member, 'he even smells like a man. Your father has a floppy piece of skin between his legs and smells like a mouse.'

Kurt would watch, fascinated yet boiling with hatred as Helena lowered herself onto the boy. He'd watch as she spread her labia and slid the boy's prick up inside her, moaning and wiggling as the urchin drove into her innermost depths. Stepmama always had to be on top. She would bark her orders to whoever was fucking her, telling him how to handle her breasts, when and where to squeeze and lick.

Kurt, forced to watch, longed to beat her beautiful creamy arse. He longed to startle her and make her afraid. Anything to stop her laughing her wicked, confident laugh. He knew he desired her and he knew that his feelings were wrong.

But there was nothing he could do. And no escape from the torture she put him through.

He never forgot the day it happened. It was a hot, midsummer day and the sun beat down mercilessly with nothing to relieve the stifling atmosphere.

From the drawing room window Kurt could see his father's two Dobermans asleep under an oak tree in the garden. He had been reading a book and he looked up to see his stepmama coming towards him across the lawn.

It was two days after his seventeenth birthday. There had been a party of sorts and a cake – the last slice of which he had been eating as he sat on the window seat and read.

Stepmama had been wearing a simple white dress, her hair, normally coiffed, now loose about her shoulders. Her breasts were clearly outlined through the light material, her nipples hard and erect.

Entering the drawing room through the open French windows, she had come up to him.

'It is just too hot for anything,' she had said. 'I don't know what to do with myself.' He had looked up at her and she had raised her hand, slowly stroking his mouth with her fingertip.

Kurt had jumped as if scalded. 'It was a piece of icing,' she said. 'You had cake on your lip, that's all.' Then she had left the room and he had tried to continue reading, but all he could think of was the touch of her fingers against his mouth and how much he had wanted to slide those fingers between his lips.

He had got up and put the book down. He had climbed the wide marble staircase and tapped on the door of her room. She had called 'come in,' and he had entered to find her at her dressing table brushing her long, red hair. Her windows were wide open but not even the slightest breeze had stirred the plain, heavy net curtains that covered them.

She had stood up and faced him and he had gone to her, untying the belt of her dressing robe, drinking in the scent of her perfumed skin. She was sticky with sweat. Stickier still between her legs as he fell to his knees and sank his face into the silken triangle of hair that parted to release the sweetest scent he'd ever known. The touch of her had forced his swollen cock even harder against the seams of his trousers till he thought he would split the material.

She'd pulled his head away from between her legs and gestured to him to get up. Then she had knelt before him and unzipped him, taking his throbbing virgin penis between her lips, anointing him with a kiss.

Kurt had reached for her breasts, rolling her nipples between his fingers and marvelling at the softness, the lushness of her as he felt the pressure of her lips around his shaft. He thought he would die with longing and then, the sweet release as the pounding in his loins turned to liquid and with a sharp, gasping series of thrusts he felt his juices shoot from him and into the back of her soft, deep throat.

She had swallowed everything, sucking his penis till his thrusts finally subsided. Then she had smiled at him and wiped her mouth. 'Happy birthday,' she had said, a mocking smile playing about her eyes.

Never again had they mentioned what had happened and never had she invited him to her room. It was as if she had stolen something from him and with the passing of time, his desire and his hatred for her had grown in equal measure.

The boys had continued to come to the house. And she continued to fuck them all, right under his nose.

One day, Kurt had hit one of stepmama's youths who had hit him back. The youth had laughed and so had Helena, and with the noise ringing in his ears and blood on his tongue, Kurt had left the house, heading for a nearby brothel which until now, he'd only ever known by reputation and the excited speculation of his schoolfriends.

He looked a lot older than his seventeen years. They didn't question him when he asked for a girl. The one he picked had long, reddish hair like his stepmama.

He had blushed at first when the girl had asked him what it was he wanted. 'I'd like to spank your arse,' he'd replied, expecting her to throw him out. But the girl, who had soft pink skin and was dressed in white lace, told him that he could do whatever he wished. He made her slip out of her camisole and kneel on the bed, keeping on nothing but her stockings and suspenders.

He'd walked all around her, looking at her little pointed tits which dangled downwards, almost brushing the white sheets above which she crouched. He'd leant forward and smelt her hair, brushing his face against her cheek. She was young and very pretty and she smelt of talcum powder. And then he'd slapped her arse, slapping it till it wobbled like a pink jelly, making her cry and gasp as she knelt before him.

His prick had got harder with each slap until he could bear the pressure no longer and with one sudden and violent thrust, he'd pushed himself between the girl's buttocks, aiming for the hidden opening, the pleasures to be found inside which had been described to him by his stepmama, in such detail.

Though this was his first ever fuck, Kurt found that control came easily to him. His strokes inside the girl's tight cavern were long and measured and to his surprise, he felt the whore shudder and moan and heard her cry out long before he finally climaxed inside her.

It was the first of many visits to the brothel on Sieben Strasse. From the start, Kurt found he had a knack of pleasing women, though he cared nothing for their satisfaction.

He liked to beat them, often coming straight from his father's house in a rage, leaving his stepmother and her latest young lover behind, their laughter ringing in his ears. Then he would beat a whore, always choosing auburn-haired girls.

Sometimes he would like two or three together, binding their ankles and hands and making them kneel so that their arses stood in the air. Not only would he restrain each girl in turn but sometimes he'd tie them together in a row, going from one to the other, sticking his cock between the upturned rump of one and then the next and the next. He liked to blindfold the girls for this little game. Sometimes, he'd unexpectedly bugger one of the girls, forcing himself inside her with no forewarning. He could feel the fear in the other two when he did this, feel their bodies tense when their comrade cried out. But often he'd simply slap their fat little arses till they reddened and he'd fuck them, one at a time, going along the line.

He always thought that all whores had orgasms until one of his schoolmates told him differently. 'They pretend,' said his chum, 'but they never do.' Kurt knew differently. His seventeen-year-old prick was made for pleasure, though his temper barred him from enjoying it himself without first inflicting pain.

With every slap, he thought of his stepmama. Even when he was grown, the image of her, long-legged and auburn-haired, never left his mind. But that was all long ago. Long before his skill with a tennis racquet had eclipsed even his skill with his penis.

Unlike the rest of the Mottlesham's lady membership, Alex hadn't rushed to take lessons with Kurt.

As a total beginner, she'd been happy simply to have a knock around with Gina, laughing hysterically when the ball shot up in the air, revelling in her own ineptitude before, as was their habit, they retired to the bar to drink too many Spritzers and then make their way back to Docklands.

Kurt had seen her, though. Politely, he'd volunteered his services, his pale blue eyes staring unblinkingly into her clear green ones. And when she'd agreed to 'maybe a couple' of lessons, he'd stood behind her on the court and guided her tennis swing, clasping her hands firmly beneath his own, his breath tickling her neck, his heart thumping against her back as he held her close.

'Relax, Alex,' he'd say as though he'd known her for years. The other women players were jealous of her, their long-suffering husbands envious of him.

Alex had got into the habit of having a warm-up with Kurt whenever he was around and wasn't teaching. He'd hit balls to her across the net and when she missed too often, he'd walk round to her, holding her at every opportunity, showing her how it should be done.

Alex wasn't a natural at tennis. In fact, she was little better than hopeless. And when Kurt was near, somehow even her limited talents would desert her. Frustrated and impatient, Kurt would grab her hands, splaying her fingers around the handle of the racquet, fixing them tightly in the correct position, telling her off for not listening to him.

One day, he dug his nails into her serving hand, just for emphasis. The slight pain made her gasp, sending a tingle through her body.

'You like that, don't you?' he'd said. 'I knew you would.' He'd smiled at her. 'If you don't listen to what I'm telling you, I'll have to hurt you some more.'

That had been the afternoon she'd known that she was crazy to have anything more to do with Kurt. That had been the afternoon she had realised she was playing with fire.

She'd gone to the club alone, hoping to find him there. It was the day after Paul had failed to make love to her and, bored and listless, she'd longed for a little excitement. She'd got her wish. But then she'd wished she hadn't. The experience on the court had shaken her, the way Kurt had taken command of her, voicing her deepest fantasies in a manner that was so matter of fact.

Alex would play games with Paul. He would smack her and tie her to the bed. But Kurt was something different. Something dangerous.

Yes, she did want Kurt to hurt her. To tie her up and overpower her, to beat her and humiliate her. The look in his eyes alone had shocked her. The fact that he *knew*.

He'd been there when she'd left the changing room to walk out to the car park. 'Alex,' he'd said and she'd turned, seeing his face just before he grabbed her, holding her face between his strong fingers as his mouth crushed against her own, his tongue driving between her teeth as they clung together, devouring each other.

She felt his mouth on her neck, his teeth biting her in sharp little nips as his fingers groped for her nipples. 'I'm going to fuck you,' he'd said, his voice quiet yet menacing. 'You know I'm going to fuck you. Now, or next week or next month I don't care . . . but it's going to happen.' His hands had moved down to cup her buttocks, squeezing her body against his prick which she could feel, hard and long, beneath his tennis shorts. He rubbed her mons against the length of it and she felt her body moisten and open, her softness against his hardness, longing to feel him slide inside. She could feel her heart racing in her chest as he stroked her neck with the tip of his tongue and she closed her eyes, her body melting. She could smell the clean, sweet smell of his freshly laundered tennis shirt and the scent of his hair as he held her ever closer. His cock was hard and ready, thumping between his tanned thighs, with only a couple of layers of cotton separating their hot and eager bodies.

But she'd pushed him away and then she'd started to run, her heart pounding as she made her way across the car park – conscious, with every step she took, of the swelling in her vulva, the taste of him in her mouth and the memory of his lips covering her own.

Her hand trembled as she fumbled to get the key in the lock of her pretty little Honda CRX. The car that Paul had recently bought her so that she could get around. Her head was swimming, her body alive with sensation.

She'd driven just a few yards along the road and then she'd parked the car. Sliding one hand inside her cotton shirt and another beneath her skirt, Alex had begun to masturbate, pinching her nipples hard while she rubbed frantically against her aching clitoris. She wanted him. She wanted him so badly she could hardly bear it.

She was wetter than she'd been in a long time and the inner folds of her pussy slipped and slithered hotly beneath her touch. Reaching into the glove compartment of the car she searched around for something thicker than her own fingers with which to pleasure herself, with which to silence the terrible longing that threatened to swallow her up. There was nothing. Nothing but need and temptation and the image of Kurt, burning through her brain.

Then she became aware of the gear stick. With the utmost difficulty, Alex manoeuvred her body until she was astride the thick, black knob. Afraid to slide it inside her in case she injured herself, she simply spread the gaping entrance to her womanhood over the familiar shape. But it was enough to do what was wanted, its roundness and hardness propelling her towards an orgasm which the pinching and rubbing of her fingers helped to hasten.

She came with a deep moan, slumping back into the driver's seat and sitting with her head in her hands as the throbbing coursed through her and her whole body ached for Kurt. Her pussy was a molten pool of longing. Kurt was all she could think of.

Alex had driven home in a daze and paced the flat, waiting for Paul to come home. And when he had – oh, the relief that he was *there* that night! – she'd fucked him like a demon, climbing on top of him and lowering herself onto his thick shaft with a shudder that shook her whole body.

It was as though she'd wanted to swallow him up. She'd ridden Paul like a rodeo horse, bucking and squeezing him deeper inside her, driving the knob of him against her womb as she crushed her clitoris against his hot prick in a slippery fever of lust, each thrust of her body making her hungrier, urging her towards an orgasm of such intensity that it wrenched a cry from her throat like that of an animal, a deep guttural moan that broke from her lips as Paul squeezed her nipples and thrust inside.

But it was a temporary relief. And when Paul had casually mentioned that he was going away again the following Tuesday and would be away for a week, she'd known she must do something to escape the trap into which she felt she was falling. She wanted Paul. She didn't want to lose him. But she knew that Kurt held the key both to the realisation of her wildest fantasies and to her destruction.

She must throw away that key. She would never go to the tennis club again. And in the meantime, she must get away. If Paul wasn't going to be here for a week, then neither would she.

Chapter 4

Mary's mother had told her that she was looking well – even though, she confided, 'you've put on a bit of weight.'

Whenever Mary's mother made a remark there was always a sting in the tail – even when she was paying a compliment. Mary stared out from behind the neat lace curtains in her mother's front room and sighed. Paul would be home by now. But she wasn't there.

The call had come last night, when Mary was preparing for Paul's arrival. Doctor Carter, the family physician, had rung to tell Mary that her mother had fallen downstairs. This time the old lady wasn't crying wolf and Mary had had no choice but to jump in her car and drive the interminable distance from Manchester to Sutton, and the small, relentlessly respectable terraced house where she'd grown up.

She'd been here for only a few hours but already it felt like months. One of the few precious weeks when Paul would be at home and now she'd almost certainly miss him. But this time, there was no way she could leave the old lady. Not till she was sure she could manage alone.

There was no point in fretting. Mary knew that even if she managed to escape in less than a week, everything was spoiled and her plans were shot to pieces. By the time she got back to Manchester, Paul would be off down south again. Gone in an instant. Leaving Mary to her work.

The lace curtains at the windows flapped in the breeze. Mary could hear the steady, relentless click of her mother's knitting needles.

Alex turned her car into the drive of Tingles Health Farm, the satisfying scrunch of gravel beneath her wheels giving way to a feeling of pleasure as the imposing facade of the gracious Georgian mansion came into view.

She had driven here in the car that Paul had given her as a surprise present. She was pleased not to have to get taxis any more. Not to have to rely on other people.

Alex parked her car on the driveway and switched off the engine with a sigh. It was good to be back. Tingles felt like home. Alex viewed it as her own private bolt-hole, the place to which she always retreated when something got her down.

She'd left the flat in the early afternoon, throwing a few essentials into three suitcases and locking the door behind her with a feeling of relief. She'd been lucky to get a booking but at the same time, she *was* one of Tingles' more regular customers.

Driving through the leafy country lanes, the memory of Kurt had come, unbidden, to her mind. She'd tried to dismiss it but even the radio at full blast had failed to banish the images which struggled to rise to the top of her consciousness.

She'd imagined herself in one of those black leather corsets she'd seen in the windows of sex shops, the ones with the unforgiving fasteners and a tight, constricting cut. The ones she'd pretended not to look at a dozen times as she'd hurried past.

She saw herself standing naked, wrapping the strange, stiff garment around her, feeling the leather grip her soft skin like a vice, the corset forcing her tits together and deepening her already voluptuous cleavage.

In her reverie she was wearing spiky, patent leather high heels and gossamer-fine stockings. A wisp of auburn hair from the bush between her legs was just visible from beneath the hem of taut leather which skirted the tops of her milk white thighs.

Breathing deeply, she saw herself walk into a room where Kurt would be waiting – like her, dressed in black – his golden hair in stark contrast to the severity of his clothes.

She would feel all-powerful as she entered the room. She would be conscious of the silkiness of her stockings, enjoying their sensuous contact as they brushed against each other as she walked. She was a sex goddess. She knew how enticing, how beautiful she looked and she expected Kurt to fall at her feet.

But Kurt simply stared at her coldly. Seated in a large black swivel chair behind a huge and imposing desk, he ordered her to walk across to him, to stand in front of him turning this way and that so that he could inspect her.

At first, her eyes flashed their defiance and though she paraded as she was bid, she held her head proudly and walked slowly, her hips swinging. Then he called her to him and telling her to turn around, he administered a stinging stroke across her buttocks with the black leather crop which had rested unseen across his knees.

The pain made her catch her breath and brought tears springing behind her eyelashes. In a voice as cold as it was steady, he ordered her to turn around and get down on her knees.

Rising to his feet and moving around her as she knelt before him, he stroked her softly rounded buttocks with the little leather tassel at the end of his crop. Then sliding the crop between the globes of her arse, he moved it between her cheeks like a violinist drawing a bow across strings.

She was frightened now, her heart racing inside her leather confinement, afraid of the menace in his voice, in his mood, in his every gesture.

But beneath the fear a deep arousal was building within her as she bent her head low and he stood over her, his breathing deep and steady.

She knelt before him in silence, the slippery film which covered her thighs and soaked into her stocking tops bearing testament to the pleasure to be found in humiliation.

Probing with his crop between the globes of her pretty buttocks, he moved around to stand in front of her, bringing his groin level with her face.

'Suck me,' he commanded. 'Unzip me. And then suck me.'

Shaking, she began to fumble with his fly, her eyes focused on the teeth of the zip. The little slivers of metal seemed locked together, releasing each other painfully slowly. At last she pulled the zip open, freeing a cock which came out of his trousers of its own accord, forcing its way into the open with a firmness of purpose which made her tremble.

Alex stared at his cock, rising from its forest of dense golden hair. A thick dagger of taut flesh, it stood proud and hard above the heavy pendulous balls which nestled beneath.

Her jaw ached at the mere thought of taking his huge penis in her mouth. But she was hungry for him. Hungry for the sensation of his prick as it moved between her lips, hungry to feel his smooth knob fill her mouth as she explored it, greedily.

Tentatively, Alex leant forward and brushed the knob of his prick with her lips. The touch of flesh upon flesh heightened her arousal and with the very tip of her tongue, she began to lick deep into the valley at the head of his penis. She closed her eyes, trailing her tongue through the slippery fluid which had escaped from the tip of his prick and now smoothed her progress. She sighed deeply, luxuriating in the musky scent that enveloped her.

Suddenly, with one thrust from his hips, Kurt filled her mouth, fucking her deep in her throat. She shuddered, sucking on his jolting penis as Kurt's riding crop toyed with the hole in her arse.

Her belly was squashed against his leg and he pressed the front of her pussy with his boot. Opening her legs in response, she held the lips of her pussy apart and rubbed herself along his leg, the feel of the shiny leather against the inner lips of her vulva sending waves of arousal deep into her womanhood.

Alex clung eagerly to him, polishing the black leather with the juices which flowed from her, crushing her clitoris against the unforgiving leather as she teased and kneaded his penis with her mouth. She sucked and licked till she felt him tense. Opening her throat, she prepared herself to feel him spurt on her tongue. But he didn't. All of a sudden, Kurt pulled his penis out of her mouth and shot his juice between her breasts, reaching down to massage the slippery fluid into her hard and eager nipples.

At each pinch and vicious twist of his fingers Alex felt her juices flow more freely. Sliding her dripping pussy the length of his boot, she spread her labia to embrace his toe, masturbating herself against his foot as he circled his polished boot inside the lips of her womanhood.

Kurt watched her closely, seeing the flush spread across her chest as her breathing quickened and her orgasm gathered pace.

Wishing to deny her the pleasure of release he dragged her to her feet then, pulling her across the room till she stood before a plain white wall into which were fixed manacles for her wrists and cruel leather straps to bind her ankles.

Buckling her tightly by the arms and then the legs, and with her face to the wall, he left her standing spread-eagled, arms and legs outstretched. Alex felt her burning forehead against the cool, smooth plaster, her pussy open and vulnerable, spread wide beneath the leather corset which barely covered the tops of her legs.

Coming up behind her Kurt lifted the hem of leather, baring her arse. Then he stood quite still. She could feel a soft breeze playing across her skin as he paused for what felt like an eternity. She could hear her heart beating. She knew what was coming. But why did he delay? Why did he torture her so!

Smiling quietly to himself, Kurt raised his crop and beat her and she cried out, squirming inside her leather prison, screaming and begging him to stop, though each sting across her skin sent a ripple of delight through her throbbing vulva, the pain of his cruel punishment bringing her close to an orgasm in which dread and desire were evenly matched.

His flaccid prick recovered itself as he beat her, rising hard and thick from its forest of blond curls.

He was behind her then, his breath tickling her burning skin as he whispered into her ear. 'I shall fuck you now,' he murmured in honeyed tones, reaching round the front of her to where her breasts were trapped against the wall, still sticky with his juices and tender from where he'd rammed them back inside their constricting garment.

Lifting them free of their leather corset once more and dragging them across its coarse seams as he did so, he brought her soft globes out into the light.

Then she felt something thick between her sore buttocks as he pinched and twisted her nipples and with a sudden thrust, she knew his cock as it plundered the darkness of her flooded cavern, a cock that filled her, length and breadth. Its huge bulbous head pushed deeper into her and . . . suddenly Alex had arrived at Tingles and as the familiar mansion came into view, Kurt melted away, the only reminder of her fantasy being a sticky warmth between her legs.

The receptionist looked up and smiled as Alex came through the heavy front door and crossed the expanse of pink carpet towards the white desk.

A little group of beauty therapists was gathered nearby studying their rotas, seeing who was booked in to give one of the forty or so treatments on offer at Tingles, 'England's premiere health spa and beauty oasis'.

'It's good to see you again, Miss Chambers,' said the receptionist. She slid a registration card in Alex's direction, reaching for the key to the room which Alex knew would be ready for her, cool and quiet, its en-suite bathroom full of the fragrant and mysterious 'flowers of the rainforest' based products for which the spa was famous.

'Anyone interesting in?' Alex whispered to the girl behind the desk. While aware that she shouldn't gossip about the spa's other guests, the girl was unable to resist the temptation.

'Jason Hannard booked in on Sunday. He's staying for ten days,' she confided quietly. Alex smiled at the girl who closed her lips in an exaggerated gesture meaning 'I really shouldn't have said that.'

Jason Hannard, thought Alex as she opened the French windows of her room, minutes later. She stared out across the lawns to the open air swimming pool, around which the empty sun loungers stood bathed in the spring sunshine, ready and waiting for summer. Jason Hannard. That should be interesting, she mused, opening her wardrobe and extracting a handful of hangers.

Chapter 5

Fame had come relatively late in life to Jason Hannard and he didn't intend to forego any of its privileges. After years as a bit-part player, part-time waiter and occasional gigolo, at the age of thirty-five the boyish-looking actor had landed a leading role in an unexpectedly successful TV series.

Jason played Giles, the sensitive, brooding and deeply troubled lover of an equally wacky doctor's wife called Amanda – a woman torn between her love for Giles and her duty to her alcohol-and-drug-dependent GP husband who, known mysteriously to Giles but not to Amanda, was slowly dying of an incurable and rather exotic kidney complaint.

Overnight, Jason Hannard, or rather Giles, had become the pin-up of women everywhere. While solicitous in the extreme to every fan who stoppped him in the street for an autograph, in his private life Jason felt he had at last been given the chance, and the means, to indulge all those appetites which poverty and lack of opportunity alone had kept in check.

'A little higher, darling,' he murmured to the girl who was massaging his leg. Swathed in towels, lying on his back cocooned and warm, Jason Hannard was luxuriating in the pleasure of embarrassing the young beauty therapist whose job it was to stimulate his muscles, expel his toxins and encourage the healthy circulation of blood through his veins and capillaries. Opening his eyes, he saw that she was blushing deeply. He flashed her his most endearing Hollywood smile.

'Mr Hannard, you're supposed to be relaxing,' she scolded, adopting her best schoolmarmish pose. His reply was to reach up and pull the pin from the back of her hair, releasing a curtain of thick, blonde silkiness. Her hair spilled forward, totally destroying the severe and businesslike composure behind which the girl had retreated on realising that she was faced with a client whose need for the relief offered by a good massage was not confined to the aching in his shoulders.

He closed his eyes again. 'You are the sexiest thing,' he murmured, growling with satisfaction as her hands moved expertly across his thigh, pummelling and squeezing his firm muscles beneath their golden skin.

Though his eyes were closed, Jason Hannard knew that she was looking at him, fancying him, her hair now loose about her shoulders, totally negating the effect created by her crisp, white uniform. Her fingers were firm and capable and he could feel his erection begin to grow beneath the towel which lay spread across his hips.

'I want to squeeze your nipples through that white uniform,' he continued, his eyes still shut. 'I want to feel them harden beneath your prissy little overall . . . and then I want to undo the buttons and bury my face in your breasts.'

'Mr Hannard,' the girl interrupted, 'please . . .' but though her voice was tinged with the requisite degree of disapproval, her hands caressed him more sensuously than ever, the long, even strokes of her fingers pressing more deeply into his flesh, her steady breathing laced with the occasional sigh.

'Touch me, darling,' he implored her, 'touch me and undo the front of your uniform . . . please . . .'

'Mr Hannard!' she replied, trying to sound shocked.

'Oh, darling,' he replied, his eyes still tightly shut, 'just look what you've done to me!' Pulling aside the towel which covered his hips, he let it fall to the floor.

Jason knew he had a magnificent cock. In the bad old days it had often seen active service as his meal ticket. And while he had allowed the pleasures of fame and fortune to go straight to his head, deep down he had never deluded himself as to the fickle nature of celebrity. But fame or no fame, his cock was here to stay. He could rely on it. And right now, it needed attention.

He had heard the girl gasp quietly when he pulled the towel aside and now he lay perfectly still, his eyes shut, his cock standing to attention, piercing the scented air.

The pause couldn't have been more than a few seconds but the anticipation seemed to go on for ever. Then he felt her fingers, cool and strong, as she wrapped them around his shaft. For a second she held it quite still as the blood thumped along its length. And then, backwards and forwards, backwards and forwards, tentatively at first then harder, pulling and stroking, her expert fingers working their magic on the thick rod of his prick as the overhead fan whirred gently.

He had so nearly come at her first touch, and was grateful for the years of practise that had taught him how to hold back. His prick was slippery now, the leakage from its tip spread along its length, making her strokes ever smoother, the pressure of her fingers and the palm of her hand moving in unbroken glides of deep sensation.

'That's right,' he said, 'oh . . . that's *so* right . . .' Opening his eyes he saw that the pretty blonde girl was fiddling with the buttons of her starched white uniform, her breathing heavy and laboured as she struggled to divest herself of her clothes while still concentrating on the job in hand.

Unwilling to move, afraid lest he break the spell, he left her to struggle with her buttons, concentrating only on the feel of her fingers pulling against his prick, sending tremors of pleasure pulsing through every pore of his skin. Jason had glimpsed her only momentarily and now he shut his eyes again, visualising her fingers with their neatly manicured nails administering the kind of manipulation which didn't appear on Tingles' official programme of therapies and curative treatments listed in their glossy leaflet.

He heard her sigh and suddenly he felt her lips – a warm, delicious sensation as they slid themselves over the hood of his penis in a smooth and moist embrace. He felt the tip of her tongue toying with the bulbous knob of his manhood and, opening his eyes, he saw that her uniform was undone. Her breasts were round and firm beneath a sliver of lace which doubled as a bra, her fat pink nipples clearly outlined by the flimsy material as she leant over him, sucking steadily.

'I can't waste all this,' he thought to himself, 'not on a blow job.' Lifting the girl's head, reluctantly, away from his prick, he sat up and kissed her deeply.

'I've wanted you for so long,' he murmured, totally ignoring the fact that he'd been at Tingles for just a couple of days. Lifting his mouth away from hers to cover her in kisses, he moved swiftly down to her breasts, pulling her bra cups down to allow her miraculous tits to spill over the top. Jason fastened his mouth on one luscious pink nipple as his fingers toyed with its double and his other hand moved across her leg, finding its way beneath her cotton uniform and up into the deep undergrowth of her pubic hair through the middle of which ran a stream which, in seconds, had turned into a torrent.

Jason looked into the girl's face. Her eyes were hazy, her mouth half-open and little gasps escaped from her lips as she bore down upon his fingers, now buried deep inside her pussy. Jason paddled in the softness which yielded to his steady probing. His fingers plunged in and out in a rhythmic simulation of sex while his thumb trailed through the folds of her pussy lips, the little flaps of skin slipping and sliding beneath his touch.

'Oh,' she groaned, 'oooh . . .' and suddenly Jason was off the massage couch and she was on it. 'One second, darling,' he said, reaching for his towelling robe and digging into the pocket for the packet of condoms he carried with him always.

With his penis carefully wrapped in its rubber overcoat, her panties were dragged off by a practised hand as Jason's prick navigated between her thighs and into the warm wetness which enveloped his straining member.

The girl grabbed his hair, pulling his mouth over her own and wrapping her legs around his back, drawing him deeper into her. 'Mmm,' thought Jason. 'Nice, tight pussy. I'll have to book a massage with this one again.'

He hadn't been so keen on yesterday's manicurist and as for the girl who'd supervised his session in the flotation tank, well, she'd been a waste of time.

He rather fancied the one who did the mud wraps, though.

He'd try and get round to her tomorrow. And then again, there was the little blonde hairdresser he'd seen out jogging the other morning . . .

Jason thrust faster as he felt his orgasm begin and reaching for one of the girl's nipples and pinching it, he felt her body throb and tighten as her vagina responded to his deeper and more urgent penetration.

Mmm. There were so many treatments to be had in this place. A chap was simply spoilt for choice.

Alex hadn't enjoyed herself so much in ages. She'd turned up at Tingles' 'Stretch 'n Tone' class to find the usual complement of lycra-clad women, a sprinkling of stressed-out executive men and much to her surprise, a few moments later, Jason Hannard. Resplendent in body-hugging black shorts and a simple white 'T' shirt, he had ambled into the class just seconds before it was due to begin, his unexpected presence sending shock waves through the assembled female company.

Though everyone had known he was staying at Tingles, the word having taken precisely an hour to get around on the day he arrived, so far he had only been spotted in corridors, moving from one treatment room to another.

For the first couple of days, he'd taken to swimming in the early morning in Tingles' Olympic-sized pool. By the third day the pool had become mysteriously busy by six am and Jason had disappeared as quickly as he'd come.

But here he was. Alex had tried not to stare, though sideways glances as the class got into its stride had shown her that yes, he was undeniably handsome. Surprisingly, better looking than on TV with his floppy blond hair and soft, grey eyes. He had an interesting face, she thought. Humorous and intelligent as well as good looking. Not her type, but she could understand why he'd become such a success.

Even before the incident that happened that fateful afternoon, Alex had been highly amused by the exercise class. Almost without exception, the women had shown off, vying with each other for Jason Hannard's attention, throwing themselves wholeheartedly into the exercises in an effort to demonstrate their litheness and fitness for whatever else he might have in mind.

Then the fat girl had fallen over. Purple in the face and spread across the floor like a beached whale, she'd attempted one exercise too many and had slid on the heels of her trainers, landing with a thump and a squeal at Jason Hannard's feet.

In true magnanimous megastar fashion he had bent down beside her and taken her hand, asking if she was all right, suggesting in his most charming manner that the fitness instructor should fetch a doctor which, dutifully, she had trotted off to organise.

The other women had gathered round and watched reverentially as Jason Hannard had removed the girl's trainer from her already plump and now badly swollen foot. There was love and devotion in the girl's eyes as she stared up at him, and that was when Alex had caught the eye of a fair-haired girl who, like her, was keeping her distance.

Alex and the girl smiled at each other, acknowledging the ridiculousness of the scene – the injured girl evidently feeling no pain as Jason Hannard and the rest of the class waited for the doctor to arrive.

Alex wandered over. The blonde was the only other female in the class who hadn't gathered around, expressing her mock concern.

'He *is* rather good looking,' Alex had remarked, quietly. 'Yes,' the girl had replied, nodding her head in the direction of the scene before them. 'It seems we all think so.' They'd smiled at each other. Then Alex had left the gym. The class was over, stopped in its tracks. Now what should she do next?

Alex had been in the steam room for about ten minutes when she heard the door open. Lifting her sleepy eyelids she saw the pretty blonde girl framed in the doorway, a towel wrapped carefully around her.

The girl hesitated and went to leave, and sitting up on her elbow, Alex heard herself say, 'Don't go.'

'I'll be disturbing you,' the girl had replied to which Alex had informed her that she wouldn't and besides, as Alex put it, 'this is Tingles' steam room, not my own private one.'

Alex smiled a smile of welcome. The girl sat down and kept her towel firmly around her.

Spread out horizontally, her full breasts covered in little beads of sweat, Alex surveyed the girl from the corner of her eye. She looked ill at ease. Self-conscious. She lacked the air of self-absorption and arrogance necessary to make an impression in a place like Tingles. And from the way she kept her towel clutched to her body, she'd obviously never been in a steam room, either. 'What is she doing here?' wondered Alex as the sweat trickled in rivulets across her skin, tickling her as it went. What is she doing here and why do I want to know?

Propping herself up on her elbow again she looked directly at the girl who continued to sit, bolt upright, and as far away from Alex as possible, on the shelf below her own.

'You okay?' said Alex.

'Fine,' replied the girl, looking awkward.

'I'm Alex,' said Alex, her full breasts swinging as she sat up and swung her legs down across the bench.

'Pleased to meet you,' said the girl awkwardly, averting her eyes from Alex's naked body. 'My name's Mary.'

Chapter 6

It was six am and down in Tingles' kitchens over three hundred fresh fruit and muesli breakfasts were being prepared. In reception, two yawning receptionists were sorting through piles of newspapers, marking a room number on each. Outside, the Tingles head gardener was having a surreptitious cigarette, barking orders at his young assistant who was clearing stray leaves from the lawns and pulling out the occasional weed which had dared to show its head overnight in the otherwise immaculate flower borders.

Mary opened her eyes very slowly and wondered where she was. Then the memory of the night before came flooding back to her and, wincing, she hid her head under the covers. But the pain and distress that she'd been expecting to flood over her simply didn't come. Hiding under the covers wasn't necessary after all.

Mary surfaced from beneath the sheets to turn her head and look at the man beside her, still sleeping peacefully. The golden hairs on his chest glinted in the sun which filtered in through the open window, bathing the room in a soft glow.

She moved a little. Felt the bruising between her thighs and the tenderness deep inside. It was a good feeling.

'I've been well and truly fucked,' she announced into the silence of the early dawn. Jason Hannard stirred in his sleep but did not wake.

Mary felt a smile playing about her lips. Had she gone mad? she asked herself. To be lying here next to a stranger, willing him to wake up and fuck her again, after all that had happened in the last twelve hours?

But she felt hungry and randy and very much alive, and the smile just wouldn't go away. All she could think of was that last night she'd had three orgasms. Earth shattering, deep and satisfying orgasms of the kind she'd almost forgotten existed.

Yes, she must have gone mad she told herself. She was mad with grief.

Jason Hannard sighed softly and shifted on his pillow. He might be about to wake, she thought hopefully.

Mary slid her hand over her belly and down to the bush of hair between her legs, stiff with the dried juices of last night's lovemaking. She probed between her pussy lips with the tip of one finger. She was wet, slippery and sore. It would hurt to take him inside her again. But it didn't matter. Whenever he awoke, she'd be ready.

It had been a crazy night, almost like a dream. She'd gone to take a steam bath in the late afternoon, the first of her life, and had got talking to the red-haired girl whom she'd seen at the exercise class when the fat girl fell down.

From the moment she'd opened the steam room door, Mary had felt uncomfortable. Ill at ease with this glamorous redhead who had lain spread out, her beautiful naked body dripping with sweat while she chatted comfortably – as if, thought Mary, they'd both been fully clothed and they'd met in a coffee shop.

But Mary had told herself not to be silly. There was nothing wrong with being proud of your body. Then something weird had happened. The girl had introduced herself as 'Alex' and immediately, Mary had experienced a curious feeling of unease.

To break the strange tension, Mary had felt obliged to talk, telling this Alex how she'd been on her way home from her mother's house in Surrey and that she'd stopped at the Health Farm on a whim, to see if she could lose a bit of weight.

'You don't need to lose a thing,' Alex had said. 'I saw you in the exercise class. Your figure's perfect.'

It was then that Mary had told the girl that she was trying to 'lose a bit' for Paul, the man in her life.

'That's a coincidence,' Alex had replied. 'Mine's called Paul, too. What kind of business is he in?'

Mary remembered the look on the girl's face when she told her. She hadn't known what was wrong but at every word she'd uttered, the girl called Alex had looked odder and odder. Mary had chattered on, nervousness making her talkative. Then the red-haired girl had started screaming, calling Mary a liar and a bitch.

It had all had a nightmarish quality about it, and Mary had felt herself unable to breathe.

Then the girl Alex had demanded to know why Mary was following her and why she was out to cause trouble. Mary had opened her mouth to reply, and then the girl had slapped her across the face.

Mary had got up then and made a dash for the door, her legs feeling weak and about to buckle beneath her. But the strange, screaming girl had stood in front of her, barring her way. Then it had all come spilling out of the girl's trembling mouth. On and on she'd talked, unceasingly, about Paul . . . *her* Paul, the man she lived with who was hers and nobody else's.

Mary had sat down again, crumpled in the vile and claustrophobic heat, her face smarting from the blow, willing the girl to get out of the way of the door so she could just get out into the air. She thought she would suffocate.

The next thing she remembered was Jason Hannard's arm around her as she stood in the corridor still wrapped in her towel. She was shivering and crying. Then she remembered laughing a great deal and asking if he made a habit of picking up strays. She was standing just outside the steam room and she could still hear the girl inside, sobbing. Then it all got a bit hazy.

She knew that she'd told Jason Hannard what had happened, though she wasn't quite sure what that was herself. She knew he'd been kind and had taken her back to his suite of rooms.

'Happens to the best of us,' he'd said. 'Men are two-timing bastards and so are quite a few women, too. You'll be all right.' And with that glib summation, Jason Hannard had dismissed the seven years that Mary had spent with Paul as if they'd meant nothing.

It had all seemed at a distance. By now, her tears had dried and Jason Hannard had wrapped Mary in one of his bathrobes. And there she'd sat, her head spinning, as she tried to come to terms with everything the red-haired girl called Alex had said.

There was no doubt about it. She and this Alex had both been talking about the same Paul. That couldn't be denied. And worst of all, Mary couldn't fool herself that there'd been some mistake. She'd seen the name 'Alex' written in Paul's handwriting a dozen times. It had never occurred to her that 'Alex' might be a woman. And suddenly, the man who Mary thought she knew had turned into a stranger . . . an insubstantial shadow wafted away on the clouds of steam which had engulfed her and the hysterical red-headed girl in a steambath, late on an otherwise ordinary Wednesday afternoon.

Mary had never felt so vulnerable as she'd felt in the steam room. And she was strangely conscious, even at the time, that her life was unravelling before her. And though the girl Alex was naked and Mary had had a towel to protect her, within minutes she'd felt stripped of everything.

So. Paul's bedsit in London wasn't a bedsit after all. Paul had a flat with the girl who'd been screaming and crying. The girl who'd slapped her face.

The weirdest thing of all was that, deep down, Mary hadn't been all that surprised. Though at first the shock had felt as bad as hearing that someone you loved had been hit by a bus, when she'd ridden the wave of panic that had flooded over her, Mary had felt nothing but a kind of mute acceptance. Not so the red-haired girl. Eventually, when she'd stopped shouting, she had sat down with her head in her hands and started to sob. That was when Mary had stood up on shaky legs and made for the door. When Jason Hannard had found her and led her away.

The sound of the girl's wrenching sobs had haunted her, even when she was out of earshot.

Jason Hannard mixed a mean Gin Fizz. In fact, he had mixed them three or four apiece, taking what he needed from a little fridge in the corner of his elegant sitting room like a conjuror pulling rabbits from a hat.

He'd called for room service, ordering Mary some smoked salmon and scrambled eggs and cutting it up for her like a child, urging her to eat. Then when she did not, he'd fed her. Obediently, she'd opened her mouth but found she could not swallow the food. She remembered looking into his handsome face and wondering why he was doing this. Wondering if he was taking notes. Planning to turn what she'd told him into a plot for one of his TV dramas.

But she didn't care. It would have been impossible to go back to her room. She decided to stay if he'd let her. On any terms he wanted.

He was handsome, he was here and she needed to be held. And the night that should have been one of the worst of her life had turned into a voyage of discovery, a pleasure trip across the mountains, valleys and peaks of a body as unfamiliar as it was delicious.

Mary pulled the sheets up under her chin as she ran the events of last night back through her mind, stopping at the best bits time and again as if replaying a video recording.

She remembered how Jason had fed her, forking small portions of food into her mouth with the utmost care. She'd been a little drunk by this time and she'd sat quite still, gazing at him solemnly like a dutiful child as he placed the food between her lips. Her visit to the steam room had left her hair wet and plastered to her head. By the time she'd finished eating it had quite dried out and, getting up and reaching for one of Jason's hairbrushes, Mary had fluffed her hair till the golden curls bounced back to life.

Then she'd gone into the bathroom to wash her face. Catching sight of herself in the mirror over the handbasin, she'd seen that her eyes were sparkling.

I'm drunk, she'd thought to herself. I'm drunk and I don't care.

It wasn't Jason who'd made the first move. Walking back into his sitting room Mary had paused in the doorway for a moment and then, as if making a decision, she had let the bathrobe she was wearing slip from her shoulders and had walked across to him, naked.

Jason had sat looking at her, saying not a word. Then he'd reached up and gently taken hold of her wrists, pulling her down to him so that her face was level with his own.

'You're upset,' he'd said. 'Are you sure about this?' In reply, Mary had pressed her lips to his. He had tasted sweet and lemony and she thought of all the gin they'd been drinking. She felt him sigh, felt the pressure of his tongue as it stroked her own. Then, the thrilling wave of sensation as her nipples came alive beneath his touch. He was brushing them oh so gently as they puckered and stood to attention, the feel of his fingers alone making her whole body ache with longing.

Then, quite unexpectedly, he had leant forward and picked her up, lifting her naked body in his arms and carrying her through to his bedroom.

Mary had thought she would die of longing as she'd lain there on her back, watching him undress. Jason was very tanned and fit-looking, his broad chest with its sprinkling of golden hairs tapering to a narrow waist. He had neat, small buttocks she noticed. She'd watched him from all angles as he'd removed his clothes. Most of all, she'd watched his cock. It wasn't erect, not at first, and it dangled thick, floppy and dark pink against his thigh. But it was long and she knew that when it swelled, it would be big. Bigger even than Paul's.

'Are you sure about this?' he'd said again and Mary had held out her arms. At that moment she'd seen his penis begin to rise, twitching into life as he climbed onto the bed and straddled her, looking down into her eyes and stroking her hair.

She hadn't been able to help herself. She'd reached up and touched his cock and as if by magic it had twitched against her fingers, swelling and throbbing into life as Mary had wrapped her hand around it and stroked it against her palm.

She could feel his beautiful cock pulsing in her hand as Jason had begun to kiss her breasts, covering them in butterfly kisses as his mouth worked its way towards her eager nipples. Then he'd begun to lick, coating first one and then the other nipple in saliva, moving between the two and flicking each in turn with the tip of his tongue in rapid, light movements that drove Mary wild with desire.

His cock was huge now, bigger even than she'd expected it to be and releasing it from her grasp, she moved both hands around his back and down to his buttocks. 'They feel like velvet,' she'd thought to herself as she'd closed her eyes.

Mary spread her legs and pressed her fingers against his beautiful arse, urging him towards her opening, poised for the pleasure to come.

She knew she was very wet, her body open and welcoming, ready to embrace him as her fingers pressed into his buttocks. She felt the knob of him brush her clitoris ever so gently then slide just inside the entrance to her gaping passage.

She felt him push, then pull back and push again, each drive of his huge cock taking him a little deeper inside her body, each determined thrust coating him in her juices, smoothing his passage into her inner depths.

He was so big that even though she was wet, it took him a while to work his way inside her. With every push, his cock reached further into her, pressing against the inner walls of her cavern, stretching and filling her completely.

He'd begun to pinch her nipples, tweaking them hard between his fingertips, each pinch sending a spasm of pleasure darting into her belly. As he pinched she felt her body open wider as Jason penetrated deeper and she felt his cock advance on its journey to paradise.

With one final, thrilling thrust he was fully inside her. Then he'd begun to pump. She could feel the pressure of his cock in every part of her womanhood from the base of his thick shaft pulling against her pussy lips to the knob of him stretching along the length of her passage.

Mary had never known, never imagined that such rich and all-enveloping sensation could exist. This was more than sex. His body inside hers was all she knew. Nothing in the world existed outside the sound of his breathing and the feel of his cock as it thrust and drove her towards a deep and almost mystical climax.

She didn't want to come. She wanted to feel him inside her forever. The pleasure of his pumping thrilled her, causing a throbbing that spread throughout her body, right down to her fingertips.

As Jason twisted her nipples her body strained towards him, reaching up, crying out for her deepest-ever fuck to go deeper still.

The fierceness of her eventual orgasm had shaken and overwhelmed her, the animal-like cries that she uttered sounding strange and unreal.

Her pussy had thumped like a beating heart as wave upon wave of pleasure had pulsed through her, flooding her like a great heat as her body tightened around Jason's prick and he'd held her and stroked her hair as she thrashed and moaned.

Within seconds she felt him tense, his rapid pumping coinciding with the gentle descent of her pleasure onto a plateau which brought her back to being merely human, merely a woman lying in the arms of a lover who had shown her the joy she was capable of.

It was only when he'd slid out of her that she realised he'd been wearing a condom. She wondered when he had slipped it on. But she could remember nothing apart from her own satisfaction.

They'd slept then. When they'd woken he had taken her through to the bathroom and run her a bath, soaping her all over with his long fingers, washing away, once and for all, the shock if not the memory of her terrible experiences in the steam room with the strange, screaming woman called Alex.

As he'd washed her, she'd guided his fingers under the water till they were inside her. In a matter of hours Mary had lost all inhibition, and with her encouragement he masturbated her beneath the foam, sliding his fingers back and forth inside her slippery, exhausted body as she rubbed her own nipples and groaned in ecstasy.

He'd dried her and then they'd made love again. And again. And afterwards they'd slept and Mary had dreamt the sweetest and most peaceful of dreams.

Mary lay quite still in the early dawn and tried to feel guilty. But guilt wouldn't come any more than despair. She'd needed last night. She'd needed Jason Hannard's laughter and flattery and kindness more than anything in the world. She'd needed his tongue on her skin and his cock inside her like she needed the air that she breathed. Even her ribs felt bruised! He'd lain on top of her for hours, his long prick deep inside her.

He'd given a strange little gasp in the back of his throat every time he'd climaxed. She'd heard the sound many times last night. It was the loveliest, sexiest sound she'd known. A sound that banished the memory of the steam room and the girl's frantic sobbing.

With a sigh, she began to think about Paul. She stared at the ceiling, knowing that her life as she knew it was over. Somehow it must have been ordained that she'd stop off at this place. That her dread of returning to an empty house would lead her to Tingles Health Farm and the strange encounter with a woman who'd ripped her life apart.

Mary was grateful to her mother for telling her that she'd put on weight. Without her biting comments and the weariness that Mary had felt on leaving the old lady, 'feeling a bit better', the meeting with Alex might never have taken place. Mary might never have known. Never have realised what Paul was capable of.

Mary pictured Alex and Paul laying in a bed somewhere, fucking. The image was clear. Her mind was clear. She tried to feel hatred but it wouldn't come. Right now, Paul seemed a long, long way away.

Mary ran her fingers over her hips. She wasn't fat. Her figure was smooth and rounded and womanly. Jason Hannard had said so as his lips had brushed the curve of her hips, his mouth moving across the smooth bulge of her belly towards the little bush between her legs. She had opened her legs wide for him, welcoming him in, her clitoris swelling and hardening in response as his tongue tasted and savoured its tip and he began to lap the juices of her desire in slow, steady licks. He had reminded her of a kitten washing its fur. She had shuddered and sighed and she had come as he licked her, his beautiful hair softly brushing her belly as his mouth lit a fire between her legs.

Mary looked across and realised with a lurch in her stomach that she wanted him again, desperately. She also felt tears running down her face. Tears she wished would stop.

No one at Tingles knew very much about Miss Alex Chambers though she was a regular visitor, usually arriving for two or three nights at a time. From her luggage, her dress and her demeanour the staff had surmised that she was obviously quite wealthy. But they knew little more than that.

Alex's air of friendly detachment combined with her distinctive beauty only added to her mystery. Aloof and lovely, she would glide through the days at Tingles, enjoying every beauty treatment on offer but needing none.

All of which made it all the more odd to find her sitting alone in the steam room, her head in her hands, crying her eyes out. Gently and without asking questions, the girl who had gone in to look for abandoned towels had asked what was wrong. Receiving no reply, she had called her superior. A doctor was summoned. Alex was taken back to her room and sedated.

Rumour got around that she'd had bad news. Someone close had been killed and they said it was her brother. Her tears were understandable. They took her meals on trays though she ate nothing. She didn't want to talk so they left her alone.

Alex had sat by the phone for two days, trying to find the courage to ring Paul. There must be some explanation for what had happened in the steam bath. There must be some simple answer that would make everything better and the pain go away. Maybe this woman was an old girlfriend who still worked for him. Or an infatuated employee with a vivid imagination. You read about women like that in the papers. Obsessives who'd go to any lengths . . .

It was about three o'clock in the afternoon when the phone sprang shrilly into life, shattering the silence and rousing Alex from the uneasy slumber that had become the best way of passing time.

Reception said that there was a gentleman to see her but he didn't want to give his name. He wanted to surprise her.

Suddenly, Alex knew that everything was going to be all right. Paul must have somehow heard about the confrontation – the woman Mary must have phoned his offices, pestering him – and he'd come rushing here to explain, to show Alex that it was all a mistake, a bad dream.

Her voice shaking with excitement, she told reception to ask the man if he'd kindly wait a few minutes and then come along to room twenty-five. Her heart racing, she rushed to the bathroom to tidy herself, to apply make-up to the shadows beneath her eyes, to make herself look like nothing had affected her. For how could she admit to Paul that she'd ever doubted him?

She was zipping herself into her dress when there was a firm knock on the door. 'At last,' she said to herself, rushing to throw open her arms, to hold him tight, to tell him how much she loved him.

She'd tried to slam the door again as soon as she'd opened it, but Kurt was too quick for her. Clicking it shut behind him, he stood looking at her. 'Don't shut me out,' he said. 'Please Alex. I have driven all this way to see you. Please.'

'Go away, Kurt,' she had replied. 'I don't know how you found out where I was, but I want you to leave. You have no right . . .'

'You look pale,' he had replied. 'What have you been doing?'

In an unsteady voice, Alex had heard herself say that she wanted him to go. That her boyfriend was about to arrive at any moment and he must leave at once.

'We both know that's not going to happen, Alex,' he said to her quietly. How did he know? she wondered. How could he guess at her misery?

'Gina told me that you were here,' continued Kurt. 'She said that you had needed to get away. I understand.'

Should she run, should she scream? That would be best but Alex wanted to do neither. Gradually, as he stood patiently looking at her, Alex felt her misery subside. Kurt had followed her here to take his pleasure. He wanted her above all others. Paul didn't want her like this, didn't need her like this. She had to face what she knew already. That Mary had been telling the truth. And if Paul didn't love her, what did it matter? What did anything matter? A wave of misery swept over Alex and she realised that if Kurt left now, once again she'd be alone.

For just a few moments she'd been happy, thinking that the nightmare of the past couple of days was over. She'd been happy thinking that Paul was here to take her home. But he wasn't. There was no release from her pain. Better just to block it out. Fuck it out of her system. Lose herself in oblivion. She couldn't force Kurt to go. Not now. It was impossible. For then she'd be left with the silence she feared most of all.

Alex began to unzip the dress she'd done up so eagerly only moments before. It fell to the ground and she stood before Kurt, naked and gazing steadily into his eyes.

'This was meant to be, Alex,' he said. 'You know that, don't you?'

Alex nodded. Somehow his gaze had overwhelmed her and she'd had to look away, turning her eyes to the ground.

Kurt walked towards her and stood in front of her. She could feel his breath against her skin, his exhalations stroking her neck, caressing her shoulders. As his breath passed across her breasts, her soft nipples crinkled into two little buds of eagerness. Kurt continued to gaze at her. Alex raised her hands to take her nipples between her own fingers, stroking them between her fingertips while he watched. Without a word, she took his hand inside her own and placed it between her legs. Two of Kurt's fingers sank into her vulva and she closed her eyes and pictured them there. They were strong, capable fingers. She'd watched as they demonstrated how to hold a tennis racquet. Now they were stretching her ravenous pussy. Alex twisted her body in circles, pinching her tits harder as she swallowed his fingers deep inside her.

'Is that good?' he whispered, to which her only reply was a dreamy groan of pleasure. Alex leant forward to touch her lips against his neck. The faintest hint of aftershave clung to his warm skin as she nuzzled against him and she felt an arm around her waist, holding her close.

She felt faint. Nothing seemed real. Alex had left the room and was somewhere else, but her body was left behind and now she could feel Kurt's fingers moving between the cheeks of her buttocks, searching for the little hole of her arse, stroking it. She was so hot for him she thought she would melt. Nothing else on earth mattered but the here and now. The taste of his skin and the promise of his cock. The thick, hard cock she'd felt pressed against her in the car park. She'd wanted it so much she'd had to run away.

Taking her hands away from her tits, Alex reached down to the front of his pants. His fingers plunged deeper into her as she opened her eyes and began, slowly, to unzip him. His cock came out of his trousers as if spring-loaded. Alex watched as Kurt rolled a rubber along its length. It reminded her of herself, rolling stockings up her legs. Even the action of putting a rubber on looked sexy. Kurt stood before her, primed for action.

Alex took his cock in her hand and guided its huge knob towards her pulsating chasm. With one deep and savage thrust he was inside her.

Alex bit her lip, the pleasure of him more than she'd imagined even in her dreams. She could feel his cock, long and firm, pushing its way up and she bore down upon him, pressing her clitoris against the base of his thick shaft.

The pleasure of being filled by him ran through her like an electric current, coursing from her tingling clitoris and up into her slippery depths. She felt the head of his swollen member ramming against the door to her womb and she knew that with just a few more thrusts, she would come. Then she felt him slip out of her as quickly as he had entered.

Alex opened her eyes to see him standing opposite her. His cock was huge and fully erect and glistening with her juices. It belonged inside her. What was he doing?

'Now we will do it my way,' said Kurt, grabbing her roughly by the wrists.

Alex's dreamy, trance-like state evaporated as she felt his

fingers dig into her and she began to struggle.

'What are you doing?' she said, but his only reply was to grip her harder, his strong, tennis player's hands making all resistance futile.

'Kurt, please . . .' she pleaded, her voice a barely audible whisper. His blue eyes were expressionless as he smiled at her. 'Shut up, you stupid bitch,' he said. 'You wanted it rough and that's how you're going to get it.'

In sudden panic, Alex leant forward and bit his hand. Kurt yelled loudly and began to swear. For a second his grip was relaxed and, pulling her arm free, she ran towards the door. But he was too quick for her. As her fingers met the door handle she saw his hand close over her own and felt his other arm slide around her waist, lifting her from the ground.

Alex kicked and struggled. This was not what she wanted, not now. Or was it? She just didn't know any more. She didn't know anything.

Kurt carried her towards the bed, throwing her roughly on her back.

'Now you will keep still,' he said, his quiet voice filled with menace as he straddled her, pinning her with the weight of his body. His cock was pressed against her belly, his thighs gripping her so hard she thought he would crush her.

'So the bitch bites, does she?' he said in amusement. 'We'll see about that . . .'

Alex could not move as he pulled her hands roughly above her head. She was aware of him fixing one of her wrists tightly to the bedstead with what felt like a stocking. He held her other wrist in an iron grip. Where had the stocking come from? she wondered. Then she remembered that she'd left a pair on the chair by the bed. She'd been about to put them on when the knock came at the door. They were black, ten denier, just how Paul liked them. She'd been going to wear them for Paul.

'Women like you are for fucking, not for making love to,' she heard Kurt say in a matter of fact voice as he began to secure her other wrist. 'That is your purpose. You have no other use. I will fuck you in any way I choose and I will do with you as I please. Do you understand?'

Alex felt the tears choking her throat. 'Do you understand?' he repeated, looking down at her with her arms spread-eagled above her. She did not, could not reply.

Kurt looked at her and smiled and Alex felt her blood run cold. Then he leant forward and began to lick her left nipple. At the touch of his cruel mouth Alex began to struggle, trying to fight him off. He stopped what he was doing and looked up at her. 'Please . . .' she muttered and Kurt smiled again.

'It's no good,' he said. She saw his blond head go down again and she began to struggle even more determinedly but the more she struggled, the harder his mouth clung to her breast, the sharper his bites became.

A wave of heat engulfed her body and despite herself and against her will, Alex knew that she wanted him. The harder she fought him, the harder he bit and the more she ached to feel him inside her, knowing how savagely he would fuck her, how completely he would take control.

Suddenly, his mouth left her breast. Her nipple was throbbing and she longed to soothe it with her own fingers, but she could not. Hardly daring to look, she opened her eyes to see him standing at the bottom of the bed. He was watching her as, slowly, he removed his clothes. He took hold of her ankles and spread her legs wide apart, tying each of her ankles to the legs of the bed. His huge cock pointed towards her like an accusing finger of giant proportions.

'I asked you a question, Alex,' he said. 'I asked you if you understood what you are for. What you are here for, on this earth.'

'Yes, Kurt, I do,' she replied, her voice choking with emotion. 'I understand.'

Alex stared up at him as he stood at the end of the bed smiling at her. She could hear herself breathing and she concentrated on inhaling and exhaling steadily, trying to calm herself as she gazed at him. She was afraid of him, though her lust was stronger even than her fear. If he would fuck her once and make her come, she knew she would be his forever.

He was right. She was made for fucking. What other

purpose did she have? And Kurt wanted her. Really wanted her. She would do whatever he wished.

Alex dared herself to look at him. She had never seen such a perfect body. It was as though he was carved out of marble like a statue in a museum. His eyes were as cold as marble but she knew that his flesh was warm, his cock pulsing with life. And despite her fear, her body was longing for his, her need overcoming all doubt, all hesitation. She felt her pussy lips open like a flower at the thought, the juices of longing flooding the dark passage that longed to close around his demanding penis. But Kurt had other ideas.

Alex watched as he walked across to the chair on the corner on which he had thrown his trousers. They were cream linen with a dark brown leather belt at the waist. She watched as he slid the belt free of the loops that held it in place. She watched as he came slowly back to the bed, running the belt through his fingers and smiling.

Alex closed her eyes as she saw him raise the belt, bringing it down with a whip-like crack against the soft skin of her thigh. The shock knocked the breath out of her, the biting, burning strokes searing her flesh as blow rained down upon blow. Sweat broke out on her skin as she struggled to ride the tide of pain through which a hot and potent pleasure was fighting its way to the surface, a pleasure deeper and stronger than anything she'd known before, whipped into life by this man who knew her darkest secrets better than she knew herself. Her clitoris was thumping wildly as suddenly the blows stopped as quickly as they'd started.

'You were about to come,' he said. 'Weren't you, Alex?' She nodded, gazing up at him as the pain in her skin began to subside. Kurt stood over her, the belt still in his hand.

'You do well,' he said. 'You please me.'

'Thank you,' she heard herself say in a broken voice as he smiled his strange, bloodless smile.

Alex gasped as she felt the leather belt brush her belly. Was he about to beat her again? The rough underside of the belt glided across her, making all the tiny, fluffy hairs of her skin stand on end.

She closed her eyes trying to prepare herself for the pain

but instead, she felt the belt move down, sliding towards her gaping pussy.

She opened her eyes. Kurt was running the belt between her pussy lips, its rough dryness dragging across the wetness of her glistening clitoris, the uneven texture of the leather sending a torrent of rich sensation into the depths of her womanhood as he moved the belt backwards and forwards.

Alex opened her mouth and groaned as he trailed the full length of the belt against her softness, at the same time lowering his body towards her. She was panting as she gazed up at him, seeing the tip of his fully erect penis heading towards her open vulva.

As the knob of him brushed against her bruised opening, Alex felt her orgasm begin, driven further inside her with every thrust from his cock as he filled her, body and mind.

This was what she'd wanted and there was no point in denying it. This cruel, fair-haired boy was all she desired. All she deserved.

Chapter 7

Mary was trying very hard to control her excitement, but failing spectacularly. After coughing and fidgeting sufficiently to rouse Jason Hannard from his slumbers he had made love to her again, the soreness inside her overcome by the pleasure of taking him between her legs and up inside her tender pussy. Then they'd had breakfast – though Tingles' pleasant, wholesome fare had seemed somehow inappropriate.

We should be eating chocolate croissants and sipping champagne, Mary had thought to herself, gazing across at the handsome man who sat opposite her, picking at his bowl of fruit salad. As if reading her mind, Jason Hannard had got to his feet and walked across to the phone. She'd heard him say something about getting the car ready.

'Could you be dressed in half an hour?' he'd said to Mary as he finished his call.

'What's happening?' she'd replied, but Jason had just smiled.

Mary had gone back to her room, aching with fear and trepidation as she opened the door. The last time she had been in this room her world had been whole. Now it was in tatters. Or was it?

Why wouldn't the feelings come? Why didn't despair sweep over her, making her unable to move, crushing her will to survive? Why wasn't she on the phone, trying to contact Paul, frantic to know *why*?

Mary couldn't answer any of the questions with which she tortured herself. She stood under the shower, wondering if she really *was* in shock, but knowing she was not.

Last night had shown her how frustrated she really had become. How much of what she needed had been absent for so long. She was a woman who needed sex – good sex, regular sex – to make her feel alive. It was something she'd always known, if she was honest. But she'd suppressed her appetites. Denied her own needs to fit in with Paul, to fit in with the life he'd carved out for them both.

Mary had stood in the shower, lost in thought, soaping her body. The touch of her fingers across her breasts had brought her back to reality, sending a sharp stab of longing into the pit of her belly.

She soaped her fingers again, lathering the bubbles across her nipples. Though they were sore with being sucked, they hardened to her touch and Mary began to tease them beneath the tips of her fingers. She felt the familiar swelling and throbbing begin between her legs as her gentle pinches grew harder and she lifted her head and murmured his name. 'Jason,' she purred to herself as the water cascaded across her face. 'Jason . . . fuck me . . . please . . .'

Sliding one hand down her belly she parted her labia with her fingertips, stroking her clitoris with her index finger and bathing it in the juices of her own arousal. The slippery wetness of her womanhood was so different from the wetness of the water that ran over her face and she enjoyed the contrast. Mary stroked the bud of her clitoris with the very tip of her fingernail. The lightness of her touch against her bruised labia aroused her till the juices from within her ran free and she felt the heat of mounting orgasm spread through her, the frenzy of longing and shuddering release making her moan out Jason's name as her climax sent its shock waves of pleasure tingling through her tired body.

She didn't want to get dressed. She wanted to go back to Jason's room and fuck him again. Right now, that was all she wanted. More than food, more than the air that she breathed. But he'd said they were going out. Where to, she wondered?

The lingerie shop just off Bond Street was quite the most gorgeous place Mary had ever seen. Cooling fans whirred noiselessly overhead as she'd stepped through its heavy glass doors and into a world she'd only ever imagined.

A simply, yet immaculately dressed woman came towards

her across the acres of cream carpet asking if she might be of assistance. Mary said she was just looking. With a smile, the woman withdrew.

Mary hardly knew where to begin. Gossamer-fine teddies, lacy bras and wisps of suspender belts cried out to be fingered, touched, tried on. And outside, *he* was waiting, reading his newspaper in the back of the stretch limousine which had picked them up at Tingles and driven them the forty or so miles to London cocooned in an all-enveloping comfort so complete, so all-embracing, it had seemed to Mary that the houses, fields and offices that they passed were somehow unreal, part of a different, harsher world to which she no longer belonged.

Jason had told her he wanted to buy her something to wear. Then they'd have lunch and if she liked, they could visit a gallery or stay in town and see a show.

Mary didn't know what she wanted, apart from Jason Hannard. Why was he doing this? Did he feel sorry for her?

He'd handed her a wad of cash and told her to 'get whatever looked good' in the lingerie shop. He would come with her to buy a dress, but he thought that her underwear was best bought alone.

'I'd love to watch you try it on,' he'd said, smiling. 'But the paparazzi, you know.' She'd nodded, in awe.

The heavy curtain of the changing room had glided across behind her and Mary had been alone. The sexiest, most provocative underwear she'd ever seen was waiting to be tried, and she found her hands shaking as she lifted garment after delicate garment off its hangers.

Everything looked wonderful. She would wear it all for him. Cream silk, black lace, dove grey clouds of nothingness that showed off her curves to perfection. She would wear them all with the stiletto heels she intended to buy later in the day.

She imagined his mouth brushing against the top of the stocking she was now sliding up her leg. Her pussy began to grow moist at the thought of his lips against her skin. Oh, how she needed him to fuck her forever! And he was here. He was outside, sitting in the most beautiful car in the world, waiting patiently to drive her on to the next delight . . .

Paul was furious. Where the hell was Mary? By now, he'd expected her back from visiting her mother. But it seemed she'd disappeared off the face of the earth. What's more, it was the end of the financial year and one of the busiest times for the business. She knew that. But she was nowhere to be found.

After putting it off as long as possible, Paul had phoned her mother. Once he'd dutifully asked if the old bird was feeling better, he had asked to speak to Mary.

'She's not here,' he had been told. 'She left three days ago.' Paul had then asked if Mary had mentioned where she was going. The old lady had replied that as far as she knew, Mary was heading back to Manchester. 'But who knows?' she had continued. 'She might have decided to make a detour. After all, I'm sure she knew *you* wouldn't be waiting for her.'

Paul had felt the annoyance building in him as he listened to the old bitch. Her voice, as ever, was full of reproach.

What was Mary playing at? He needed her back at base. She was well aware how much there was to be done.

'If she calls, would you tell her I'm anxious about her? Worried that she's okay?' Paul had continued.

'Of course,' Mary's mother had replied. 'If I speak to her I'll pass the message on.' Paul knew she was lying as they hung up.

That was three days ago. Where was she? If Mary didn't show up soon, he'd have to hire a book-keeper.

Paul felt very aggrieved, sitting alone in the flat. Mary had disappeared and so, apparently, had Alex. Driving back from Manchester early, he'd expected to find Alex waiting for him. But now it seemed even Alex had gone walkabout. According to Gina whom he'd met in the corridor, Alex had gone off to her health farm. Paul supposed he shouldn't mind. After all, she wasn't expecting him home so soon. In fact, once he'd got used to the idea it seemed like a bonus to be alone. He could work from the flat for a few days, undisturbed. He'd even be able to phone Mary without being overheard by Alex. He'd had it all planned, all set up.

All he needed was to contact Mary in order to get things organised. But now this.

At first, he'd forgiven Mary when she hadn't shown up. After all, her mother had probably driven her crazy and if she needed a night away, then fine. But she'd been gone all this time! If this was some kind of stupid protest she was making, he thought, what the hell was he supposed to have done?

The restaurant had pink linen tablecloths and huge, tulip-shaped glasses into which a waiter was pouring chilled Chardonnay. Mary's menu had no prices on it. It was printed with the day's date, April 25th.

I'll remember this day, this time, this lunch for the rest of my life, she'd thought to herself. I'll remember it when I'm old and all my juices have dried up. But that was a long way off yet, she thought, smiling to herself. Just sitting opposite her lover, simply breathing the same air as he did made her wet and slippery. She looked across at Jason and thought how happy she felt. A fragile, temporary happiness that was all the more precious for being so.

A waiter stood at her shoulder. 'Avocado mousse and Dover Sole to follow,' she said to the waiter. Jason Hannard squeezed her hand. For a moment last night, he'd felt guilty. When first she'd lain in his arms, clinging to him, her orgasm wracking her body, he'd felt that maybe he was taking advantage of her. After all, she must be deeply unhappy.

But then she'd grown playful and bold – demanding, even – and the sheer joy she'd shown in their coupling had convinced him that he'd done nothing wrong. This pretty girl had sucked him inside her greedily. His cock had lost itself to her charms and much to his surprise, his heart had soon followed. And now she was about to enjoy her lunch with as much relish as she appeared to enjoy everything.

'I expect you're tired after all that shopping.' He smiled at her in amusement. Mary pictured the back of the car which by now was full of bags of the most expensive kind. Thick, glossy carrier bags with silk handles. Everything swathed in tissue paper. She pictured unwrapping her presents back at the health farm, shedding tissue all over the floor.

She'd longed to ask Jason why he was doing this. Why he had decided to make her so happy. Women fell at his feet. He could take his pick. So why her? she wondered. Instead, she simply smiled and squeezed his hand in return.

Jason Hannard had enjoyed his morning every bit as much as Mary. Of all the women he could so easily seduce, she was the only one for a long time who'd excited more than his lust.

She'd come to his arms last night willingly and openly, wanting nothing more than to be loved.

As he'd held her and touched her, he'd discovered an innocence he'd forgotten could ever exist. There'd been no performance, no attempt to impress him with her sexual skills, her repertoire of tricks. The hunger in her was fierce and exciting. Most of all, she'd been in bed with *him*, not Jason Hannard – superstar.

Mary had had only one lover in her life, she'd told him so without embarrassment. He'd felt privileged to touch her smooth skin, her soft golden hair. Her arse was like a smooth and rounded peach. He'd longed to bite it.

Jason had felt himself wanting to protect her, to wrap her in his arms and keep her safe. He knew what it was like to be exploited and deceived. Just being an actor taught you that. Some women deserved it. This girl did not. The tale she'd told him when he'd found her hunched and shaking outside the steam room was shocking, even by Jason's standards. But now she was okay. And she was eating her lunch with as much real pleasure as she'd shown throughout the entire morning. He was tired of women who picked at food. Whose every gesture and pose was painstakingly polished. Mary was something different and he loved her for it. He'd take her back to the health farm and dress her up and fuck her again. He had to leave quite soon, but he'd spend the time he had remaining locked in her arms and buried in her body. Beautiful tits and a tight little pussy. Jason Hannard felt his cock give a lurch. *The man she lived with must be mad,* he thought to himself as he drained his glass and called for the bill.

Mary didn't know how she'd make it back to the health

farm with her parcels intact. Like a child waiting impatiently for Christmas morning, she'd begun to poke and prod the bags as soon as they got back in the car, as soon as they drove off.

Jason Hannard had suggested putting her shopping in the boot but she'd have none of it. So many beautiful things, she hadn't wanted to let them out of her sight.

'Please,' she said, 'let me just show you the lingerie I bought.' Jason had smiled benignly and nodded, amused by how easy it was to make her smile.

Mary reached delightedly for the glossy black carrier with its silver lettering, delving into its depths and fishing out a pair of exquisite black silk French knickers and a suspender belt.

'They look very good on me,' she whispered naughtily into Jason's ear. Her blonde curls brushed his skin as she turned her head. He felt his prick begin to swell uncontrollably.

'Put them on,' he said. Mary looked at him, startled.

'I can't,' she whispered. 'Not in here . . .' She turned to look at the back of the chauffeur's head. His eyes were on the road, his mind on the journey.

Jason Hannard leant forward, pulling down a blind which covered the window separating the driver from the back of the car.

'But he'll *hear* us,' Mary had protested, a flush spreading across her cheeks, a smile playing about her lips.

Jason Hannard took her hand in his own and placed it against the front of his trousers. He was rock hard. Mary sighed and shrugged in mock resignation. She began to unfasten the front of her dress.

'Close your eyes,' she said quietly, 'and only open them when I tell you I'm ready.' Jason Hannard began to unzip his fly, fingering his swollen cock as he settled back against the leather seat, his eyes tightly shut as he listened to the rustling and shuffling which indicated that something rather delicious was happening.

'Don't open your eyes,' Mary whispered and then, 'Oh, no . . . we've stopped at a traffic light. I'm half undressed. People will look in.'

Jason Hannard smiled at her discomfort. 'You forget,' he said, 'the windows are tinted. No one can see you. Except me.'

'Don't look, don't LOOK!' she pleaded with him. Jason felt his cock swell in his hand. 'I'm nearly ready,' she said. 'Just a few seconds more.' Then, suddenly, 'You can open your eyes.'

In all his years of filming, screwing around and generally living the life of an urbane and sophisticated man of the world, Jason Hannard had never seen anything so lovely as the sight of Mary, sitting on the floor of the stretch limousine dressed in black silk.

Gift-wrapped and gorgeous, her eyes were sparkling and her breathing heavy and he could tell that she was as turned on by the outfit she was wearing as he was.

Her lips were slightly parted and her eyes were shining and she sat with her legs stretched out in front of her, her ankles touching, her knees kept coyly together. The palms of her hands were resting on the soft beige carpet which covered the floor of the car and she was smiling at him, her eyes dreamy and full of desire.

Jason moved forward and knelt beside her. He could feel the vibrations of the car's engine as he reached out and touched the lace which trimmed her French knickers, his fingers following the contours of the pattern, touching silk and then the flesh beneath, according to the curls and whorls of the lace trim.

He could smell the sweet fragrance of her warm pussy. He leant closer to her, resting his cheek in her lap as he nuzzled his face against her rounded belly, drinking in her scent and the warmth of her body.

He sat up. 'Take your knickers off,' he said. 'Please.' Mary smiled and manoeuvred her body, leaning on the palm of one hand and pulling the wisp of silk down over her stockinged legs with the other. She threw the panties onto the seat at the back of the car. Now he could see her suspenders, black against the creaminess of her warm skin, framing the tops of her thighs and the triangle of golden curls which nestled between her black-stockinged legs.

Leaning back on his knees and steadying himself against the movement of the car, Jason spoke again. 'Spread your legs,' he said. 'I want to see you.'

Mary reached across for his hand and took it within her own. Closing her eyes, she kissed the back of his hand in a gesture of total obedience and humility. He looked at her. Soft and blonde and lovely.

Jason moved back and rested on his haunches as she opened her eyes and smiled at him, bringing her knees up until they touched her body. Holding his gaze unfalteringly, she spread her legs, moving her feet apart so that he could see her, so that he could see inside her pussy, pink and fragrant like the inner petals of a rose.

He eased his trousers down over his hips, discarding them on the back seat of the limousine where they lay covering the French knickers that had landed there moments before.

With the speed and fluency that comes with practice, he rolled a condom the length of his prick and positioned himself opposite Mary, a smile playing about his lips.

Bringing his legs beneath the bend of her knees, he sat opposite her, his hard and eager penis just centimetres away from the wet warmth of her parted bush. The scent of her pussy came up at him in waves, each whiff of her sending a rod of steel through a cock which was already throbbing with intent.

Jason sat quite still. As the car moved gently it gave an occasional lurch and every now and again the brakes were applied, slowing the huge limousine as it took a bend or the driver changed gear.

Jason leant on his hands, allowing the movement of the car to dictate every lurch of his body. His prick was tantalisingly close to the opening of Mary's vagina. So near, yet so far. So good to delay the moment.

The car slowed. It jolted him forward and the knob of his prick brushed against Mary's open bush. He felt her shudder as his penis bathed its head in the pool of slipperiness into which he longed to plunge. But Jason sat quite still. Mary was breathing heavily. Then the car took a bend and he felt the head of his penis sliding along the inner lips of her labia, meeting the crinkly, moist flesh, sending his nerve ends into overdrive and sending the most exquisite sensations coursing through his prick and down to his throbbing balls.

They hit a straight bit of road. The gentle rhythm of the car rocked him backwards and forwards, dipping the head of his penis just inside the opening of her dripping passage, only to pull him back again as the movement of the car dictated the rhythm of his tentative explorations.

He looked at Mary. He could see that she was as excited as he was. He smiled at her and she lifted her hands towards him, sliding her two index fingers between his lips. He sucked them and she pulled them out of his mouth, reaching into her black lace bra and spreading the slick saliva across her hard pink nipples, squeezing and rubbing her tits in a swoon of ecstasy and delicious frustration.

Suddenly the car braked sharply and Jason felt himself tipped forward, his prick sinking into Mary's soft body with one smooth glide. This time he couldn't pull back. He was deep inside her and they were both about to come, sitting on the floor of the limousine, locked together.

Jason straightened his legs beneath her and she tipped forward, spreading her body on top of his as he lay on his back.

He felt the softness of her pussy lips pressed against his groin as her vagina tightened around him and she began to slide up and down his prick, pushing him further inside her with each panting thrust as he felt the throbbing in her intensify. His cock touched the gaping mouth of her womb and he drove harder, his fingers reaching up to pinch her nipples through the lace of her delicate black bra.

'Fuck me, Jason,' she breathed into his ear. 'Fuck me hard, fuck me deep, fill me and fuck me . . . I want you . . . I want you . . .'

He loved to hear her talk dirty. There was something so pure, almost virginal about her that hearing her beg for it turned him on.

'What do you want?' he teased her.

'I want you to fuck me deep in my pussy. Please . . .' she panted, her voice coming in gasps. Her body came down on him again, her pussy tighter than before . . . or was it that his cock had grown even bigger? As she pushed harder still, engulfing him with her gloriously greedy body, Jason felt himself pushed to the edge of orgasm.

His cock began to tense, jerking and driving deep inside a body which seemed to be sucking him in with every movement, drawing him towards the exquisite moment of release which had been so deliciously delayed.

He felt the spasm begin inside her as the cry escaped from her parted lips. As she came, she rubbed her face against his cheek, grasping his earlobe softly between her teeth and sighing into his ear.

Jason licked the sweat from between her breasts as Mary gave one final shudder. A moan of such complete satisfaction broke from her lips that he reached up and stroked her cheek, looking into shining blue eyes that were awash with tenderness.

'Beautiful girl,' he said as with a sudden burst of rapid pumping, he came with a muffled groan. They lay together, exhausted, locked in each other's bodies as the limousine glided along country roads. Jason could smell the sweet smell of grass filtering in through the window as he felt his penis grow limp and begin to slide out of Mary's satisfied body.

The chauffeur coughed discreetly and announced that they were nearly home as the limousine began its stately progress along Tingles' meandering drive. As the car ground to a halt, Jason was zipping himself into his pants. Mary smiled at him as he reached across and kissed her hand. He'd really miss this girl, he thought, much to his surprise.

Chapter 8

Alex had heard that a spell in a flotation tank was one of the most effective ways of relieving stress. In the last two days she'd tried crying, getting blind drunk and walking around the grounds of Tingles for hours at a time. But nothing had worked. Surely the tank must have some effect?

Kurt had stayed with her for a day and a night and then he'd left as quickly as he'd arrived. He felt confident that within a matter of days she'd turn up at the tennis club. But right now, he had things to do.

'I understand,' she'd replied meekly when he'd told her. She'd watched him walk towards his car. He hadn't even turned his head as he'd driven away, though it had been all she could do not to run after him, to beg him to stay.

She knew she should leave Tingles. Go back to London. Sort things out. But that woman Mary was still here. Alex had seen her. Could she go without talking to her, without knowing more?

Maybe it had all been just a bad dream. Maybe the woman would tell her she'd imagined everything. Maybe, she thought, the flotation tank might ease the burning in her brain.

Alex lay in five inches of saline solution kept at blood temperature. The door of the tank was shut and she was floating in total darkness, her head supported on a small inflatable cushion. She couldn't feel her limbs. She couldn't see a thing. Weightlessness, warmth and total absence of all external stimulation. Yet her mind continued to race and rest would not come. What was she to do?

She felt she'd like to lie in the tank forever. Though the calm and peace she ached for eluded her, at least it was dark. At least, here, she could avoid the stares of Tingles staff, the sympathetic enquiries as to how she was feeling. They'd all thought her boyfriend had come to take her away. They'd all felt relieved. But he had gone and she was still here – and now she felt awkward on top of everything else.

With a sigh, Alex sat up and opened the door of the tank. She climbed out and reached for a towelling robe, blinking in the daylight.

The beauty therapist whose duty it was to sit outside the door when clients were entombed in the tank, was amazed. 'Miss Chambers,' she said, 'your session isn't even half over.'

'I'm sorry,' said Alex, 'I just couldn't stand it.'

Mary had returned to her room and was hanging up her new clothes when there was a gentle knock on the door. Laying the black linen Paul Costelloe jacket she had just unwrapped carefully on the bed, she walked across to open it, humming softly to herself. The woman from the steam bath stood there, her hair wet and plastered to her head. Mary felt her stomach lurch.

'I've come from the flotation tank,' she said, irrelevantly. She wasn't shouting. She wasn't worked up. She didn't look as though she would lash out again. She just looked awful.

'You'd better come in,' Mary replied.

Sitting on the edge of Mary's bed, surrounded by acres of tissue paper and carrier bags, Alex said nothing. Then, as if emerging from a trance, she looked around her.

'You've been shopping,' she said. 'I like to go shopping.' And then, much to Mary's discomfort, Alex began to cry.

Tears poured down her face and she sobbed uncontrollably as if her heart would break. 'I'm sorry,' she said. 'I'm sorry I hit you. I feel so embarrassed but it was all such a shock. Such a terrible . . . shock.'

Before she knew what she was doing, Mary found herself on her knees beside the girl, holding her hand and muttering, 'come on . . . it's all right,' as if to a child.

'This is bizarre,' she thought to herself. 'This whole business is crazy.' Alex reached for one of the pieces of tissue paper that lay strewn around, and blew her nose on it.

'Hey,' said Mary, 'I've just had a very expensive jacket

wrapped in that.' Through tear-stained eyes, Alex looked at Mary crouching beside her and smiled.

'A fine mess we've got ourselves into,' said Alex, trying to lighten the atmosphere and at the same time, control her sobs. Mary ignored Alex's pathetic attempt at levity. 'Not us,' said Mary quietly. 'It's Paul who's got us into a mess.'

'But what are we going to do?' asked Alex hopelessly. 'After what happened I wanted just to leave here, never to see you again, but I *had* to speak to you. To tell you, ask you . . . oh, I don't know . . .'

Mary looked at Alex. Yes, she was quite lovely even with wet, straggly hair and swollen eyes. She could understand what Paul had seen in her. But why had she come to Mary's room, asking advice? What made her think that Mary had any more answers than she did?

'Do you work?' Mary said suddenly and unexpectedly to Alex, getting to her feet and walking around the room.

'I did,' she replied, 'when Paul first met me, but I gave it up. I wasn't much good.'

'So what do you do now?' asked Mary. There was a pause.

'Oh, I don't know,' Alex replied miserably. 'I play tennis. I go out for lunch. I wait for Paul to come home.'

Mary looked at the girl and despite everything, she felt sorry for her. So the beautiful, apparently confident creature she'd first set eyes on three days ago was a woman who spent her time eating out and staying in, waiting for Paul.

Mary knew how all-consuming Paul could be, how much attention he demanded. And it was this girl's job to give it to him, in return for which he kept her in flashy clothes. Poor cow.

'Are you going back to him?' Mary asked.

'I don't know,' Alex replied.

'No,' said Mary. 'Of course not.'

She'd been pacing the room uncomfortably. Now she stopped.

'If you don't go back, where will you go?' Her words had a profound effect on Alex, who appeared to crumble beneath the weight of the question.

'I've no idea,' she replied quietly. 'I have nowhere to go.'

Mary looked at Alex, damp and dishevelled. For the first time she saw the full depth of her despair.

'Then don't leave,' Mary heard herself say. 'Why should you just walk out? Stay there . . . if you can face it. Stay there and think things through.' The women looked at each other. Alex wiped her eyes and sniffed. 'Your flat . . . is it comfortable?' Mary continued.

'It's Paul's flat,' Alex replied. 'And yes . . . it's beautiful. But it's not mine. It was all there . . . before I was. Long before.' The words stung Mary as if Alex had hit her again.

Paul's flat. So he'd had it all set up before this girl had even come on the scene. How many other women had there been before Alex, Mary wondered. He had it all worked out, all neatly arranged. Paul's flat. The bastard.

'Listen to me,' Mary said, kneeling once again beside Alex. 'Go back to Paul's beautifully furnished flat and stay there. And don't say a word to him, do you understand? I'm not sure what we're going to do but neither of us is going to leave as things are. It's just not right. Not right at all.'

She looked at Alex who appeared to be miles away.

'Alex . . . are you listening?' she said. It was the first time Mary had used her name. Alex looked startled, her big green eyes opening wide.

'Neither of us is going to quit just because of what's happened.'

Alex nodded, looking nervous. 'Whatever you say,' she murmured. 'Whatever you think is best.' She paused. 'Do you still love him?' Alex whispered, her voice cracking.

'I'm not sure,' said Mary truthfully, 'but right now, that doesn't matter at all.'

Jason Hannard was to star in a new series of *Heartbreak Hospital* which was scheduled for transmission in November. Filming would start in a week's time, before which he had a whole series of meetings to get through.

There was lunch with his agent, an interminable chat with the series' producer, wardrobe fittings and who knew what else. In addition, he had two daytime chat show appearances lined up, designed to whet the appetites of adoring housewives everywhere.

Playtime was over. Jason was going back to work. 'All good things,' he thought, 'must come to an end.'

He was sad to be leaving Mary. He'd even thought of asking her to be his regular date, of going public about their relationship. But the thought of all those women out there waiting for him, all those opportunities he would miss, had won the day. Besides, it would be a lousy career move. Jason had worked too hard to see his popularity plummet because he wanted something as trivial as a private life.

He'd tried asking Mary what she was going to do about the lousy situation with her boyfriend. She'd told him she really didn't know and that he wasn't to worry.

'I'll be watching *Heartbreak Hospital* in the autumn. I won't miss an episode.' The idea had made him inexplicably happy and he'd held her close.

Jason knew that for the first time in a long time, he'd been in love. Mary had made him lower his defences, if only a little, and he'd relished every moment. He'd enjoyed buying her clothes, enjoyed the light in her eyes when he'd shown her so many beautiful things and told her she could have what she wanted. Her boyfriend was rich, that much was obvious. It was also obvious that he was mean to her, or the little expedition to Bond Street that Jason had organised would not have thrilled her so.

She'd loved all the silly, frilly things he'd picked out for her and he was glad. She'd worn them all for him, posing with all the relish of a child showing off her dance steps. Mary was innocent, lovely . . . yet at the same time, with a cool-headedness that was more than mere affectation. A strange, complex girl, Jason felt sure she would survive the situation with her boyfriend. He hoped she wouldn't be damaged in the process.

He was leaving in the morning and he'd told her so. There'd been no fuss and no scene. She'd simply put her head on his shoulder and whispered, 'I'll miss you.' Then she'd disappeared to her room, knowing he had things to organise.

He had planned a farewell supper and asked her to come to his suite at seven. It was now a quarter to, and the cold supper that Tingles' chefs had prepared specially was carefully laid out in his fridge. Chicken in aspic, salmon mousse, six types of salad . . . he'd serve it himself. He'd feed her again like he did on the night she first came to him.

Mary tapped quietly on his door at exactly seven o'clock. There was no pretence with this woman, Jason thought. No being late to make an impression, no silly games.

She was wearing a simple shift in pale blue silk which matched her eyes exactly. Her blonde hair fell about her face in fat, ripe curls and her cheeks were flushed.

'Sit down,' he said. 'Would you like a drink?' But Mary simply stood in the middle of the carpet, smiling a dreamy smile.

'What is it?' said Jason, looking at her closely. He'd never seen her look so beautiful and he felt his resolve falter at the thought of giving her up.

'I don't want to sit down,' she said. 'I don't want anything but you.'

Mary raised her hands and reached for the zip at the back of her dress. It fell to the floor with a swishing sound and she stepped out of it, standing before him in dove-grey lace, her breasts rising and falling, sending waves of perfume carried to him on the warmth that emanated from her skin.

Mesmerised, Jason watched as Mary walked across to his bed. She sat down, bringing her knees up in front of her with the soles of her feet flat against the bedspread. 'Look,' she said, a wicked grin on her face as she spread her legs, crossing her feet in the lotus position so that her pussy was open wide.

'Straight down to business,' he thought, his excitement mounting.

By now he was sitting at the foot of the bed, just inches from the beautiful creature who was pleasuring herself for his delight and her own.

As her fingers moved across to stroke one nipple he saw its tip transform, as if by magic, from a fat and generous bloom into a hard little bud, tightening beneath her touch.

Jason could feel his cock straining inside his trousers as he watched her pinch her tit, the fingers of her other hand now trailing lazily between the open lips of her womanhood, spreading the slippery film which had begun to flow from deep inside as excitement gripped her in waves of ever deeper longing.

Jason reached for the front of his pants and released his prick. Oh, that felt better! He began to stroke and squeeze its swollen shaft as he gazed at her. Mary was now rocking backwards and forwards on her fingers, paddling them inside the folds of her pussy, still tantalisingly hidden from his view behind the fine lace of her French knickers. He got up and moved towards her, kneeling before her on the floor.

He could feel the heat from her and smell the fresh ripeness of her womanhood, the scent of her own arousal throbbing through his senses, hardening his prick as he came close to her. With the utmost gentleness, Jason took hold of Mary's hand, pulling it away from her body. He held her wet fingers to his face, breathing in the smell of her as he kissed her palm.

'Lay on your back,' he whispered. Mary smiled and moved further up the bed.

He climbed onto the bed beside her and looked down. One of her beautiful breasts was still encased in her lace brassiere while the other poked its little pink nipple over the top of the bra cup. It looked like it was peeping out, winking at him, and Jason leant over it, squeezing the nipple between his lips, feeling it harden as he circled it with his tongue.

Mary made a soft purring sound and squirmed beneath his touch. He lifted his head and looked into her eyes.

'I want you so much,' she murmured. 'So very, very much.' Jason brought his face down to her belly, stroking his cheek against her warm skin. With the tip of his tongue he dipped into the well of her navel, pulling her French knickers over her hips as he did so. He moved his mouth outwards, nibbling her hip bones as Mary gave a moan of pleasure and spread her legs, urging him with every gesture of her body to enter her, to quench the longing.

He moved his mouth down, down towards the curly bush

between her legs, covered by its wisp of dove-grey lace. He could see the wet stain of her arousal at the crotch of her French knickers, turning the pale grey lace to a darker hue.

Jason curled his tongue and, pulling the sticky wisp of silk to one side, slid its tip into the opening of her pussy. She was so wet! Jason dipped his tongue into the pool of her then pulled back. He spread a trail of her juices across the inner folds of her labia, feeling her shudder with every tiny movement of his tongue against the most sensitive parts of her body. She thrust her hips towards him.

Easing her panties down her legs he slid them over her feet and dropped them on the floor. Then he reached up and unhooked her bra, releasing her breasts into the warm evening air.

He got up and walked to where the Tingles staff had left the buffet he had ordered earlier. He picked up a bottle of walnut oil intended for their salad dressing and walked back towards the bed.

Mary smiled as he unscrewed the cap and poured a trail of oil from between her breasts down to her navel, leaving a little pool. The oil glistened and slowly, Jason began to spread it with his fingertips.

Her nipples slipped and slid beneath his touch, feeling rubbery as the oil coated them, bouncing beneath his fingers as he stroked and pinched them into the hardest of pink pebbles. He spread the oil across her chest, down her belly and onto her golden pubic curls, coating them, making them shiny and springy.

Jason parted the thick, fleshy cushions of her pussy lips and looked inside. Her clitoris was deep red and glistening with the juices of her arousal. He leant forward and touched it with his tongue, hearing her sigh and beg for relief as she spread her legs wider apart.

His penis aching as if it would burst, Jason buried his face deep inside her hairy mound, drowning in the smell and softness of her as he began to nibble and suck, pressing her folds against the pubic bone beneath, sending her into a frenzy of need.

Mary began to moan his name. With one deft movement

he dressed his pulsing prick in the little rubber evening jacket that stood on the bedside table. Just in time.

He felt her nails digging into the back of his head and heard her animal-like cries and suddenly his face had left her open legs and his mouth was covering her own, she was on her back and his cock was probing for her opening as she spread herself in welcome.

Sliding and skating around the hairy entrance to her chasm, at last the knob of his prick found its way and with one firm thrust, Jason was inside her.

Mary's legs wrapped themselves around his back and her pelvis tilted upwards. Jason moved his hands under Mary's arse and lifted her further off the bed so that his plunges into her demanding pussy were long and deep.

She was the best fuck he'd had in years and what's more, he really liked her. What a shame he had to leave. But not yet. The night ahead was going to be a long one.

Chapter 9

Alex parked her car in the underground car park and switched off the engine. For a moment she sat quite still, wondering whether or not to turn the key in the lock once again, swing the car around and drive out into the daylight.

Would it be the simplest solution to the confusion that she felt or simply the coward's way out? And where would she go if she did decide to make her break for freedom? An anonymous rented flat somewhere. And then what?

Mary had told her to stay put. To return to the flat and to stay there. Maybe it would be easier to do as she was told, if only for the time being. With a sigh, Alex got out of the driver's seat and locked the car. She'd leave her bags for now and come back for them later.

Alex let herself into the flat. The kitchen smelt of freshly ground coffee and the kettle was still warm. Alex knew that she could only have missed Paul by half an hour. An hour at the most. During the last couple of days she'd phoned the flat at times when she felt sure he wouldn't be there, leaving falsely cheerful answerphone messages saying how much she was enjoying herself and that she hoped he'd ring her back.

Once, in the middle of the morning, he'd answered the phone. She was horrified to find that he'd actually been at home and with thumping heart, she'd hung up straight away.

He'd left messages for her at the health farm, with precise times for her to call him back in order to reach him. She'd have to tell him that the messages hadn't been passed on. That the fact she'd failed to catch him on all the occasions she'd rung home had been nothing more than an unfortunate coincidence.

The flat looked much the same as always. Somehow, if it

had been reduced to rubble or consumed by flames, Alex could have coped. But the sense of orderliness was almost unbearable, making a mockery of her confusion and pain.

She walked into the kitchen. Paul had loaded his breakfast things neatly into the dishwasher. The smell of coffee was strongest in here and she thought she would be physically sick. She wandered aimlessly into the bathroom. She could smell his aftershave and an even worse wave of nausea threatened to engulf her.

She could smell him, she could feel him . . . and his almost tangible presence made her weak with misery. 'What can I say to him?' she wondered, flopping dejectedly onto the sofa. 'How can I pretend that everything is the same?'

The phone rang. With sinking heart, Alex got to her feet and walked across to the coffee table.

'Hello?' she said in a small voice.

'It's Mary,' said the voice at the other end.

Alex was glad she'd given this woman her phone number even though by doing so it proved to her that the whole world had gone crazy. It must have done. Because right now, the person who should have been her worst enemy was the one she needed to talk to most of all.

'Are you all right?' said Mary.

'No,' Alex replied. 'I feel sick.'

'You looked rough before you left,' said Mary. Then after a pause, 'Is Paul there?'

'No,' said Alex.

There was another pause, this one more awkward than the last.

'I think you need to get some sleep,' said Mary. 'It will make you feel better. It really will.'

'I suppose so,' said Alex. 'There's nothing else to do.'

'Well, sleep, then,' said Mary. 'And remember what I told you.'

'Yes, I will. Thank you,' Alex said, replacing the receiver.

She dreamt she was being fucked from behind and she could feel her body being lifted from the bed. There were fingers, strange yet familiar fingers pinching her clitoris and a cock was sunk into her, pumping furiously. It was a dream of pain and pleasure and all of a sudden Alex opened her eyes to find it wasn't a dream at all.

'I've missed you, baby,' she heard Paul say. 'Why didn't you answer my calls?'

'I tried to call you,' she said, but she knew he wasn't listening.

She was lying on her stomach and he was on top of her, his cock immersed in her vagina. She felt the rhythm of his plunges dragging her body backwards and forwards so that her nipples rubbed against the sheet beneath as he rammed his prick between her legs.

She'd always loved it when he fucked her like this, using her body as nothing more than an object of gratification. She had been sleeping on her stomach, sleeping deeply. He must simply have walked into the bedroom and seen her there, lying naked on top of the duvet, her legs apart.

The thought of being taken in her sleep turned her on, the urgent demands of Paul at his horniest banishing all other thoughts from her mind. She felt him twist her clitoris between his fingers and she rammed her body against his own in greedy response.

'Tie me up,' she whispered to him. 'Tie me up. Please.'

Paul slid out of her and she lay quite still, her eyes once again tightly shut. She wanted him. Despite everything, she wanted to feel him inside her. But she wanted to be fucked, not taken lovingly. Making love with Paul was more than she could bear.

'I left you messages,' he said, 'at the health farm.'

Paul came back to the bed. She felt him lift one wrist and then the other, tying them to the bedstead. He was using one of her silk scarves to secure her and he tied her very tight, making any kind of movement virtually impossible.

'Where are you going?' she said as once again he slid off the bed.

Paul's reply was to take hold of her ankles, binding them together as tightly as he'd fixed her hands. What was he thinking of? He never tied her legs like this. Usually, he spread them apart so he could see as well as feel what he was doing.

'I have a treat for you,' she heard him say. 'I think you'll enjoy it. Just relax, Alex. Relax . . .'

Paul began to stroke her arse. Slow, gentle strokes that followed the contours of her shape, soothing the nerve endings in her skin as his fingers caressed her body.

'I missed you, baby,' he said. 'Oh, so much . . .'

Suddenly she felt a soft and delightful sensation moving slowly down her back, travelling the length of her vertebrae and coming to rest in the little hollow at the base of her spine. The feeling was exquisite. Alex closed her eyes as she felt this tantalising sensation move in circles. She felt like a kitten arching its tail when it's stroked.

'It's a feather,' whispered Paul. 'The pleasure before . . .'

Alex didn't listen to what he was saying and she didn't care. The tendrils of the feather's quill had mesmerised her and she could think about nothing but the touch of its quivering tip as it brushed her skin, sending shivers of sensation which coursed their way through her body in tides of deliciousness.

She was completely relaxed, which was why the sudden sharp smacks which rained down on her arse from Paul's outstretched hand came as such a shock, waking her abruptly, stopping the breath in her throat.

'Paul, no!' she cried but he didn't hear her, lost as he was to all but the pleasure of seeing her rounded and quivering arse turn from pink to red as he struck it, time and again, with his flattened hand.

Paul knew that the more he beat her, the more aroused Alex would become. And so would he. Watching her struggle, watching her try to break the bonds that fixed her to the bed, was all part of the pleasure. And he wanted her as excited as he was. He had a treat in store.

Alex felt the sweat break out on her forehead as Paul's blows bit viciously into her skin. Her arse was burning and there was nothing she could do to escape the blows, nothing but succumb to the familiar pleasure that swept over her, the dark and aching pleasure that she sought and found, skulking inside pain and nestling within humiliation.

Suddenly, as quickly as he'd started, Paul stopped beating

her. She felt a finger burrow its way between her tightly-clenched buttocks and slide easily into her chasm. Paul gave a grunt of satisfaction.

'Naughty baby,' he said. 'Naughty baby to ignore my phone calls. Now I'll have to force myself inside you. Your legs are tied so tightly I'll have to prise you apart. I'm going to enjoy that.'

So will I, thought Alex as she felt his hands take hold of the cheeks of her burning arse, pulling her apart so that his cock could make its way towards her vagina, fighting past her clenched thighs until the knob of his prick had found the entrance to her tightly constricted womanhood.

Alex couldn't move, couldn't refuse or even respond to his thrusts, could do nothing but lie on her belly with her hands above her head and take the punishment that Paul had decided to mete out. For punishment it was.

He was fucking her hard and viciously, like a dog with a bitch. Fucking her for all he was worth while he held her nipples within his cruel fingers, pinching and twisting them while she moaned, each cry from her lips encouraging him to drive harder, reaching further into her trussed-up body with his relentless prick.

The orgasm began in the very depths of her belly, quickening as it flooded her body with its urgent pulse.

She felt as though Paul's cock was driving each spasm deeper into her, each thrust fuelling the pleasure which consumed her with its heat.

As he felt her come he began to slow his thrusts to long, languid movements. Alex's body gripped him within her hungry grasp and she came, sobbing and throbbing, her face buried in the pillow in front of her.

Her moans tipped Paul over the edge and he felt his cock respond to the wave upon wave of contractions with which her body massaged and encouraged him. He came as Alex's orgasm reached its height, his balls slapping hard against her buttocks, his fingers digging into her slim waist as he held her tight and rammed himself home, punishing her for her neglect, her failure to be at the end of the phone at the moment he decided to call.

'Please,' he heard her say, minutes later. 'Please, Paul. Untie me now.'

He had been lying on top of her, half asleep, the weight of his body putting pressure on her arms, making her bondage too painful to bear.

With a yawn, Paul reached up and untied the bonds that held her to the bedstead. Then, climbing off her, he rolled Alex onto her back.

'Now the ankles. Untie me, Paul.'

'Only if you let me tie your hands up again,' he replied.

'Why?' she said.

'Because I have a present for you.'

Alex felt a jolt of excitement in her stomach. 'Okay,' she said, slightly reluctantly. 'Okay.'

Paul smiled as he tied her hands above her head. This time he spread them out wide. She was on her back now, watching him. Then he untied her ankles. But what was he doing? Then she saw. He had produced a fat rubber dildo and was stroking it, running his fingers along the length of the huge, ribbed monster.

'Oh, no . . .' she said.

'It'll be fine,' replied Paul. 'If you're wet enough.'

'But it's . . .' Paul ignored her and moved off the bed, walking into the adjoining bathroom. Alex heard him turn on the shower. What the hell was he doing? Seconds later he came back and Alex felt a stab of excitement shoot through her. His prick was hard again, the veins on its surface standing out like gnarled ropes. How could something so ugly be a source of such fascination she wondered, not for the first time.

His thick and angry prick was all she could see, all she could think about. His betrayal, his duplicity counted for nothing. For now, his penis was the centre of her existence.

Paul came across to the bed and untied her, pulling her to her feet. He led her into the bathroom and towards the shower.

'What . . . ?' she began, but Paul simply glared at her, his eyes giving her a warning, telling her to shut up.

Pushing her into the shower he lifted her arms above her

head and tied them to the shower fitment. The warm water cascaded down her body, past her thumping heart, rolling down her thighs and twirling around the gold-plated plug which, along with all the other fixtures and fittings in Paul's flat, was the most expensive available.

He stood close to her in the shower and she watched as he began to soap himself. Paul lathered the black hairs on his chest, washing his muscular shoulders and then moving his hands on down to his manhood which he cleansed with the utmost care, soaping the pendulous pouch of his scrotum, rolling the heavy balls between his fingers as Alex watched, her pussy melting with desire as the water poured over her.

She watched in fascination as he began to soap his prick, the little white bubbles of foam with which he coated it in startling contrast to the thick rod beneath. How she longed to take him in her mouth, to roll his foreskin backwards and forwards beneath her lips, to feel his balls slide against her tongue.

But she could not move. She could only watch as he fingered himself and his prick grew thicker still, rising from between his thighs in a series of thrilling little jolts.

With one hand on his penis, Paul leant across and began to rub soap into her skin. She jumped as if struck, his touch sending spasms of desire through every pore of her skin as his fingers spread scented foam across her tightening nipples.

She saw him lean outside the shower, reaching for the black rubber dildo. 'Look, my little baby,' he said, stroking it across her nipples, bringing it up to her lips for Alex to kiss.

The glass walls of the shower were steamed up and Alex felt herself locked in a prison, though one that she felt was of her own making. She knew what a bastard she was with. She also knew that right now, at this moment, it didn't mean a thing.

Paul was stroking her now with the rubber dildo, trailing it through the rivulets of water which ran down her body. The feeling of it against her skin was delicious, the thought of its rough, ribbed surface inside her, too exciting to bear.

'Push it into me, Paul,' she whispered. 'Push it into me slowly. I want to feel it inside me.'

It looked bigger than any man, yet Alex felt ready for its strange embrace. The bigger the better, she thought as she felt its fat, ugly head nosing against the open mouth of her vagina.

Chapter 10

Mary had left the health farm soon after she had telephoned Alex. She had a long drive ahead but the prospect didn't worry her in the least. It would be good to have time to think. Jason had said goodbye to her that morning and had handed her a note, telling her not to read it until after he'd gone.

She'd put it in her bag and left it there unopened, keeping it for later, holding it as a kind of talisman against whatever might befall her when she arrived back in Manchester.

She had dressed in some of the clothes that Jason had bought her. With her expensive outfit and the exquisite perfume she was wearing, Mary felt cocooned and safe, protected somehow against the outside world.

Even as the miles slipped away and familiar landmarks came into view, the thought that she was returning to the house she shared with Paul somehow didn't register. All she could think about were the events of last night and this morning, running the memory of Jason making love to her through her mind time and again, anxious to keep the images from fading.

The tops of her thighs felt tender as though she'd strained the muscles and she could feel the lips of her still-swollen pussy squashed against the gusset of her panties. She was on a straight stretch of road in top gear. Moving the fingers of her left hand up her leg and under her skirt, she pushed the damp crotch of her panties to one side and began to touch herself. She was still as wet as she'd been last night and her fingers slid easily into her pussy. Pulling them backwards and forwards between her clitoris and the entrance to her slippery chasm, she felt the familiar heat build within her.

Mary wiggled in her seat, trying to move her body so that

she could sink her fingers inside herself up to her knuckles. Suddenly she heard a car hoot its horn, a loud, insistent racket that brought her sharply back to reality.

Lost in her reverie and the pleasure of arousal, Mary had wandered into the fast lane of the motorway, meandering along at forty miles an hour.

The sudden shock of the car overtaking her pulled her back to the present and she grabbed the steering wheel with both hands. It was dangerous to mess about behind the wheel of a car. But in the back of a sleek, black limo . . . that was something else. She smiled at the memory.

All the lovemaking of the past few days had tired her and she was pleased that this was so. She felt that Jason was still with her, still inside her. Even as she pulled up outside the house, the memory of his kiss goodbye was stronger in her mind than her fear of the hurt that she knew was waiting for her, the pain that had been kept precariously at bay with the happiness of the last few days.

She put the key in the lock and walked into the hallway. I'm home, she thought wearily. She looked around. The house she'd left such a short time before, the place in which she'd invested all her dreams, seemed like an empty shell.

There was dust on the windowsills. The hall carpet needed vacuuming. So what? she thought. Who's interested? The only thing that seemed real to her was the outfit she stood up in and the smell of her pussy on her fingers. Jason loved to kiss her fingers when they'd been inside her. He loved the outfit she was wearing, too. He had chosen it for her. The shop assistants in the pretty boutique in Brompton Road had made eyes at him as he waited to see Mary emerge from the changing room, her excitement at the way she looked, the way she felt, so strong you could almost reach out and touch it. Jason had stroked her sleeve, she remembered. She touched it now. Touched the jacket where his fingers had been. It was a simply cut two-piece in fine burgundy wool. It fitted her perfectly, making the most of her new, slimmer figure. He'd touched her jacket and then he'd followed her into the changing room and lifted her skirt, sliding his tongue between her legs while she'd squirmed in pleasure, panicking in case a shop assistant came in. How will I feel when I take this outfit off? she wondered. Opening all the doors that led off the hallway she began to peer into each room. Everything looked the same. But it wasn't. It had changed forever. Though she still didn't know what to do about it.

She felt that the beautiful clothes she stood up in were a barrier between her and all she surveyed, their softness strong as armour, protecting her from the present and the future. She couldn't change back into her old clothes or resume her old life. Paul had torn her life apart at the seams and there was nowhere to run from this bitter truth.

Jason had loved her and cared for her and made her look better than ever. She'd stay that way. She'd diet and exercise if needs be, and she'd wear only the finest, the best, the most flattering outfits she could buy. After all, Alex dressed well. Paul could afford it. He could pay.

In the past, Mary had never bothered. Those days were gone. The clothes that were practical for work could be thrown out. Paul could buy her a dozen new designer outfits.

She opened the phone book, looking for the number of Manchester's most exclusive hairdresser – one she'd heard about but had always felt too self-conscious to visit. Yes, they could see her the following morning for a blow dry and a manicure. In the meantime, she couldn't stay in the house. She may as well go back to work. For the afternoon at least.

Jason Hannard had never seen nipples like them. He'd noticed them clearly outlined through the girl's tee shirt, but it wasn't until closer inspection during the lunchbreak on the first day of filming that he'd managed to get a good, close look. Amazingly thick and long, they stuck out like miniature wine bottle corks from the mid-points of breasts that were otherwise fairly standard, attached to a body that was far from unpleasing.

By now, Jason was used to the ready availability of women who, once they'd recognised him, seemed instantly happy to throw caution and knickers to the wind. But it never ceased to fascinate him how easy it had become. Today it was a production assistant, bent over the desk in an empty office. Tomorrow, who knows? It was better than eating a fattening lunch though, and he really *had* wanted to touch and taste the girl's extraordinary nipples in the flesh. She'd been only too willing to let him, proferring her tits and then her pussy for Jason to suck before he slipped inside her for a quickie. But even as he unzipped his trousers, he wished it was Mary he was about to enter. Mary had been real. An extraordinary girl and what's more, he really liked her. Maybe he'd see her again.

He'd left her a note. If she ever wanted or needed to find him, he'd told her how.

When Mary walked into the office in the middle of the afternoon, for once the girls in the accounts department fell silent.

She'd been gone about a week and a half, no one knew where, and though there were many questioning glances when the door opened and she appeared, she'd gone straight to her desk without any comment.

She was almost unrecognisable, they'd all agreed in the canteen an hour later. In fact, she looked fantastic. Incredible. Something extraordinary had happened, they all felt sure. But for now it was clear that Mary wasn't letting on. They'd all known that Paul had been less than pleased about her absence. He had phoned from London expecting her to be at her desk and on discovering that she had failed to appear on two consecutive days, had attempted to cover his confusion. He pretended that he had 'forgotten' something, indicating that he would be able to get in contact with her elsewhere. But they weren't fools. They knew that somehow she had gone missing and that he was as in the dark as they were.

Mary was aware that she owed the girls some kind of an explanation. Sitting at a desk piled high with notes, invoices and faxes all marked 'urgent', she knew that she would need to enlist their help. She hadn't spoken to Paul. She had no intention of trying to contact him. She still had no idea of what she really intended to do or say and, for now, was acutely conscious of the fact that she was simply going through the motions.

Mary looked up to find Jinny standing in the doorway, holding a cup. 'I thought you might like some coffee,' she said, hesitantly. Mary indicated for her to come in and sit down. 'How did the wedding go?' she asked.

Jinny smiled. 'Fantastic.'

'I hope,' said Mary, 'that Paul hasn't made life difficult while I've been away?' As the words came out of her mouth she realised that it was the first time she had ever said anything about Paul that was less than totally loyal, less than completely supportive.

'He whinged a bit,' said Jinny, emboldened by Mary's new and unfamiliar tone. On seeing that her words made no difference to Mary's expression, she smiled and added, 'and he phoned us as well . . . from London. He was furious you weren't here. Then later, he sort of said that he knew where you were.'

'Well, he didn't,' replied Mary. 'Nobody did. If you want to know, I've been playing hookey at a health farm.'

The phrase sounded so ridiculous that both women burst out laughing.

'You look wonderful,' said Jinny, 'whatever you've been playing, you look great.'

'Well, I'm back now,' said Mary, flushing with pleasure. 'And I'm going to need your help to sort out this little lot.'

Gina knew that Alex had come back from the health farm and that Paul, too, had been at home. She'd seen both their cars in the underground car park and had been expecting Alex to call. But when Gina knocked on Alex's door the following morning, it remained unanswered, though the lights were on in the flat. Thinking that the two of them must be 'at it', she beat a hasty retreat, amusing herself instead by paying a visit to one of her husband's string of restaurants where she proceeded to enjoy an early lunch and a heavy flirtation with one of the waiters. She knew that news of her visit would get back to her husband quicker than you could grill a kebab. He'd be furious and jealous. Naturally, she'd protest her innocence. It all helped to keep him on his toes.

Alex eventually answered the phone to Gina at 3pm. She

told her she'd returned from the health farm the night before and that Paul had left again for Manchester that very morning. 'I was in when you knocked earlier,' she said. 'Paul had only just gone. I didn't feel like answering the door.'

'He's been here all week,' said Gina.

'He was busy . . . he had to leave,' replied Alex.

'So he hung around for a quick bonk and then off again,' said Gina. There was a silence at the other end of the phone. 'I'm sorry, Alex,' she said. 'I should never have said that. It's none of my business.'

Alex sighed. 'Let's just forget it,' she said.

It was a cool afternoon, but that didn't worry Gina. 'I'll pick you up in half an hour and we'll go and have a game of tennis,' said Gina. Alex was still smarting from Gina's earlier remarks, but she decided that even Gina's company was better than being alone.

'I don't want to go to the Mottlesham Club,' said Alex.

'Okay,' replied Gina, brightly. 'We'll go somewhere else.'

Alex seemed entirely oblivious to her surroundings as she sat beside Gina in her pretty car with the windows wound down. Gina wondered if Alex might have had a massive row with Paul about his comings and goings, but whatever the reason for her friend's muted response to her constant chatter, Gina was glad. Alex was totally preoccupied. So with the help of a circuitous and evasive route, Alex hadn't noticed until it was too late that they were heading for the Mottlesham Tennis Club after all.

When they turned to go through the gates, Alex appeared to snap out of her reverie.

'Oh, no,' she said. 'Gina, I *told* you . . .'

'But you *had* to come,' Gina replied. 'There's been such gossip! I've just *got* to find out and so have you. It's the hottest thing in years . . .' Gina pulled up and parked her car. 'Something's been happening with Kurt and some woman . . . a member . . . we're all *mad* to find out who. Come on, Alex . . . we don't have to play tennis, but we can't miss out on this . . .'

Kurt had known she'd come back from the moment he left

her. Known that her addiction to pain and punishment was growing stronger and that the more he fed her hunger, the more she would be his to do with as he pleased.

When he saw her step out of Gina's car he thought that his first action must be to punish her for staying away so long. He needed to punish her more than he'd punished any woman. He would take her to depths of enslavement she'd only ever imagined and she'd be his, for exactly as long as he wanted.

He watched the two women as Gina began to lock the driver's door. It appeared that there was some tension between them. Gina was raising her voice and Alex was waving her hands around. Then he saw Gina turn her back and walk off towards the club house.

Alex stood and watched her go. Then, looking as though she didn't know what to do next, she began to walk down the drive towards the exit.

Kurt watched her as she moved. Her body swayed with a natural grace, her red hair moving like a sheet of silk about her shoulders.

He noticed how pale her skin was. He saw the haunted look in her eyes. Why was she trying to leave? Where the hell did she think she was heading?

Kurt followed her, moving among the foliage that lined the drive, keeping out of sight till he was level with her. Then he caught hold of her arm.

Alex gave a cry and turned her frightened gaze in his direction. 'Where are you going?' he said.

'Home,' she stammered and then, as if the word made no sense, 'I don't know.'

'I suppose Gina told you they're all gossiping,' he said as he pulled her off the drive and into the shade of nearby trees. 'But they know nothing. They are stupid women, Alex. Spiteful, irrelevant women. I despise them all. Every one of the bitches. They are fucked by their ineffectual husbands and fucked by the world when their husbands trade them in for a younger model. But they think they're fine. They think they can make eyes at me and when they find they cannot, they gossip.'

Alex tried to pull her arm out of Kurt's grasp but he held her tight. 'Don't struggle, Alex,' he said. 'You know it's no good.'

'Please, Kurt,' she said quietly, but he pulled her closer. His lips brushed her cheek, touching her gently.

'It's okay,' he said, 'relax,' and, holding her face between his hands, he pressed his lips softly against her own. They stood beneath a darkening sky, the wind rustling through the trees and bushes which hid them from the view of the club house. Alex was glad that the wind was blowing, its chilly breath cooling her burning face.

Kurt pushed his tongue into Alex's mouth and curled it around her own. His lips moved in circles, pressing softly then hard, his tongue meeting hers, crushing her resistance.

His penis squashed against her thigh and he remembered what it felt like driving it into her, plundering her body, overcoming her.

His hands moved to either side of her face and he applied a slight pressure to her temples. He moved her mouth away from his and looked into her eyes. Without a word, Alex sank to her knees on the grass. His penis had made a huge bulge in his tennis shorts and she knelt in front of it as if in awe.

He watched as with the utmost care, Alex slid her long fingers inside the front of his shorts, touching cotton until she came in contact with warm flesh, a thick tube of smooth warm flesh, soft as a baby's skin, hard as steel.

Kurt gave a jolt as her fingers reached his penis. He watched her close her eyes as she continued her explorations, moving her fingers downwards until she could cup his balls in her hand. They were large and close together and she balanced them in her narrow palm where they spilt over the edge, heavy yet strangely fluid as he felt them move against her thrilling fingers.

Kurt's reddened cock was sticking out the front of his shorts at a perfect horizontal angle, the foreskin taut and stretched back, its bulbous tip shiny and smooth at the end.

Kurt looked down at Alex, kneeling before him on the grass. He leant forward and touched her hair. Startled by his unaccustomed gentleness, he saw her jump as though she'd been hit.

'Steady,' he said as if talking to a highly strung animal. 'It's okay . . . steady.'

The wind had begun to blow more strongly and Alex gave an involuntary shiver.

'Unbutton your shirt,' he ordered her. Alex reached up and opened the buttons. 'Undo your bra,' he went on. She reached behind her and slipped the hooks.

Kurt took a step towards her till the tip of his cock was touching the front of her chest. Holding it in his hand he guided it across her skin, using it to pull the bra strap from her shoulders. Her breasts were rising and falling and he knew she was struggling to control her breathing.

He fixed his eyes on her nipples. They were taut with arousal, their tips rising from circles of puckered pink flesh in deep contrast to the milk-white globes which rose and fell in time with her beating heart. 'Like the cherries on the cake,' murmured Kurt, touching each nipple in turn with the tip of his forefinger.

'Scrape up some earth,' he said to Alex. She looked up at him, the fear in her eyes more pronounced. 'Earth,' he said, nodding towards a flower border just a few yards away. Alex went to pull her shirt across her breasts. 'No,' said Kurt. 'Go like that. Crawl on all fours.'

Without a murmur, Alex leant forward and placed the palms of her hands on the ground. Then as she was bid, she crawled on her hands and knees towards the flower bed, her breasts dangling in front of her as she made her way across the cold grass. Kurt followed her, watching her tits as they swung, watching her long fingers as they sank into the grass, spread out like strange, elegant paws.

Alex looked up at him. 'Earth,' he said. She dug her fingers into the ground. The earth was cold and hard but with some difficulty she scraped and scooped a handful of damp, dark soil mixed with leaves, a muddy mix which she held in her palms. 'Give it to me,' he said. With the utmost care, Alex tipped the black mess into his upturned hands. 'Now, come here,' he said, 'and kneel.' Alex knelt in front of him as before, his prick level with her face.

'Open,' said Kurt, pushing his penis against her mouth.

Reluctantly, nervously, Alex pursed her lips and began to touch the tip of his cock with her tongue. 'I said open,' said Kurt thrusting his thickening manhood between her teeth, flattening her tongue as its head brushed the roof of her mouth. Again she closed her eyes. She began to suck steadily.

Kurt moved closer, still spreading the black earth between his hands. He hesitated, enjoying the contrast between its dark, uneven texture and the smooth white skin of the woman who knelt before him.

He held the earth in his palms, moulding it like a potter working with clay. He pressed it against her breasts, scraping it across the tender tips of her nipples. The earth was gritty and sharp and he knew he was hurting her. He knew, because as he began to rub it against her tender skin she began to suck harder, responding to the pain with a sudden surge of desire.

She moved her mouth backwards and forwards, exerting as much pressure as her lips would allow along its length as she sucked. He rubbed the earth harder into her breasts, each tiny particle and grain tormenting her as it scratched and scored her with its roughness. He could feel her arousal, the urgent need in her as her velvet mouth pulled against his penis, drawing him on until he could hold back no longer.

He wanted to beat her. Beat her and fuck her and leave her sobbing upon the grass. Most of all, he wanted to humiliate the beautiful bitch who so reminded him of his stepmama.

Kurt rubbed the earth harder and harder into her breasts, feeling its scraping particles scratch the tender skin of her nipples, leaving her streaked and caked with mud. Why did he need the bitch so badly? Why did she have such a hold over him, body and soul?

As he felt himself begin to come he tore his penis from her lips and shot his juice upon the cold spring grass, turning his back on her, leaving her kneeling there. Then he walked away. Alex called after him but he ignored her. He thought of her, bewildered and streaked with mud. She was filthy, cold and kneeling on the grass, unfucked. There's more than one way to punish . . . thought Kurt as he tucked his cock back in his shorts and headed for the club house.

Mary had felt terribly embarrassed. She'd been sitting at her desk, crying quietly, only to look up and find one of the lorry drivers standing opposite her, a time-sheet in his hand and a look of bewilderment on his face.

She should have been working. There was a lot to do, but somehow she hadn't been able to settle to the demands of any kind of task that required even the slightest degree of concentration. She hadn't heard the driver knock, so engrossed had she been in the letter that Jason had written and given to her on the day they parted. Until now she hadn't been able to bring herself to read it. And now she had, it had had precisely the effect she'd anticipated, bringing feelings and memories flooding back.

But why was she crying? 'When you open this letter, picture me as I write to you,' it had begun. 'Picture my fingers holding a pen, and then think of them inside you. I will seal the envelope with my tongue . . . though I'd rather be licking your nipples and tasting your skin than tasting glue.'

There was no getting away from it. Jason Hannard had a one-track mind and that was half the reason Mary loved him. Making love to Jason had been one of the happiest experiences of her life. So why was she crying?

'If I close my eyes,' he'd gone on, 'I can smell the warmth of you lying next to me in bed. As I write, you are still with me and it is early morning. Now I am moving beneath the sheets, sliding down the bed till my face is level with your little furry forest. You are still asleep, Mary, my love, and the forest is all mine. The scent of you is strongest down here under the covers and if I get close enough to the forest I can see your little pink animal poking out of the undergrowth. I long to stroke the little creature, but if I do so you will wake. The creature between my own legs is rampant and throbbing. He longs to rub noses with the little animal in the forest and I know he can wait no longer. I bring him up to the edge of the forest and lead him gently to the little creature that is yours alone. They touch and you wake. You smile. As soon as you move there is a clearing in the forest. A deep ravine with a waterfall. I plunge into the undergrowth and the forest closes around me. It is a rainforest. Warm and wet.'

As she read, Mary could feel Jason deep inside her, his glorious prick sliding backwards and forwards in the long, steady strokes that thrilled her so. She remembered a time when he'd knelt over her and brushed her breasts with the knob of his prick, stroking the very tip of each nipple between the cleft of his manhood as his fingers stroked and circled her clitoris with a touch that was so light she could hardly feel his fingers through the throbbing that they caused.

Jason had known exactly how to turn her on with his soft, gentle movements that drove her wild with need, making her crazy, making her beg him to fuck her and fuck her hard. And he would. In the blink of an eye his slow, easy manner would change and Jason would hold her firm, ramming her full of his throbbing cock as he held her arse cheeks beneath his long fingers. Pumping deeply inside her, he would lick her tits and bite her nipples till they were red and sore, squashing their puckered little points between his lips as he held her waist, gyrating and circling her body around his prick till he felt the pleasure in her explode. He would push her harder against his prick then, making sure that she felt him in every part of her, making sure that she'd never forget . . .

Mary's clitoris was thumping away like a drumbeat as she read Jason's words. Now, she could see herself on her knees as he parted the cheeks of her arse and nuzzled between her legs, licking up and down the crack of her arse before stopping to tease her protruding clitoris with little flicks of his tongue, before . . .

Jason had made love to her in the letter and he had written about how much he would miss her. He'd told her that if ever she needed help, he'd be there. He'd enclosed his private phone number and she knew that she was one of the privileged few to have it. She felt flattered. And from the tone of the letter, she felt that he was here with her in the room and that she had only to look up to see him there. The letter reminded her how much she missed him. But when she had looked up, it had been to see the young lorry driver, covered in confusion at the sight of the woman who gave him his instructions, sitting crying. Without a word, he'd reached into the pocket of his jeans and handed her a handkerchief. It was a linen handkerchief of the finest quality, white and faultlessly ironed. Mary had taken it gratefully, smiling at the man. 'I'm sorry,' she said. 'Bit of a family problem.' The driver had smiled at her, his dark eyes crinkling with good humour. 'I'll wash this and return it,' she said, folding the fine handkerchief and then putting it in her bag. He nodded.

By the end of the day the accounts department was, seemingly, back to normal. Mary had re-acquainted herself with what was happening, who had to be paid, who was being laid off or taken on and how each division of Paul's complex business empire had fared in her absence. There were dozens of cheques waiting for her signature. After a titanic struggle with herself she was back in control, both of herself and her emotions. Yet when she returned to the house alone that night she felt a sudden stab of loneliness that made it impossible for her to rest. Paul hadn't phoned, either in the office or at home. He must be in London. He must still be angry with her for disappearing.

Pouring herself a large glass of white wine from the fridge, she decided to ring Alex. It didn't matter if Paul was there, Mary would simply hang up. Tapping the sequence of numbers into the phone that would make her call untraceable should Paul answer, Mary dialled the Docklands flat that she'd never seen but had imagined as clearly as if she lived there.

The answerphone took her call. 'Hello. This is Paul and Alex. Sorry we're not in. Leave a message.' Despite the fact that by now, Mary had fully acknowledged, if not accepted, Paul's duplicity, to hear Alex's voice confirm the situation on tape was deeply disturbing. Mary slammed the phone down, her hand shaking. She wrote down the words that Alex had spoken and stared at them. The words were sharp and clipped, so unlike the answerphone message that she'd recorded. She pushed the 'answerplay' button on her own machine. 'Paul and Mary are so sorry that we can't come to the phone right now, but do leave a message and we'll call you as soon as possible,' it said.

She liked the tone of Alex's message. Straight and to the point. She never knew why she did it but without hesitation Mary pushed the 'record' button on her own answerphone, changing her own message to the words that Alex had used in the tone that Alex had said them. 'Hello. This is Paul and Mary. Sorry we're not in. Leave a message.'

Then, for some strange and unaccountable reason, Mary re-dialled Alex's number, knowing instinctively that it would be answered. The phone was picked up and she heard Alex's voice, sounding far away.

'Alex? Are you all right?' said Mary at which point the girl at the other end burst into tears.

'No,' she sobbed, 'I'm not. I'm going crazy. I just don't know what's happening to me.' Between sobs she told Mary about Kurt and how he had followed her to Tingles. She told Mary she'd seen him again, and that he'd humiliated her.

'What do you mean?' said Mary and Alex had hesitated.

'He ties me up and he uses me,' she said. 'He humiliates me and I go back for more.' Mary had a sudden picture in her mind of Alex, bound with silk scarves and with her legs wide apart. She had seen Alex naked and could picture just what she would look like with her red bush parted and her clitoris poking out. Mary imagined Alex to have a long, thin clitoris. She imagined it reddening and hardening with arousal. She saw herself touching it, hearing Alex groan with pleasure . . .

Much to her dismay, Mary felt a gentle throbbing between her legs as the picture formed in her mind. With a huge effort, she dismissed it.

'Mary?' said Alex. 'Are you there?'

'Yes,' she replied. 'Yes, of course.'

'I don't know why this is happening to me,' said Alex. 'Maybe it's because of . . . what's been going on. With Paul, I mean. With both of us.' Then, as if in explanation of her behaviour she added, 'Paul isn't here. He's never here. I can't be on my own.'

'Where is he?' said Mary, suddenly alarmed.

'He left this morning,' replied Alex. 'Said he was going to see to some business in Scotland. Said he'd be gone for a couple of days.'

Mary breathed a sigh of relief. At least he wasn't on his way back to Manchester. Not yet. She couldn't face him yet.

Alex sounded in a very bad way and Mary was glad she'd phoned. But she didn't really understand what Alex was doing with her tennis coach. He humiliated her and most disturbing of all, from the strange way that Alex had described it to Mary, she enjoyed it.

'Could we meet sometime?' said Alex. 'I need to talk to you so badly.' Mary's heart sank. She had enough problems of her own to sort out right now but at the same time she felt it would be impossible to refuse, to turn her back.

She was inextricably linked to this girl who was sobbing at the other end of the phone. This strange, disturbing girl whose life was so deeply mixed up with her own. Their destinies were connected and in some peculiar way she couldn't yet define, she knew that her happiness was dependent on Alex's. And hers on mine, thought Mary, and hers on mine.

Chapter 11

Mary knew that any time now, Paul would return. She didn't know how she would face him or what she would say. In the meantime she believed that if she could hold onto just a tiny measure of the happiness she'd felt with Jason and draw strength from the memory, she would have the courage to face anything.

The thought of Jason warmed her. He'd given her back a delight in her own smooth and voluptuous body, a delight that she'd almost forgotten.

It was the memory of Jason that now took her to the hairdressers, the manicurist and the beauty salon. It was the thought of his mouth on her skin that persuaded her to add expensive oils to her bath. It was the recollection of his tongue against her thigh and between her legs that persuaded her to wear stockings, throwing away the bundle of tights that cluttered up her lingerie drawer, forever.

There was still enough work to keep Mary at the office late into the night but she had decided that, whatever was to happen between her and Paul, there were better things to do than to play the martyr. She left the office at five-thirty sharp. She exercised. She slept well. The bloom of awakening that had lit up her entire appearance remained with her. She nurtured it like a fragile flower, knowing that without love it would soon fade. She still felt Jason close to her. Every time she smoothed her gossamer-fine stockings along her legs or pulled on one of her soft designer suits, he was there, gazing at her, telling her how lovely she looked.

So it was that Paul walked into Mary's office at three o' clock one afternoon and found, not Mary sitting at her desk, but a voluptuous blonde, her head bent over a column of figures, her full breasts outlined by a starkly simple and very sexy business suit.

'Excuse me?' he said and the girl looked up. The shock for both of them was equal and for a moment, neither spoke. Mary took her glasses off very slowly and laid them on the desk. They were new. Black frames. Very sexy, Paul thought.

'You haven't phoned,' said Mary.

'I've been busy,' Paul replied, feeling like a schoolboy being interrogated by his headmistress.

'I see,' said Mary, looking him straight in the eye. Paul wasn't used to this. Usually when he turned up unexpectedly, Mary would jump to her feet and fetch him coffee. She'd witter on about how tired he must be feeling, her concern for his well-being totally wiping out her own preoccupations, eclipsing her own fatigue.

Often on these occasions, Paul would look at her eyes and see the dark circles that spoke of late nights in front of the computer, of a woman who cared about keeping his business running like clockwork, of a woman whose devotion extended to self-neglect. Mary's clothes were always neat but never thought about. Her hair was always well cut, but never well styled.

But all he could see before him now was a clear-eyed girl, perfectly groomed and expensively dressed, who stared at him from beneath mascara'd lashes, her gaze unfaltering.

'How's business?' he said, meeting fire with fire, hoping to throw her into confusion, hoping to force her to admit that her time away, wherever she had been, had put them all behind.

But neither a sudden rush of guilt nor an apology was forthcoming.

'Okay, I suppose,' she said. 'I haven't been here all that much.'

Paul didn't know how to handle this. He took a seat opposite her. Mary saw that he was fiddling nervously with a ring on his finger. It was the one she'd given him last Christmas.

'Mary,' he said, as coolly as he could manage, 'can you tell me what's happening, please? You disappear without trace for I don't know how long, and now . . .'

He simply couldn't find the words. He looked at her again. She looked dazzling, beautiful. He wanted to fuck her.

'I went to a . . .' Mary checked herself suddenly as the words 'health farm' prepared to spill out of her mouth.

'I went to an hotel,' she said. 'On the way back from my mother's house. I was very tired so I took a few days, just for myself. Then I bought a few clothes and came back.'

'And the business?' said Paul.

'As you see,' she replied, 'it's still here.' She could see that he was totally confused and she loved it. When she got up some moments later to leave the room, his eyes followed her, taking in every inch of her body.

His attention, despite her best intentions, excited her. She knew he wanted her. His lust was almost tangible, creating an unfamiliar tension in the office, an undercurrent of uncertainty which pervaded every room.

Mary whispered to Jinny, 'Don't tell him where I've been. I don't want him to know.' Jinny giggled, her eyes wide. Then Mary went back to her desk and after another couple of failed attempts to put her on the spot, Paul went to his.

At five o'clock Paul went looking for her. 'She's gone to the gym,' said Jinny. 'And then I believe she's going to the hairdressers. She said she looked in on you but you were on the phone. She said to tell you she'd be at home by eight.'

Paul pulled up in the driveway of his house at exactly eight o'clock. For some inexplicable reason he hadn't wanted to be late tonight. Thinking about Mary's strange behaviour, he hadn't been able to concentrate all afternoon.

Some remarkable, fundamental transformation had taken place in Mary and he couldn't figure out what it was, or how it had happened.

A few nights in an hotel, she claimed. But it was more than that. Much more.

As Paul parked the car he was brooding deeply, wondering when all this 'gym' and 'hairdresser' business had begun. Then suddenly he realised. This was all an elaborate charade to make him toe the line. To make him get home on time and behave.

Naturally, she'd have left the office early to go home and

cook him dinner. Like she always did. A perfect meal, down to the last detail.

But when he opened the door, there was no smell of cooking. Instead, he saw Mary, looking even more beautiful than she'd seemed earlier in the day, standing at the top of the stairs. She was wearing a simple, sleeveless black velvet dress. Huge gold and diamond clusters sparkled in her ears, highlighting her subtly made-up face which was framed by a soft mass of pale golden curls.

'You look lovely,' he said, unable to find the words to describe the strange mix of emotions that were assailing his senses.

'I've booked a table at *Chez Phillipe*,' said Mary, 'for nine o'clock.'

Where was the welcoming fireside, the homemade casserole and Mary, slopping about in her leggings like a faithful sheepdog? Paul put his case down in the hall. 'I'd better shower and change quickly then,' he said. 'I won't be long.'

Paul stood in the shower and thought about Mary and the black dress she was wearing. He'd never seen it before. It looked fabulous and very expensive. What was she doing while he was showering, he wondered.

He pictured her, cool and elegant, sitting in their dining room sipping a gin and tonic. Yes, that was what she'd be doing. Or maybe she'd be in their bedroom, touching up her make-up. Or she could be touching up something else . . .

As the water poured down his body Paul pictured Mary going to the drawer in the bedside table and taking out a strange, smooth, white object. It was fat and thick and when she pressed a button, it began to whirr softly.

He saw her lift one of her elegant legs and place her foot on the small stool that stood in front of her dressing table. In his mind, she was sliding the hem of her dress up along her leg and slipping the white, whirring monster beneath the black velvet. Black stockings, black dress, white dildo, smooth as marble. Paul felt his cock twitch and swell as his imagination took flight.

In his fantasy, he was on his knees beside her, looking up her skirt. She was wearing the finest, gossamer thin stockings and a tiny pair of black briefs which she now eased to one side so that the crease between her pussy lips was clearly visible to him. Now she was parting those beautiful cushiony lips with the head of this thick, whirring monster. Surely she wasn't . . . oh, yes!

Paul felt his cock grow hard as he pictured Mary dipping the head of the dildo into the mouth of her open chasm. He could see very clearly now as it drove into the pinkness and she pulled it backwards and forwards, each time sliding it a little deeper, dragging it back so it emerged coated in a slick of her juice . . .

He was very close to her now. He could see the opening of her pussy as the white dildo invaded it, stretching her body as the slithery folds of her womanhood circled it like pink coral.

He could hear her moaning as she stood there in her elegant dress with her leg on the stool and the crude, mechanical object shoved up inside her. Her other hand had come down and she'd slid it beneath the rim of her pants and was tickling her clitoris with her fingers as she pushed the dildo in and out, moaning and writhing and sighing as she teased and tweaked and whirred herself towards orgasm.

Paul felt himself grow hot, though the water cascading over him was cool. He looked down at his prick, watched as the hood of his manhood slid backwards and forwards under the pressure of his fingers.

She was beautiful and he wanted to go downstairs and fuck her. He wanted to pull the velvet dress up over her arse and spread her face down across the dining table. 'That should rattle her composure,' he thought as the white juice squirted from him and he gasped, rubbing his cock in hard, jerking movements as the water ran down his body.

Paul had felt disturbed all evening. He was behaving in a way that was unfamiliar, and he seemed to have no control over his actions.

Chez Phillipe was crowded and bustling with Manchester's most fashionable crowd – familiar faces from the nearby TV station, sporting celebrities and models that even Paul, with his limited knowledge of the social scene, recognised immediately.

Paul found himself ordering champagne, wondering why anything else would have seemed somehow inappropriate. Dinners out with Mary, which were fairly infrequent, usually meant a trip to the local Chinese or Italian for something simple with a bottle of house white. They usually took their work with them and would be discussing figures and business plans over the tagliatelle, oblivious to all but their combined efforts to improve profits and cut costs.

Tonight, any talk of business would have been impossible. Paul was alive to his surroundings, noticing everything, from the speed and efficiency of the laughing waiters to the deliciousness of his dinner. Most of all, he noticed Mary.

In all the years he'd known her, Mary had never flirted. But tonight she was stroking the stem of her wine glass, gazing straight at him and talking, talking . . . about anything and everything other than work. Yet despite her chatter, he knew that some kind of barrier had descended, shielding her true feelings from his penetrating gaze.

Mary had always been an open book. Now, he felt, there was artifice in every move she made. What had happened while he'd been away? For the first time ever, he began to regret his long absences. He saw men glance at her as they passed the table. He'd have to keep a closer eye on her from now on.

Paul asked her to dance, leading her to the small and intimate dance floor, its polished wood surface reflecting the light of the candles which flickered on every table.

He held her close, breathing in the familiar smell of her perfume, enjoying the feeling of her body pressed against his.

With a sudden start, Paul realised that the perfume Mary was wearing was familiar, but it wasn't hers. It was Alex's perfume. The one she always wore.

He could feel the little buttons of Mary's suspenders pressed against his leg. Mary never wore stockings. At least, he'd never known her to. 'Strange,' he thought. Strange and disconcerting.

The bill for the evening was enormous and though she saw it, Mary didn't bat an eyelid. They went home. As they walked into the hallway and closed the door, Paul felt like a kid on his first date. He leant across and touched her arm. 'Mary,' he said. She turned to face him and he held her. He kissed her. He felt her lips respond and her mouth open as his fingertips sank into her scented hair and his tongue slid into her mouth.

Then, without a word, she broke away from him and went upstairs. Paul went to the kitchen for a glass of water. His hand was shaking. Then as if on automatic pilot he locked the front door as usual, and followed. It was as though he had taken some powerful and dangerous drug. His senses were heightened, he noticed everything from the thick pile of the stair carpet beneath his feet to the soft breeze that ruffled the curtains at the landing window. Then he was there at her bedroom door. *Their* bedroom door.

He opened it slowly and entered. Mary was standing by the bed and for a moment, all he could do was look at her. The moon was shining through the half open window, bathing her in a muted light. It was a warm, clear-skied night and standing perfectly still he could hear the distant and unearthly call of a fox. The smell of grass drifted in through the window.

'Come here,' she said.

Obediently, Paul moved closer. He could smell her perfume more strongly now, rising in waves from her skin. She was wearing a cream lace slip, its thin straps accentuating the beauty of her shoulders, its elaborate trim heightening her femininity and highlighting the curves that lay beneath.

She was breathing steadily and he leant towards her, touching her cheek with his own. Mary did not respond. She simply stood still in the moonlight. 'Like a beautiful statue,' he thought to himself.

Paul traced the shape of her shoulders with the tips of his fingers, touching her as if she were fragile and about to break. She shivered at his touch and gave a small sigh in the back of her throat.

Moving his fingers down her silk-clad body, he realised

how much weight she'd lost, how curvaceous she'd become. She wasn't thin, but shapely and womanly; her breasts rounded and firmer somehow, her waist more pronounced, her belly a small and pleasing protrusion.

He moved his hands inwards till he could feel the familiar triangle of hair beneath the silk, its little curls parting as he groped for the opening between her legs. As he explored her, easing her pussy apart with his fingertips, he felt the smooth material slide against the softness of her inner lips, following her most intimate contours and staining her slip with her feminine juices as he began to rub her.

Paul got to his knees and put his tongue against the wet patch on her slip. He could feel the outline of her clitoris through the material. He knew that he had only to lift her slip to touch her completely, but there was something strangely pleasurable in resisting the urge to do so. He pulled his mouth away and fingered her once more.

The material was sticking to her clitoris now and he was flicking the tiny bud with his fingernail, enjoying the tension that he could sense within her which somehow was heightened by the wisp of silk that separated them.

Her slip had worked its way between her inner lips and through it Paul could see the contours of her womanhood, clearly outlined by the silk which clung to her folds and crevices.

As his fingers continued to rub and scratch her, his other hand strayed to the hem of her slip, moving underneath the pale material and up her leg, feeling the smooth skin beneath his touch. She was very warm. The heat increased till he was stroking the insides of her thighs, the touch of dry flesh giving way to a slippery trail as his fingers bathed in the juices which ran from her, spreading around the bush of golden hair which guarded the entrance to her secret passage.

He would move his fingers inside that honey-sweetness and open her body wide, ready for the deeper and more penetrating explorations of his manhood which now stood ready to burst the zip of his fly, like water against a dam.

Suddenly she moved away. Pulled back. Her action was

strange, shocking almost – like a sudden rejection, a slap in the face.

'Mary,' he said 'Mary . . .'

She stood just yards from him, staring at him. Then slowly, with a peculiar half-smile on her face she came towards him again, standing very close.

Somehow, he couldn't bring himself to touch her, so rapid and unexpected had been her withdrawal. He could hear her breathing, he could feel the heat from her like a magnetic force field.

'Move to the bed,' she said, 'and lie on your back.' With his penis poking out of his trousers he did as he was told, wondering what she would do next, hoping that she would lower herself straight on top of him, swallowing him inside her tight pussy, drawing him into the scented mystery of a body that since that afternoon, he'd longed for like never before.

He closed his eyes and lay there. She was watching him. He could feel it. Then he felt the bed move as she climbed onto it beside him. The next thing he knew was her fingers easing his pants and his trousers down over his legs. He lay quite still. At the touch of her lips against his stomach he thought his body would explode with need.

He felt her hand move down to take the straining sac of his scrotum between her cool fingers, sliding his balls back and forth in rhythmic motion. Her lazy, almost indifferent handling of his testes caused him to tense, his prick hardening till he felt the pressure and excitement to be almost unbearable. He longed to dig his hard prick into her body . . . her mouth, her pussy, even the tight little arse that he'd become so conscious of today, now that she'd taken to wearing her skirts so tight.

He wanted to fuck her into submission, to bathe her in his sperm, to rub it into her tits, her hair, to fill her mouth and her pussy, to overcome whatever it was in Mary that had sought, of late, to defy him.

But he knew that if he made even one movement to overcome her she would reject him with a coldness which, until recently, he'd never believed her capable of.

He closed his eyes and felt her lips teasing him, running backwards and forwards over the knob of his prick. His body gave an involuntary jolt and she moved back, the thrust of his hips meeting only the velvet night air.

She was going to do it her way and at her pace. Paul tried to control the aching in his prick as slowly, agonisingly slowly, she began to lick his penis, covering every inch with her thrilling tongue.

He could see her blonde head in the moonlight, working her way the length of his prick in long, firm licks from the forest of black hair at its root down to the straining tip, giving a flick with her tongue across the knob of him before returning to begin all over again.

Painstakingly, methodically, she covered his prick with her steady, even licks, this time pausing to take his balls between her lips and knead them till he thought his cock would burst with pressure.

'Please, Mary . . .' he whispered in the semi-darkness. 'Get on top of me.'

She seemed not to hear him, intent on her task, but a moment later he felt the delicious and tantalising licking come to an end.

Panting, he propped himself up on his elbows. He could feel her saliva evaporating, cooling his burning prick as it did so.

'I want to fuck you so badly,' he said. Mary smiled her strange half-smile and swung her body over his, thrusting her pussy towards his face, its rich scent mingled with the disturbing scent of a perfume which until today had been Alex's alone.

He felt her mouth slide over his cock once more, though this time she was sucking hard, her fingertips kneading his balls as she did so.

Her pussy was open, beckoning, and Paul leant forward and buried his face in the folds of her glistening labia, stabbing his tongue into damp hair before finally sinking into the well of her womanhood.

She was sucking him hard while his licks inside her pussy became deeper and more penetrating and his body tensed in uncontrollable response. He wanted to hold back, wanted to wait until he was inside her. He wanted to be inside her, tasting her not with his mouth, but with his prick. She was his. His alone.

Suddenly, Paul felt an unaccustomed wave of jealousy and possessiveness and at that moment he knew he was about to come.

As if by telepathy, he felt the muscles in Mary's vagina begin to contract in waves, pulsing out their message of pleasure and release as the pressure of her mouth on his prick grew harder.

With a huge shudder he came deep in her throat while her orgasm broke inside his mouth, her clitoris throbbing against his lips as his tongue drove against the walls of her vagina, licking her out as she pressed her hips down, smothering his face in the scented stickiness of her hot and tingling womanhood.

Moments later, Paul lay in the darkness still breathing in the musky perfume of Mary's body, still tasting her, still wondering why he hadn't fucked her, why she hadn't let him.

She had taken what she wanted and though she had satisfied him, he longed for more. Something that for now, it seemed she wasn't willing to give.

Paul lay still for a few minutes and then he leant across and touched her. 'Mary,' he whispered. She did not reply. Still wearing her jewels and make-up, she lay sound asleep.

Chapter 12

Dan Simmonds was one of thirty lorry drivers working for Mason Long Distance Haulage Co. The other men regarded him as something of an oddball and, though the girls in the office cast appreciative glances in his direction whenever he passed, for the most part he kept himself to himself.

Olive-skinned and with soft, wavy hair, Dan had a full and generous mouth, dark expressive eyes and a perfect Roman nose. Handsome, if somewhat exotic, he combined a brooding masculinity with a delicate, almost feminine quality which women found intriguing.

Strangely, he seemed almost oblivious to his attractions. His beauty meant nothing to him and his entire lack of self-consciousness, on this score at any rate, made him even more attractive. On a more basic level the girls in Mason's accounts office had noticed that Dan had a beautiful bum. He often wore jeans and dazzling, white shirts. Strange for a lorry driver but very nice, they all agreed.

The cab of his lorry was full of books and play scripts piled alongside the heaps of maps and empty sweet wrappers which every lorry driver seemed to accumulate.

He could often be spotted sitting in his cab reading, his long fingers caught up in his dark hair as he rested his head against his hand and concentrated.

There was never a copy of *The Sun* to be seen in his cab. The newspapers he read were the arty-farty ones and he didn't even have any dirty magazines or pin-ups of girls stuck against the dashboard.

Some of his fellow drivers thought that this was evidence enough of the fact that he was a 'poof'. He was untidy, yes, but fastidiously clean . . . a trait that many of the older men regarded with the deepest suspicion.

No matter how far he'd driven, no matter how much loading or unloading he'd been involved with, Dan always appeared at the depot in a spotlessly laundered shirt. Strangest of all, he didn't blow his nose on bits of loo roll like the other blokes, but carried perfectly ironed linen handkerchiefs which never seemed to get dirty.

'Mummy's boy,' they muttered darkly. 'Big poof.' They resented his presence and went quiet when he walked past. Until, that was, the day the fight broke out. The day that little Tommy Deakin went berserk.

It was the old, old story. One of the drivers had been caught having an affair with the wife of another, visiting her when her husband was away on trips and she was at home, bored. The trouble was, the cuckolded man was Tommy Deakin. Tommy Deakin, who had once upon a time been a legendary flyweight boxing champion. Tommy Deakin, tough as leather and vicious with it. They said that Tommy had killed a man when he was in the ring. He wouldn't speak about his boxing days and if anyone pressed him on the subject, his eyes would cloud over and they'd soon get the message that it wasn't wise to push their luck. Sensible men were wary of Tommy Deakin. He was a man who didn't take anything lightly. And he'd been made a fool of.

He'd known nothing, hadn't even suspected. Then one day there'd been a last minute change in the shift rota and Tommy Deakin had returned home to find his wife dolled up to the nines, waiting for the arrival of Sam – one of Tommy's oldest friends and the best man at his wedding.

Tommy had gone to Sam's home looking for him. His distraught and frightened wife had said that Sam had just left on a trip. On the off-chance, Tommy had gone to the depot to find Sam there collecting the present he'd bought for Tommy's wife. It was an item of lingerie in crimson nylon trimmed with black lace which he'd been unable to leave at home for obvious reasons. Tommy had grabbed the garment from a frightened Sam. It had a split at the crotch. Tommy imagined Sam fucking his wife while she was dressed up in this tart's regalia. Much to his fury, the idea of his oldest friend pumping away inside his wife turned him on. Sam had been dressed up in his best and reeked of aftershave. The sight of him added fuel to Tommy's blazing temper.

Tommy had already knocked out three of Sam's teeth by the time Dan arrived for his shift. The other men had stood around watching, not knowing quite what to do and secretly enjoying the spectacle. They hadn't wanted to interfere, they'd told Dan. Tommy was small, but very strong.

Dan hadn't hesitated. What he did and how he did it became the talk of the depot for months afterwards and from being a figure of mild derision, Dan took on the status of a hero.

It turned out he was a martial arts expert. A black belt, so they said, in one of those lethal oriental ways of fighting.

Whatever he was, he'd separated the two men swiftly and for long enough to stop Tommy from slaughtering his erstwhile friend. Afterwards, though, he wouldn't talk about it other than to say that the whole business had been 'regrettable.' They still thought he was a bit strange and talked like a BBC announcer, but they never again laughed at his fastidiousness or asked why he listened to Shakespeare in his cab instead of the local radio station like any 'normal' bloke. Two of the younger men even went so far as to join a local martial arts club. Watching him in action had been fantastic. 'Like Bruce Lee,' they'd said. 'Just like Bruce Lee.'

It had been his father's idea for Dan to get an HGV licence. He had told his son, quite wisely as it turned out, that if he insisted on pursuing his ambition to be an actor then he would most likely be in need of something to fall back on.

For once, Dan had listened to his father's words, and lately, he'd been very glad that he did – for all sorts of reasons.

It was the pinnacle of most actors' careers to play Hamlet. Dan was to play the Prince just three years after leaving drama school and though he felt himself to be relatively young and inexperienced, he knew he had something to bring to the part other than a faithful mouthing of the lines or a pale imitation of some of the great performances he'd seen on stage or film.

Admittedly, the production was to be staged in a small, not-quite-fashionable theatre in an outlying suburb of Manchester that hadn't as yet been discovered by 'serious' theatre critics. But Dan knew he was able to change all that. He had a few good contacts, he had limitless enthusiasm, he knew he had talent and, until two days ago, he thought he had the money needed to stage the production.

Three locally-based companies had been sponsoring the play. Then one of the major names had dropped out and, robbed of the kudos of appearing alongside this internationally famous retail chain as a 'patron of the arts', so did the other two, each of which had pledged five hundred pounds each.

As it was, right from the outset, the production had been designed to be presented on a shoestring. Props and scenery were kept to a minimum, the only real extravagance being Dan's hand-sewn Hamlet costume in black velvet.

Dan had been working as an HGV driver on and off since he left drama school. He was a 'casual', working as and when his acting commitments allowed.

When the chance had presented itself, Dan would audition for TV commercials. He'd appeared in thirty-second spots for coffee and breakfast cereals, and in one, had actually been given two lines to say. He'd had the odd walk-on part in TV dramas and a couple of good understudy roles in mainstream theatre. At one time, he'd been in rep for a whole year, working regularly.

Compared with most young actors, he'd been lucky. He'd saved a little of the money he'd made, though not much. But now he was glad of even this amount.

If he put every penny he had into Hamlet, there'd be just enough to stage the production. Polonius and Ophelia were willing to stump up some money between them. A couple of the soldiers had pledged a hundred pounds each and Laertes had a valuable watch he said he'd be willing to pawn. All together, they might just about make it to opening night.

Dan hadn't enjoyed working for Mason's. Though he'd met Paul Mason on only a couple of occasions, he had taken an instant dislike to the dark-haired entrepreneur who wandered around the depot in his hand-cut suits, saying little and missing nothing.

Paul Mason was charming to his female employees, but totally indifferent to the drivers who worked for him. Still, Dan wasn't exactly driving lorries for fun, so what did it really matter?

But then there was her. The woman who, apparently, was Paul Mason's long-time girlfriend. The woman who ran the office. The one he'd found crying over her desk.

Of course, he'd seen her before, but only in passing. But ever since that day he hadn't been able to put her out of his mind and he didn't know why. He knew lots of women; beautiful, talented women who one day he knew would become great actresses, loved by millions. He worked with them all the time. But there was something totally compelling about this girl, sitting behind her desk in her frightfully expensive suits. To Dan, she'd looked like a child dressed up for Christmas in her best frock. He'd handed her his handkerchief and wondered if he'd ever see her again.

Then, quite unexpectedly she had appeared in the depot. The other men had watched her in silence as she'd walked across to him and handed him his handkerchief back. She'd smiled and said, 'thank you,' and walked away.

When the other men quizzed him, he'd told them she'd had a piece of grit in her eye and he'd lent the handkerchief to her when he happened to be in the office. 'Bit of grit,' they'd repeated afterwards with a knowing leer. The handkerchief became his most prized possession. Washed and ironed and smelling faintly of some intoxicating perfume, Dan had taken it out of his pocket some time later and examined it as if looking for clues. Then he'd taken to carrying it every day, even during rehearsals for *Hamlet*, feeling that things would go well if he had it near him.

Sometimes when he was lying in bed alone he would think of Mary and imagine himself wiping her tears away. Then she would lift her face up to his and he would kiss her mouth. He knew what she would taste like, how her lips would feel against his own. He imagined unbuttoning her shirt, the blue silk one she'd been wearing the day he found her crying. He saw himself trailing the handkerchief across her breasts. He saw her nipples harden and heard her tell him how much she wanted him inside her. Silly, really, to have these fantasies. She was Paul Mason's girlfriend – though he couldn't imagine why.

Towards the end of rehearsals, Dan felt very much in need of a good luck charm and the handkerchief never left his pocket. He was dog tired, sometimes driving all night for Mason's and rehearsing the following day. But he'd get there. He'd do it. He felt that this was to be the performance of his life.

He wanted to invite Mary to the first night. But how could he? What would she think? Yet he knew that without her there, there would be something lacking. Was he crazy, he wondered? He didn't even know her. He decided to stick his neck out. She'd reject him, of course. Possibly have a quiet word with her boyfriend and Dan would find that work for 'casuals' like himself had suddenly dried up. How would she react? He had no way of telling. But, as with everything else he'd ever done, he thought he'd take a chance.

Alex had decided to catch a train to Manchester. Though before now she'd taken not the slightest interest in Paul's business in the north, she decided to see it for herself before telling him that she was leaving him.

She had no reservations about seeing Mary again. In fact she rather looked forward to it. Mary, she felt, was her only ally. Her only true friend. And it was better that everything was out in the open. Better that Paul's deception should cease, here and now.

Alex felt sure that when it came to a showdown, Paul would decide to stay with Mary. Strangely, she didn't resent the fact. Mary had so much more to offer him than she did. She was accomplished, she ran his business. Everything about her was somehow stable, permanent . . . to be depended upon.

In truth, Alex didn't want to fight for Paul any more. Her hurt was too deep, his betrayal too complete. She'd hoped that Paul would keep her safe but he'd turned out like all the rest. And now she wanted it all to come to an end. Before he came back to her again, wanting to make love.

Despite the unhappy purpose of her journey, Alex enjoyed travelling by train. Comfortably ensconced in first class, she made her way to the restaurant car soon after the train had pulled out of Euston and ordered the best lunch on the menu, with a half bottle of a rather good Sauvignon Blanc to go with it.

The phone number of Paul's haulage company was easily obtained through Directory Enquiries. Alex had never known the name of it until Mary had told her and for some strange reason, had never asked Paul what his Manchester business was called. It simply hadn't been a part of their lives. It had never occurred to her to mistrust him.

Alex took a large gulp of wine and dialled on her mobile. 'May I speak to Paul Mason, please?' she said as soon as the phone was picked up. 'Tell him it's Alex.' There was a pause. Alex could feel her heart racing and for a moment, her resolve failed her. What would she do? Where could she go when she left him? She had no money of her own, nothing . . .

A voice came on the line. A familiar voice. 'Alex, is that you?' said Mary.

'Yes,' she replied. 'I'm on the train. I'm coming to Manchester.'

'Why?' said Mary. 'Alex, what on earth are you doing?'

'I can't stand this any longer,' said Alex. 'I just can't. That's all there is to it. When I get there, I'm going to come and see him. I'm going to tell him I'm leaving him. I don't want him, Mary. He's yours, always has been. I was just a diversion.'

She heard Mary sigh. 'He's not here, Alex,' she said. 'He went back to Scotland this morning. He'll be away for three days.' Alex went silent, hearing nothing but the sound of her own blood rushing in her ears and the gentle and rhythmic movement of the train as it sped along the track.

'Listen,' said Mary. 'Wait for me at the station. I'll come and pick you up. Do you hear me, Alex? Don't go anywhere. Wait for me.'

Once the penny had dropped, Gina wondered why it had

taken her so long to put two and two together.

It had all started when one of the women at the club had got wind of the fact that Kurt had been 'messing about' with one of the lady members – though no one had any idea of who it was.

Apparently, Kurt had made a chance remark in the men's changing room – a remark which had been reported back and exaggerated with all the feverish creativity characteristic of those who are either terminally bored or incurably envious.

Gina was furious with herself. She should have realised who the woman was long ago. The only one who had treated Kurt with total indifference was the cleverest of all. The bitch! Now it was all so obvious.

First of all, Alex had bolted to the health farm, which, though in itself not unusual, had happened with a rather suspicious urgency. Then since she'd returned she'd been acting strangely – particularly the other night when she'd objected so strongly to being brought to the tennis club.

It was Alex! Kurt was sleeping with Alex. And now she had disappeared completely and without a word. Gina decided to go to the club and if Kurt was there, make sure that he knew that his little games had been found out.

Gina dressed in her most flattering suit and took even more care than usual with her make-up. She would confront the beast in his lair and see what he had to say for himself. At the same time, she'd make sure he understood she was a force to be reckoned with. After all, he was only an employee of the Mottlesham, whatever his father did for a living.

With all the righteous indignation to which, as a respectably married woman she felt she was entitled, Gina set off in her dark green Mazda sports car, determined to confront the Mottlesham's tennis coach, in the process causing as much trouble for her friend Alex as was possible.

Gina had decided that it would be easy enough to pretend that her actions had been prompted by the best possible motives.

In truth, she was bored. She was jealous of her friend who had a young and handsome lover at home and someone on the side into the bargain. Alex wasn't entitled to all this, thought Gina. Alex was greedy and needed to be taught a lesson. Besides, thought Gina, a little diversion of the muck-raking kind would help to lift her spirits.

The clubhouse was deserted, the grille at the front of the bar firmly locked. It was five o'clock on a weekday afternoon and the ladies' afternoon club had already left. There was at least an hour to go before the first of the evening players turned up be-suited and stressed out, ready to slip into shorts and whack away the frustrations of the day on the pristine grass courts. But right now, all was quiet. In the distance, Gina could see one of the gardeners cutting a hedge. But apart from that, no one. Gina had driven here on impulse, not thinking clearly. She now realised she should have waited until later in the hope of catching Kurt between lessons.

She could always hang around, but if she did so she knew that her resolve would fail her. She needed to walk straight into the club and straight up to him, all guns blazing.

But what was she going to accuse him of? Unprofessional conduct? Too pompous. Taking advantage of her friend? Yes, that sounded better. It was the sort of accusation of which everyone would approve. That would do nicely. But did she have any proof? Not really, but Gina knew that her instinct was reliable enough. She'd chance it. Even if she'd got it wrong, it was worth the gamble. Anything to add a *frisson* of excitement to her increasingly dull life.

Gina sighed as she surveyed the empty club house and turned to walk away. Then in the distance, she heard the sound of running water and decided to find out where it was coming from. Maybe someone had left a tap on.

The door to the men's changing room was ajar and the noise was the sound of a shower. There was someone in there and Gina pushed the door open, hovering on the step, trying to see inside.

Gina was twenty-five, but for the last three years the only male body she had seen was that of a fat, fifty-year-old lecher with a prick the size of a thumb and a belly that almost hid it from view. Her husband had made her rich and, she believed, respectable. But she loathed him. Most of all she loathed the fact that she was trapped, knowing that her life-long habit of flirting was tolerated, but any real evidence of infidelity on her part would mean instant banishment from access to Marcos's bank balance, his flat and the pretty little car she now bombed around in.

Gina had been madly jealous when Paul had presented Alex with her own car only weeks before. The long-suffering Marcos had been despatched to buy her a car of her own the very next day. She loved the sporty little Mazda and the freedom it gave her. But lately she'd begun to feel that the freedom she'd craved so completely was illusory and that her marriage, which had always been a sham, was rapidly becoming too much to endure.

From her vantage point just inside the door, Gina knew that she couldn't be seen. Besides, the man who was showering had his back to her. 'A pity,' thought Gina, though his back and his beautiful wet buttocks were enough to keep her enthralled. She watched as the water ran across his shoulders and down, caressing his bum, pouring like molten silk across a golden body, hard as iron.

The man was blond and Gina felt her stomach give a lurch as she suddenly realised that she was looking at Kurt. Sometimes, he gave tennis lessons in the afternoons and no doubt had recently come off court.

'He's beautiful, is he not?' said a voice at her side. Gina jumped as if scalded and turned quickly towards the voice. 'I don't blame you,' it said, 'even I would be tempted to watch.' The man in the shower was not Kurt, for Kurt stood beside her, smiling his mocking smile.

'I was looking for . . .' Gina began, then her voice trailed off. All her resolve had deserted her and her pre-planned speech had flown from her mind.

'It would be foolish to ask what it is that you want,' said Kurt, 'for that much is obvious.'

Gina felt herself blush and with a muttered, 'Excuse me,' went to walk away.

'Don't do that,' said Kurt, taking hold of her arm. 'I hate to think of you having had a wasted journey. Don't go yet. I want to know if I can help you.'

Gina felt the pressure of his fingers and a stab of lust shot deep into her belly.

'And how could you possibly help me?' she said, her voice shaking.

'I think we should discuss it, don't you?' said Kurt, leading her back into the changing room and shutting the door.

The water had stopped running. The man in the shower had emerged, a towel wrapped around his waist. He was rubbing his pale blond hair and looked up, somewhat startled to see a woman.

'Steve,' said Kurt, 'this is Gina. She wandered in here looking for a friend and was about to leave when I found her.'

Kurt and Steve exchanged glances. A smile played faintly around Steve's lips.

'I'm delighted to meet you, Gina,' said Steve, extending a still-damp hand.

'Steve,' continued Kurt, leading Gina to a nearby bench, 'is one of my star pupils. You don't recognise him because he's not a club member, but I give him the occasional lesson here when things are quiet. A little against the rules, I know, but I'm sure you won't tell. Will you?'

Gina looked from Kurt to Steve and back again. Two blond gods and she was alone with them. She felt scared and randy as hell.

Steve sat down next to her on the other side from Kurt. Gina was aware of the sun streaming in through the window of the changing room. She knew that she should get out into the fresh air and clear her head. She shifted slightly in her seat and felt the dampness between her legs.

Steve smiled at her and edged closer. Her heart was pounding, her clitoris thumping wildly, sending its messages to her brain, fixing her to her seat as if super-glued.

'Of course I won't tell,' said Gina. 'I won't say a word,' she continued, her voice cracking as she watched Kurt lift his fingers and brush a strand of hair from her face. He paused, then trailed his fingers down her neck. Gina shuddered.

'Why so nervous?' asked Kurt. 'We only want to be friends. Is that okay, Gina?' Her throat too dry to speak, she nodded.

His hand was reaching for the buttons at the front of her jacket and Gina sat quite still, her heart racing.

She felt her own hand being lifted and carried. She felt the touch of damp towelling and she realised that Steve had moved it, placing it in his lap. Gina paused. 'Do I want to do this?' she asked herself, but she knew the answer. Gina began to move her fingers across Steve's lap till she found the bulge at the front of the towel and grappling beneath it, she found his hard penis, still damp from the shower. She began to rub.

Gina closed her eyes, thoughts of her husband passing through her mind which she instantly dismissed. She owed him nothing. She'd sacrificed too much for too long. And besides, she was willing to lose Marcos, the car, everything. She was prepared to sacrifice the life she'd worked so hard to build. Anything rather than leave now. She'd rather die.

It was all like a dream. Gina felt that everything was happening in slow motion as she squeezed Steve's prick and Kurt's mouth travelled across her flesh.

She felt the mood change suddenly. It was as if an unspoken signal had passed between the two men for the next thing she knew was the feeling of being lifted under her elbows and pulled to the floor. She knew that the two men were about to fuck her for one was pulling her bra off while the other was forcing her legs apart and she couldn't tell which was which.

'Hold her,' said a voice. Then she heard remarks about her body, voices talking about her as if she was not there. Gina was nothing to them. Just a body. But she didn't care. She wanted sex with both of them. Sex was all she needed, all she ached for.

Gina felt a mouth against her tits and fingers probing her pussy. The finger-fucking was deep and hard, knuckles crushed against her clitoris as whichever man it was delved deeply into her wetness as if grasping for something just out of reach. Were they Kurt's fingers or Steve's inside her? She didn't know and the fact that she didn't know thrilled her.

She pictured herself lying on the floor, her legs coarsely pinned apart as the two men took their pleasure. She wanted them both. She longed to be fucked to oblivion with no need to finish herself off with one of the array of pathetic sex aids she kept hidden from Marcos in case her need of them made him feel slighted, his masculinity called into question.

Two men, even three would be fine . . . she knew that, now she'd finally admitted to herself just how frustrated she was, she really didn't care. She just wanted a cock inside her. She needed someone young and virile to make her feel alive again, to make her feel like she used to in the old days before she sold her body and soul . . . for what?

Her nipples were being squeezed and then she felt a mouth exploring them, soft and damp as it nuzzled and sucked the puckered skin till her whole body cried out to be penetrated. All too soon the magical mouth pulled away and she felt the familiar shape of a prick against her lips.

'Open wide,' said a voice. Was it Kurt's? She couldn't be sure for she kept her eyes tightly shut, knowing that she had gone too far to go back and fearing that despite her need, if she saw what was happening she might feel trapped.

She had never meant for this to happen. Not really. Not quite like this. But she knew in her heart that she had come here looking for more than a chance to challenge Kurt about Alex.

But however much she may or may not have been responsible, it had happened so suddenly and now she was powerless to do anything but lie there and take it, enjoying her own vulnerability, turned on by the danger of exploring the unexplored, the unknown thrill of fucking two men at once.

'Open, I said,' the voice repeated, pushing his prick hard against her lips. Gina opened her mouth and took the penis which slid straight to the back of her throat.

'Aren't you going to fuck her?' said the other voice, followed by a grunt of agreement. Her tits were being squeezed and her mouth was full of cock as Gina felt her legs being held wider apart. A rock-hard prick began its probings, dipping its head into the bush of hair that stood guard at the entrance to her passage and then with a sharp and sudden thrust, diving into the pool of her longing which for years now had been barely disturbed by even the smallest ripple across its surface.

'She's tight . . . fucks good,' said a voice as Gina felt her legs being lifted and placed against the shoulders of whoever was fucking her. He was plunging so deep, stretching and filling her as the other man was plundering her mouth. Suddenly she felt the cock in her mouth tense and the back of her throat was bathed in sperm. She heard the man between her legs shudder and knew that he too was about to come. She heard him cry out and he began to drive faster, coming in a burst of swearing and cursing in German. So she was being fucked by Kurt. It was Steve who had shot his load into her mouth.

Gina opened her eyes to see Kurt pulling a condom off his prick. There was sperm trickling from her lips. Both men stood over her now, their perfect, naked bodies beaded with sweat, their pricks flaccid and resting against their legs, their blond heads turned towards each other.

'Have you finished with her?' said Steve.

'I'm not sure,' Kurt replied. He reached down and pulled Gina to her feet. She was sticky and sore between her legs and for a moment had trouble standing. Taking her by the wrist, he led her into the shower.

'Open your mouth,' he commanded and meekly, she did as she was told. The water poured into her mouth, its little jets bouncing across her tongue, the rivulets running down her breasts, soothing her bruised nipples.

Kurt's prick had been huge within her and Gina could feel the unaccustomed tenderness deep inside.

'What do you want to do with her?' said Steve, walking into the shower room to see Kurt lathering and soaping her body. 'Let's dry her off first,' said Kurt, wrapping Gina in a huge white towel.

Kurt rubbed her down, making her nipples tingle as the towel scraped across her breasts. He looked at her body and then, as if deciding he had better things to do with his time, shrugged. 'Go home, Gina,' he said. 'Go home to your husband.'

Gina felt herself becoming angry. 'I had no climax,' she

said. 'I didn't come. You both did, but I didn't. If you're going to fuck me, at least fuck me till we're all satisfied.'

Steve laughed and slapped her on her naked arse. 'You see, Steve,' said Kurt. 'See how demanding and spoilt these bitches are that I have to work with?'

Gina knelt on the floor on all fours. Her legs were shaking, her bruised pussy wet and open. 'Come on,' she said. 'Fuck me, the both of you.'

She felt a stinging slap across her arse and then a prick pushed up inside her. It was Steve this time, pulling in and out of her in long, slow plunges. He was tweaking her nipples as he thrust, and Gina knew that this time, she would reach the zenith of her pleasure.

Even in her wild teenage years she'd never fucked two men at the same time. It felt good. Better than good. In a moment, Kurt's huge knob would follow that of his friend and she would take everything they could give. But Kurt hadn't wanted her a second time. Not like he wanted Alex. Gina knew he'd fuck her simply because she was there and she was willing. Bastard. Hateful bastard.

Mary arrived at Manchester Piccadilly just in time to see the train from Euston pull into the platform. Alex was one of the last passengers to alight, and Mary was shocked to see how pale she looked. Translucent, almost.

Alex had brought no case with her, intending to stay only for a few hours. She looked young and vulnerable walking along the platform, clutching her handbag, her manicured and lacquered nails in contrast to the pale skin of her long fingers.

'Come,' said Mary, putting her arm around the girl without even thinking. 'I'm going to take you home and we're going to have a talk. I think you need to think a bit before you do anything drastic.'

Alex looked at her, alarmed. 'Home?' she said. 'Not your home. Not . . .'

'I told you,' said Mary, 'he's away. Scotland, so I'm told. Don't worry.' Alex heaved a sigh and her shoulders seemed to droop. 'Okay,' she said, as if resigned to her fate.

* * *

Mary and Paul lived in a modern, semi-detached house in a prosperous suburb of Manchester. Paul had chosen the house and though Mary would have preferred an older house, and one that wasn't the same shape and size as all the others in the avenue, over the years she'd used every moment of her limited spare time to make it beautiful.

It was late spring. Already, the garden was showing signs of its summer potential. Colour and fragrance were waiting to burst out into the air and the herb garden was preparing to run wild as it did every summer. The swifts which built their nest in the garden shed every year had already laid their eggs and were sitting patiently.

Alex stood in the kitchen and stared out into the garden. She was silent, her eyes full of tears.

'It's nothing like this,' she said, 'the flat in London . . .'

Mary had made a cassoulet. She opened a bottle of rich, red Barolo wine and stood it on the kitchen table. Alex looked like she needed a drink.

'Wine?' said Mary, but Alex seemed not to hear her. 'A drink?' she repeated, somewhat embarrassed by the other woman's reaction to the house. She'd expected Alex to regard her surroundings with quiet amusement, comparing the suburban neatness of Mary's home with a flat which, Mary imagined, was extremely smart. But Alex had looked at everything with a kind of strange awe. 'This is . . . a real home,' she said quietly. Mary didn't know what to reply to this odd comment and busied herself with opening a jar of olives.

Though the days were warm and the early mornings misty with the promise of heat, Mary still lit a fire in the evenings to banish the lingering hint of chill that was all that remained of what had been a long, cold Manchester winter.

Sitting Alex by the fireside she busied herself in the kitchen, checking on the dinner and putting French bread in the oven to warm. The smell of cassoulet filtered through to the room beyond, where Alex had slipped out of her shoes and now sat on the floor, her knees brought up beneath her chin, the glass of wine that Mary had put in her hand held in front of her, reflecting the light of the fire in its ruby depths.

With the meal finally under control, Mary came to join her. 'Now,' she said, sitting beside Alex on the carpet, 'tell me.'

The red wine coursed through her veins and Alex began to relax, telling Mary of Paul's recent, flying visit and how she had awoken to find him lying on top of her sleeping body, his penis inside her.

'I didn't want him,' she said and took a huge gulp of her wine. Mary looked at her closely. 'Are you sure about that?' she said.

'Of course I'm not sure!' said Alex, her voice raised in misery. 'In bed . . . sometimes . . . well, I can't help that. But that's not enough. Not any more. I've been wondering what to do, where to go. I feel that I'm losing my grip and it seemed that to come to Manchester and to tell him that I knew everything might help to clear my head.'

'Really?' said Mary. 'And why is that?'

'Because it's honest,' replied Alex. 'And if I don't do something soon, I think I'll go mad.'

Mary sat for a while, staring into the fire. Then she sighed. 'Alex,' she said. 'It isn't you who's been dishonest. But it seems that you want to destroy everything on the grounds that anything is better than uncertainty. Are you sure that's true?'

Alex began to cry quietly, the tears rolling down her cheeks. 'I don't understand you,' she said, 'not for a moment. Look what he's done to us. Both of us! How can you begin to think of staying with him? How can you tell me to do the same?'

Mary held her glass to the flames and warmed it. 'For that very reason, Alex,' she replied quietly. 'He's done such harm to you and me that we have to be careful not to do any more to ourselves.'

'But this *is* harming me,' said Alex. 'This situation is harming me very much.'

Mary put her hand on Alex's arm. 'Give me a little more time to think things through,' she said.

'Time for what?' Alex replied, wiping her eyes. 'And why should you try and work out *my* problems?'

'Please,' said Mary. 'Don't do anything you might regret. We've got to sort this out without ruining our own lives in the process.'

'I think that my life is ruined already,' said Alex softly. Mary didn't jump to contradict her. 'Why?' she said. 'Why do you say that?'

Alex took another swallow of wine and began to talk. She told Mary about the succession of dead-end jobs she'd gone through since leaving school, about her useless attempt at a hotel management career and how Paul, so she'd felt, had come along at just the right time. Then she told Mary about how things had started to go wrong. How lonely she'd become . . . how Kurt had come into her life. 'But he hurts you, Alex,' said Mary, her eyes troubled. 'He hurts you and I don't understand why you are with him.'

Alex smiled, noticing the frown that furrowed Mary's brow.

Mary appeared so grown-up, so capable, thought Alex. And yet in some things she was just a child.

'I'm with him *because* he hurts me, Mary. Don't you understand? I like to be beaten by him. Tied up by him. It's what turns me on. I like to be treated like . . .'

'Like nothing,' said Mary.

Alex smiled. 'Don't you and Paul ever play games?' she said. Mary looked confused. 'I don't think so,' she replied, shifting uncomfortably. 'Not like you mean.'

Getting to her feet, she said she would go and check on the dinner. Alex had never seen her look so awkward.

Alex felt a little drunk and for the first time in weeks, a wave of something resembling contentment engulfed her. Crying had done her good. Being with Mary was good. She felt at peace here, cared for by beautiful, innocent Mary. Mary with her fluffy blonde hair and unshakeable sense of right and wrong. Idly, Alex wondered what Mary looked like with no clothes on.

The meal was delicious, though Alex was aware of a tension in Mary she hadn't noticed before. Mary waited on her like the perfect hostess, refilling her glass, checking that all was as it should be, fluttering around like a teenager with her first-ever boyfriend.

Mary's face was flushed and her eyes were shining. She brought coffee into the sitting room and the women sat again by the fireside, its crackling and spitting having given way to a deep red glow from which came only the occasional hiss or sputter.

It was apparent that Mary had been embarrassed by their earlier conversation and Alex enjoyed her discomfort, sensing the other woman's awareness of her own naivety laced with an inquisitiveness which Alex found exciting.

So, Mary and Paul never played games. Mary had never been tied up or had her neat little arse slapped. Alex drank her coffee and wondered what Mary and Paul actually did in bed. The missionary position, I expect, she thought. Yet there was something about Mary that hinted at a far greater potential for pleasure.

Mary was sitting on the floor beside Alex but this time, at a carefully considered distance. She was close enough not to be unfriendly but far enough away for there to be no possibility of contact, no sudden touch of a knee or brush of a hand against a breast should either of the women decide to adjust her sitting position or make a sudden move.

She fancies me, thought Alex, feeling suddenly more worldly wise than her companion. She's gone all fluttery because she's curious about what I've told her. And she fancies me.

Alex glanced at Mary out of the corner of her eye. Mary's face was flushed in the firelight and her body was tense. A picture came to Alex's mind of Mary laying on her back, legs wide apart. Alex with her head between Mary's thighs, savouring the salty taste of her pussy. She'd relax, then, thought Alex. I'd make her relax.

The open fire was mesmeric, the flames shooting up the chimney in tongues of gold and deep red with the occasional burst of blue. Alex knew that she wanted Mary. Wanted to touch her, wanted to sleep with her. She also knew that Mary had never been with a woman. That much was obvious – and heightened the exquisite pleasure of seduction.

'Kurt ties me up,' she said suddenly, breaking the silence. 'He ties my hands tightly and beats my arse. He pinches my nipples hard and the pain adds to the pleasure. I'm always wet, very wet before his prick comes anywhere near me. I need to be. He's huge. And I can't get enough.'

Alex glanced at Mary again and saw that the flush in her cheeks had spread down her neck. 'I'm wet between the legs just thinking about him,' said Alex. 'He's a wicked, dangerous bastard but somehow I just can't break free. And Paul—'

'I don't want to hear,' said Mary, interrupting suddenly.

'I suppose I'm just a tart,' said Alex. 'I need sex. I can't live without it.'

'You're not a tart!' Mary snapped at her, the vehemence of her tone surprising them both.

'Then what am I?' said Alex, looking Mary straight in the face. Mary looked away from her and blushed. 'You're an intelligent and capable woman. And a very beautiful one.'

'So are you,' said Alex. Mary blushed again. 'Do you have any music?' Alex asked over the gentle hissing and spitting of the fire.

'What do you like?' Mary replied, visibly relieved to be changing the subject.

'I think,' said Alex, wickedly, 'something romantic. I feel very relaxed . . . just sitting here.'

Mary got up and moved across to the CD player. The voice of Alison Moyet filled the room and Alex put her glass down and lay on her back.

'Is that okay?' said Mary, lowering herself to the floor, though still keeping her distance.

'It could be better,' said Alex, sitting up on her elbow. She looked at Mary and thought again how very pretty she was. Pretty and somehow innocent with a freshness that not only Paul found seductive.

Mary was looking at her questioningly, her big eyes like those of a giant fawn. 'The music could be better,' continued Alex, deciding to take a chance, 'if we were listening to it in bed.'

Mary looked down at the carpet and ran her fingers through her hair. For a moment neither spoke. Then Alex lifted herself up and onto her knees and moved across to Mary. She thought that Mary might have pulled away, but this time she did not. Reaching up, Alex touched the soft golden curls that framed Mary's face. 'This is madness,' said Mary, 'I'm not . . .'

'No,' whispered Alex. 'Neither am I. But I need you tonight. As much as you need me.'

Mary sat quite still for a moment and then heaved a great sigh. Her shoulders seemed to relax. 'I'm so wet for you,' Alex said. 'You and no one else.'

Alex turned Mary's face towards her own, touching her lips against the other woman's cheek. She felt Mary turn her head slightly, presenting the rest of her face for kissing. There was no hesitation in her action now, no hypocritical mock protestations.

Alex lifted her index finger and traced the outline of Mary's lips. She shivered as Alex's finger made contact. Alex slid her hand beneath Mary's chin, lifting her face towards her own.

Closing her eyes, Alex pressed her mouth against Mary's parted lips. Their tongues met and intertwined and Alex felt Mary's body straining towards her. She felt hands in her hair, felt her head being lifted away and guided down towards Mary's breasts. Nuzzling between the buttons of a silk shirt, Alex's face came in contact with warm flesh and she put out her tongue, licking the little patches of skin that she could reach in the gaps between the buttons.

Taking Mary by the shoulders, Alex lowered her gently onto her back. Leaning over her, she began to undo her blouse, peeling it back as if undoing a precious parcel.

Mary was breathing heavily, the glow from the fire lighting her skin as Alex reached behind her and undid her bra. The scent of Mary's warm skin was delicious. Mary lay before her like a banquet waiting to be devoured. Her fat red nipples had puckered, her smooth, generous breasts lay spread like two milky cushions waiting for Alex to rest her head against them. But that would come later. First she would suckle these beautiful breasts with all the skill and sensitivity that only a woman could show towards another.

Alex knew what it would feel like as she flicked each of Mary's nipples in turn with her wet tongue. She knew the thrills that would course through her lover's body, how she would bring her to the edge of paradise with her tongue and her fingers alone.

Alex leant forward and recognised the scent of her own perfume. Curious, she thought as she brought her face closer. Slowly, Alex poked out her tongue and stroked it across Mary's right nipple. She felt her shiver and heard her groan softly in the back of her throat. 'I want to put my tongue between your legs,' she whispered as, taking each nipple between her lips in turn, she smeared them with lipstick as she caressed her new and unfamiliar lover with the utmost gentleness.

'I've never . . .' murmured Mary, stroking Alex's sheet of silken hair. 'It's okay, I know,' Alex whispered in return. 'But let me make love to you. Please . . .'

Alex was aware of nothing but the dreamy expression in Mary's eyes as she undressed her. The bush between Mary's legs was soft as cashmere and as Alex removed Mary's panties, the other woman parted her legs, revealing the tiny tip of her pink clitoris peeping out inquisitively, inviting attention.

'Go on,' she said. 'I want you to. I want to feel your mouth down there. Go on . . . go on . . .'

Alex reached down and took hold of Mary's nipples, squeezing them both between her fingertips.

'Fuck me,' Mary moaned, 'fuck me with your mouth . . .'

Yes, thought Alex, I knew she would be like this. She watched Mary squirm beneath her touch, the smell of her pussy mingling with the rich waves of perfume that rose from her skin.

Alex leant forward and kissed Mary deeply. As she did so, she became aware that Mary was reaching for her shirt buttons, pulling Alex's shirt from her and tearing at her bra. Mary's excitement was deeply arousing to Alex and quickly, she struggled out of her remaining clothes. Within seconds, both women were naked, the flickering flames of the fire silhouetting their soft contours as nipple brushed against nipple and tongue intertwined with tongue.

Kissing her lover's eyelids, her nose, her mouth, Alex then ran the flat of her tongue from Mary's breastbone down between her breasts and on down the whole length of her belly, stopping tantalisingly short of her open pussy.

Mary gave a deep moan of need and desire and Alex lowered her face between Mary's legs, aware of the familiar smell of pussy which was at the same time strangely exotic, rich and intense, the other woman's groans of pleasure and need setting her clitoris throbbing.

Flicking her tongue over the tip of Mary's clitoris, Alex heard her sigh and then open her legs wider still, revealing the glistening folds of her vulva which released a hot wave of heady scent. 'Lick me,' she murmured huskily. 'Please, Alex . . . I can't stand it.'

Alex plunged her face into the unfamiliar softness, aware as she did so of Mary's fingers on her breasts, pinching and rolling her nipples which hardened in response.

She tasted good. Alex began to explore with her tongue, following the slippery course of Mary's pleasure to the dark, wet cavern at its source. She knew what felt good when Paul licked her out and determined to treat Mary to the same delights.

Spicing her gentle sucking and licking with hard little nips, Alex felt her respond, the river between her legs turning to flood as she moaned and begged for more.

She's ready, thought Alex, turning Mary over onto her stomach and pulling her up onto her knees. Mary knelt, still and patient as Alex came up behind her. Bunching three fingers together Alex drove them into Mary's gaping, wet cavern covering Mary's body as she did so with her own, covering her like a dog covers a bitch.

Mary cried out with pleasure as Alex wrapped her other arm around her belly and groped between her pussy lips, trapping her slippery clitoris between two fingers and pinching it as she finger-fucked Mary from behind. Alex felt Mary's vagina begin to throb around her fingers, tightening around them as she plunged and slithered in the darkness of Mary's hungry pussy, her manicured nails stretching the walls of Mary's cavern which tightened in response to her driving thrusts.

Mary's pretty arse seemed to be pointing in defiance at

Alex and with one deep thrust, she pulled her fingers from Mary's passage, wiping them across her buttocks. 'Now,' she said, 'it is time for punishment.'

Alex began to slap Mary's arse, gently at first, but with each stroke, hitting her harder, forcing a cry from Mary's lips which by the fourth or fifth hard blow, had turned into a groan of pleasure.

Alex was pinching her own breasts as she slapped, the excitement of hitting this woman blending with a whole mix of emotions she fought to control. But she could not. Lust and desire were edged with a need for revenge on this creature who had, unwittingly, turned her world upside down.

Alex's blows became harder and faster until she was slapping Mary uncontrollably, beating her for all she was worth, watching her pink arse turn to bright red as the blows rained down.

She heard Mary give a deep, guttural cry and suddenly Mary had swung her body round, grabbing Alex's now stinging hand and stuffing the girl's fingers once again deep into her pussy.

The beating had brought Mary to an orgasm which she rode out against Alex's trembling knuckles, her own fingers clasping her punisher's breasts as her hungry tongue drove into Alex's mouth.

The gentle creature had turned into a wildcat, her body streaked with sweat and her eyes glittering sharply. She's magnificent, thought Alex as the last of Mary's shudders subsided. She's more than I could ever be. And I think I love her.

'You are going back to work,' said Mary some time later as they lay in bed, curled in each other's arms. 'Oh, am I now?' replied Alex, amused by Mary's bossy tone.

'I'm not joking,' Mary said, her voice taking on a serious tone. 'The way you live . . . the way you've told me things are . . . you'll never find any real satisfaction in that crazy kind of life.'

'Oh, I don't know,' said Alex, a lascivious grin playing

about her lips. 'It isn't so bad . . . could be worse.'

Mary shot Alex a mildly disapproving look. Changing the subject, Alex leant across to kiss Mary's breasts. 'So you liked a bit of punishment, then?' she said, beginning to tweak Mary's nipples between her fingers. All discussions of work were at an end. 'Yes,' said Alex, looking up from her task. 'I thought you might.'

Mary managed to get her key in the lock and open the front door just in the nick of time. She reached the telephone at the fourth ring, just a split second before the answer machine switched on and interrupted the call. Paul sounded unusually harrassed when they spoke. 'I rang earlier,' he said, 'and got the strangest message.'

'It's just the same as it's always been,' said Mary, ignoring the fact that she'd re-recorded it only days before, copying Alex's words and inflections precisely. The idea of Paul being confused by hearing Alex's own phraseology recorded in Mary's voice, amused her.

Paul had said that he wouldn't be back for another few days. His business in Edinburgh would keep him in Scotland for a while longer, but he'd get home as soon as he could. It was an awkward conversation, full of difficult pauses. Mary wondered if he had another woman in Scotland. 'By the way,' he said. 'Where were you when I phoned? I rang this morning at eight.'

'I set out for the office very early,' she replied, 'and got stuck in a traffic jam. There'd been an accident. Tail-backs for miles.' Mary was alarmed at how easy she found it to lie.

She could hardly tell Paul she'd been driving Alex back to the railway station. That his other lover had spent the night in his Manchester home, making love to her.

Just the thought of what had happened sent a fresh flood of moisture into Mary's already-sodden panties. Propping the phone against her ear she fumbled between her legs and began to masturbate while Paul droned on about the office, the new sales targets – all the stuff she was no longer interested in.

Deep down, Mary knew she wasn't a lesbian. But she

wouldn't have missed last night for the world. She loved Alex, felt responsible for her. And from the moment she'd dropped her at the railway station, she'd begun to miss her.

They'd hardly slept the night before and by six o'clock the following morning, Mary had climbed out of bed and was sorting through her wardrobe, pulling out outfit after outfit, searching for something she could give Alex as a gift, something beautiful that she could wear next to her skin in memory of the time they'd shared.

Both women had known that their night together had been a one-off, but the bond that they had forged was one that would not be broken. No one could come between it, especially not Paul. They would support each other, whatever happened.

Mary had pulled out the cream slip she'd worn the last time Paul had made love to her. 'Take this,' she'd said. 'It will suit you perfectly,' and Alex had smiled her beautiful smile. Then Mary had shown Alex some of her dowdier clothes and laughed at some of the things she used to wear. 'If you've no use for them, can I take them?' Alex had said. 'I'd like to wear them in front of Paul. See if there is any reaction.'

The request seemed rather curious but Mary agreed, folding them into her spare suitcase. Then she'd prepared breakfast and taken Alex to the station. Much had been said, much decided.

Sitting at her office desk some hours later, Mary felt a great wave of loneliness sweep over her. She feared for Alex, worried about her. And most of all, she missed her.

Mary had enjoyed being spanked the night before, more than she'd ever dreamed possible. But she was still worried about Alex and the man called Kurt, knowing that their sex games went further than spanking.

It was foreign territory to Mary and she knew that it was really none of her business. But Alex was unhappy, that much she realised. And her unhappiness wasn't all the result of the situation with Paul.

Mary had been disturbed to discover that Alex and Paul played 'games'. In all their time together, Mary had had no idea of this side to Paul's character, of this need in him. I know nothing, she thought. I have lived with him all these years, but I know nothing.

Alex had looked more relaxed when she left than she had done when she arrived the night before. She'd hugged Mary, holding her close, then she'd disappeared along the platform.

Mary had been genuinely sad to see her go and had returned to her car with a heavy heart. What would have happened before she saw her again, she wondered. Could they resolve their impossible situation without too much hurt?

The morning had dragged interminably and Mary had hated even being in the office. She had gone for lunch and had returned to find an envelope propped up on her desk, lodged between a paperweight and a small bunch of wild flowers which had mysteriously appeared out of nowhere.

Opening the envelope she was surprised to find that it was an invitation, handwritten and signed, 'From Dan, whose pleasure it was to lend you my handkerchief.'

Mary had looked at the invitation and laughed. *That's all I need*, she'd thought to herself. *To go and watch a lorry driver play Hamlet.*

Chapter 13

Kurt hadn't been able to get Alex out of his mind. Though he had wanted to punish and humiliate her for trying to run away from him, his little escapade with Gina had shown him how much other women now bored him.

Gina was pretty and had a good figure and a nice, tight pussy. She was also randy as hell. But fucking her had been nothing more than a way to pass the time and without the added *frisson* of sharing her with Steve, he doubted if he'd even have bothered.

He hadn't wanted to spank her or to do any of the things that really turned him on. Those were no good any more with anyone but Alex. The bitch had ensnared him, body and soul. Kurt knew he needed her but he hated her at the same time. No one had made him feel this way before. Not since the shadowy days of his youth when Stepmama had lured him to her room and the seventeen-year-old Kurt had stumbled precociously into secrets which no boy of his age had any business knowing. Not since then had he felt such excitement. Even now, he could remember the hazy, hot day all those years ago and the memory of Frau Helena as her lips touched his body and he discovered, for the first time, the pleasure to be had in the embrace of a beautiful woman.

Kurt had tried phoning Alex but had got the answerphone. In desperation, he'd phoned Gina. 'She's gone away, I believe,' Gina had answered icily. She'd put the phone down, burning with fury and humiliation. Kurt had fucked her and still he was calling her about Alex. She hated him. She hated them both. Somehow, she would get her revenge.

Mary had done what she'd vowed she never would, and had

phoned Jason Hannard. Lonely and vulnerable, she simply wanted to hear his voice and much to her delight, he'd been at home.

Apologising profusely, stating the fact that she knew that his number was only for emergencies, Mary confessed that she'd simply wanted to talk to him and she hoped she wasn't being a nuisance.

Jason's voice was as rich and comforting as she remembered, and closing her eyes, Mary felt once again wrapped in its warmth. He told her all about the filming, making her laugh with tales of small disasters, entertaining her with off-the-record stories about the other members of the cast, whilst at the same time delicately editing out his own adventures, sparing her the details of his latest conquests.

He hadn't minded her calling. He'd loved to hear her voice. And when he asked and she told him that the situation with her boyfriend was still unresolved, he sounded concerned. 'Let me know,' he said, 'and if there's anything I can do . . .'

Make me happy again, thought Mary. Take me away from everything, take me away from Manchester and from Paul forever. Instead, she told him about Dan Simmonds' invitation to watch him star as Hamlet, hoping to amuse him with tales of her rather less impressive artistic connections.

Much to her surprise, Jason didn't see the joke. 'I'd go,' he said. 'You might enjoy it.'

Mary told Jason that she thought it would be truly awful. 'I know the boy,' said Jason. 'I've seen him act. Truly awful he is not.'

Curiosity, boredom, Jason's words or a mixture of all three . . . Mary didn't quite know what it was that prompted her, but the following night she found herself sitting in a draughty theatre waiting for the curtain to go up on one of the greatest tragedies ever written in the English language, a play she hadn't seen since she was at school. She hadn't formally accepted or even acknowledged Dan's invitation and had only finally decided to go to Hamlet at the last minute. The thought of returning to the house alone had been too depressing.

Jason had said this might be worth the effort so, clutching her programme she had made her way to her seat, trying to ignore the moth-eaten velvet curtains which would soon part to reveal one of Paul's lorry drivers striding about the stage in tights.

Jason had been kind about Dan, that was all. She'd make mental notes and use them to amuse Jason next time they spoke. She knew she shouldn't ring him again, that his life and hers had overlapped only briefly and she should leave it at that. But the thought that she *could* phone him if things got too bad was something to cling on to. Something to take away the pain of loneliness so clearly highlighted by Alex's recent visit and all too hasty departure.

From the moment he strode onto the stage, Mary knew that all her preconceptions had been mistaken. From the second he opened his mouth and his deep melodious voice rolled forth, filling the theatre, captivating the audience, Mary knew that she was in the presence of someone very special.

Dan was that rare breed of actor who can single-handedly suspend an audience's disbelief, turn minutes into seconds and hours into minutes, transforming an audience so completely that they leave the theatre blinking as if half-awake, deep in thought and changed fundamentally and forever.

Wizard, magician . . . Mary longed for the play to go on, savouring each word he uttered, willing it not to end.

When Hamlet made his final speech and died, she felt tears well up in her eyes. The closing speeches had barely finished when she and the rest of the audience were on their feet, the rapturous applause promising never to stop as Dan and the the cast took curtain call after curtain call.

He was magnificent and he'd invited her to witness his triumph. She'd been churlish enough not to even bother to answer his invitation. But now she'd make up for it.

Mary made her way backstage determined to apologise, determined to make some excuse for her rudeness in not acknowledging his invitation, determined to tell him how marvellous he'd been.

Dan's dressing room was small and cluttered and filled with people, all talking at once. Perched on his dressing table and still in costume, Dan was talking animatedly, waving his arms and spilling wine everywhere as he did so. He appeared not to notice.

Mary stood in the doorway and hesitated, thinking that it might be better to see him next day at the depot, to speak to him quietly and tell him how much she'd appreciated the invitation and enjoyed the performance. But then he looked up and saw her. His handsome face flushed with pleasure and he got to his feet, pushing his way through the crowd gathered around him, his hand outstretched.

Reaching her at last, he pulled his hand back, suddenly shy of touching her. 'Please,' he said, 'come through. Have a drink. I'm so glad you came.'

'I've never seen such a wonderful performance,' she said a minute later, clutching a glass of cheap, warm plonk. It didn't matter. It couldn't have tasted more delicious.

Dan looked genuinely pleased. 'I didn't think you'd be able to make it,' he said. 'I told them not to sell your seat, under any circumstances. I hoped that even if you were working late you might get here for Act Two.'

'I was here for the whole play,' Mary replied. 'I didn't miss a second. My days of working late are over. I only stay at the office these days if I really have to.'

'So I've noticed,' said a voice at her side. Without looking around, Mary knew that Paul stood beside her. Slowly, she took another sip of her drink and turned to face him.

'Paul,' she said. 'I thought you were in Scotland.'

'Well, I'm back early,' he said. 'Come on, we're going.'

Dan shot Mary an embarrassed glance and with a polite nod, he disappeared into the crowd. Paul took Mary's arm and led her out of the dressing room and through the back-stage passages in silence.

Once outside the theatre she stopped dead in her tracks. 'What are you doing here?' she said.

'I wanted to see what you get up to when I'm away,' he replied, 'when you should be working.'

Mary felt the temper rise in her throat. He cared about

nothing but the business. If she wasn't chained to her desk making him money, he wanted to know why. What's more, she felt deeply insulted. He'd found her talking to another man and still all he could think of were his profit margins. She wished she'd been wrapped in Dan's arms when Paul saw her. She wished Paul knew about Jason Hannard and the fact that she was good for more than keeping his books straight.

Mary strode off up the road, stopping to hail a taxi. Catching up with her, Paul jumped in as the taxi sped off.

'What do you think you're playing at?' he demanded, his voice full of fury.

'I'm going home and I'm going to bed,' she said. 'You can go to hell.'

He'd never seen her like this. Her eyes were blazing and her manner defiant.

What had gone so wrong? He'd intended this evening to be special and now it was completely spoiled. But it was all her fault. If she'd been where she should be, none of this would have happened.

Returning to the office a day early, Paul had intended to surprise her, to whisk her off once again to *Chez Phillipe*. He'd been thinking about making love to her all the time he was away in Scotland. And if she needed a flash restaurant to get her going, then that was okay. Paul had been tantalised and fascinated by her behaviour the last time they'd been in bed together. She'd excited him in a way that was different. Their usual, mechanical routine of lovemaking had given way to something more interesting. But now he wanted to experience the pleasure she'd denied him. The pleasure of being inside her. He only had two days at home on his way down south and this time he wanted to be sure. He'd even bought her a little present. A pair of earrings. Women liked that kind of thing and she seemed to be taking more of an interest in her appearance these days.

When Mary hadn't been at the office he'd demanded that Jinny tell him where she'd gone. Then he realised that he wouldn't be able to find her at the theatre till the performance was over. She'd be sitting in the dark watching, according to Jinny, one of the damned lorry drivers strutting up and down. What the hell was Mary up to?

Paul paid the cab and walked into the house behind her. 'Why Shakespeare?' he said.

'Because,' she replied, 'one of your drivers was in it and it's good public relations.'

'Waste of time,' said Paul and Mary looked at him, thinking how much she despised him right at this moment. It didn't occur to him, not even for a moment, that there might be a different motive for her going to watch a young virile man than for the good of the business.

She thought about Dan. Yes, she did fancy him. A lot. She hadn't realised it until that night. Until she'd seen him on the stage.

'If you're going to bed then I'm coming with you,' said Paul.

'I don't want you,' said Mary. 'I just want to be left alone.'

Paul took hold of her by the wrist. 'I don't know what's happened to you lately,' he said, 'and frankly I don't care. But I came home early to take you out to dinner and you weren't here, and now you expect just to push me away because you're tired after your evening of culture. Well, you're out of luck.' Mary looked at his sneering face. 'Fuck you and fuck the business,' she said and turned her back on him, climbing the stairs wearily.

The first thing she felt was Paul grabbing her arms and then he was dragging her into the bedroom. As he pushed her onto the bed she saw him pull off his tie, at the same time climbing on top of her, pinning her down. 'Don't you—' she said, but he put his hand over her mouth, winding his tie around her wrists and pulling her arms above her head, roping her to the bedstead.

Mary began to struggle, fuelled by a sudden feeling of hatred for Paul that was so strong she felt it would choke her. Last night in this bed she'd made love to someone tender, someone who cared for her. And now this bastard was on top of her and she needed all her strength to fight him. To fight his deceit, his cruelty, his hypocrisy.

She bit his hand and with a yelp he pulled it away. 'You

bastard,' she said, 'You utter bastard.' Paul sat on her legs, holding them tight and she watched him tear open the front of her jacket. She was wearing one of the suits that Jason had given her and she heard it rip, watching the buttons fly off, watching Paul pull the jacket open.

She felt his mouth on her breasts. He was biting her viciously, not in the usual tender way and she struggled even harder, repulsed by the feeling of his lips against her skin . . . her bruised and tender body which such a little time ago had been caressed by Alex.

She hated him. But mixed with her hatred was a hatred of herself, for Mary knew that this humiliation she was suffering was laced with pleasure, that his vicious bites were turning her on and that when he forced his cock inside her, he would find her body wet and willing.

But I hate him, she thought. How can this be? Fighting him and fighting herself, Mary began to struggle harder. He could barely hold her and now she became aware of a change of mood, aware that his temper was rising as he struggled to keep her still.

'You bitch,' he snarled at her, grabbing her body and turning her onto her side, pulling the belt from around his waist as he did so.

The first blow took her breath away and she screamed out loud. He'd got to his feet now and was standing over her, whipping her with his belt. He'd undone the zip of his trousers and she saw his cock sticking out the front, rock hard and deep red. He had a bigger erection than she'd ever seen before and she knew that she wanted it inside her, thrust up to the hilt.

He was beating her viciously and without stopping for breath, each stinging strike of his belt cutting into her flesh, making her gasp. Gradually, as his strikes built up to their climax, the burning pain in her skin gave way to a deeper and even more urgent sensation and Mary knew the pleasure that Alex had tried to describe to her, tried to hint at through the spanking she'd given Mary the night before.

As he dropped his belt he grabbed the cheeks of her arse, pulling her apart like splitting a ripe fruit. He was inside her with one forceful thrust, sliding easily into a body that was slippery and open, more ready than she'd ever been to welcome the full force of his angry pumping.

She felt something scratching her inner labia, burning into the softest and most sensitive folds of her body, sending electric shocks of pleasure up through her womanhood and into her silky depths.

She imagined it must be his zip, for he was still wearing his trousers, such was his haste to get inside her body, such was his need to fuck her.

Mary worked her body closer to the source of her pain and pleasure. Pushing hard against him she twisted her arse in frantic circles, squeezing him against her, feeling him deep and thick inside as she took his cock from every angle. Her vagina tighten around him like a coiling snake, her body causing him to swell still more as he grew huge within her hungry passage, her cries and moans driving him on. Paul rammed his knob against her womb, fucking her wildly and viciously, reaching into her deeply as if to drive out her defiance.

She came before he did, the fierceness of the contractions around his cock more intense than anything she'd known with Paul in all their years together. But there was shame in her coming and she hated herself for being so excited by this man who had so wronged her.

He was a bastard and she loathed everything about him. But still she panted and opened herself to his proddings, straining greedily against him till he had tipped her over the edge, till she was throbbing deep inside, coating his hot prick with the juices of her angry lust.

He tried to kiss her as his orgasm began but she turned her head away. She closed her eyes. She could see a much happier image than Paul's face. Jason was standing before her, smiling. Then Dan came into the picture and the two men stood chatting and laughing together. She couldn't hear what they were saying and she strained her ears to catch their words. But she knew they were talking about her in a way that was kindly and concerned. She wanted to run towards them both, to escape the shameful throbbing that filled her body.

She heard him moan and felt his body tense. She thought of Hamlet's mother. I'm just as much a whore as she was, thought Mary, and closed her eyes.

Paul opened the bedroom door and came in carrying a tray. As Mary sat up in bed bleary-eyed, he laid it across her lap. Fresh orange juice, croissants, coffee . . . and next to the plates and cups a small gift-wrapped box.

'I bought this for you yesterday,' he said. 'I was going to give it to you last night.' Mary unwrapped the box while Paul looked on. 'Thank you,' she said. 'They're beautiful.'

The earrings suited her perfectly and she put them on while he poured her coffee.

'About last night,' he said. 'I'm sorry. I acted outrageously.'

'Well, I was a bit embarrassed . . .' she said, 'after all, I have to work with these people when you're away.'

'I wasn't worried about the play,' he replied. 'I meant . . . afterwards.'

Mary didn't intend to let Paul off the hook lightly. 'What do you mean?' she said sweetly, spreading butter on her croissant.

'I was . . . violent with you. I've never been like that before. I'm so sorry,' he said. 'Are you all right?'

'I liked it,' she said. She looked at Paul and saw the confusion in his eyes. He hadn't wanted her to like it. Not Mary. This wasn't what he expected from Mary.

'I was just angry,' he said. 'But now I feel deeply ashamed. I don't know what got into me. Can you forgive me?'

Hypocrite, she thought. You beat Alex all the time. It's part of what you do. Your 'games'.

'I said I liked it,' replied Mary, wiping crumbs from her mouth. Paul looked at her strangely. 'Well,' he said, 'if you say so.'

Mary had lain awake for most of the night, thinking about what to do next. For once, prompted by anger, Paul had given way to his natural instincts but she knew that in the morning he would apologise.

She knew he wanted her sweet as apple pie, controllable,

biddable and totally reliable. The faithful woman who ran his business and cared for his needs with whom sex was predictable and as comfortable as a pair of old socks.

He also wanted Alex – wild and neurotic, insecure and entirely at his mercy in a different way from Mary. But equally dependent on him. Equally reliant on Paul to give a meaning and a purpose to her life.

Mary wasn't sure how she was going to go about it, but she knew that everything was going to change. Paul was so sure of himself, so wrapped up in his own concerns that, though it had been staring him in the face, it still hadn't occurred to him that Mary might have been seeing another man.

She had returned from the health farm totally transformed both in looks and attitude and he had simply taken it in his stride. For this, she hated him most of all. By the time she had finished, she would make sure that he never took another woman for granted, ever again.

Mary was wrong. Paul Mason went to work that day feeling deeply disturbed. He'd beaten Mary the night before, trussed her up and whipped her arse and she had responded with a greater degree of sexual arousal than he'd ever known.

Mary, who was usually prone to blushing, had met him on equal terms, her body demanding satisfaction as blatantly and hungrily as . . . as Alex.

Where was the undemanding girl he'd known for what seemed like forever? Her underwear was silk, her body smooth and lithe and she even smelt like Alex. Where had that come from? And why, after so much hard work, had she suddenly lost interest in the business? She didn't want to talk about it. She no longer seemed to care what he wanted, what he needed.

He was going to have to leave her to go back to London. For the first time ever, he felt less than happy, less than confident about what he might find on his return.

When Paul had left for work, Mary got up and showered, pulling on some casual clothes and heading off to the post office. She wanted to get the earrings Paul had given her in the post as quickly as possible, to make sure that Alex received them before he arrived back at their flat.

Mary would enclose a note suggesting to Alex that if challenged, she should tell Paul he bought them for her. She should insist that she'd had them for a while, and seem insulted that Paul had forgotten they were his gift.

She hoped that Alex would be wearing one of her more subdued, 'Mary-like' outfits when Paul returned. She'd given her a selection of clothes that Paul had seen time and again. To see Alex dressed like Mary might confuse and disturb Paul, might help to make him as uncertain of himself as he'd made the women in his life.

Paul had seemed disturbed enough by the answerphone message Mary had recorded. Maybe there were other ways to undermine him. A plan was hatching in her mind and, though as yet the details were vague and unclear, an idea was taking shape. An idea that would pay him back for everything he'd done.

Dan knocked on Mary's door at three o'clock in the afternoon. It was two days after his triumphant performance and he had a favour to ask of her.

He felt shy and embarrassed, not least because he hadn't seen her since the unfortunate incident with Paul Mason. Added to this, he feared she'd think he was taking advantage in asking for time off at such short notice.

Mary flushed when she looked up and saw who it was. Dan seemed very different in his ordinary working clothes, but equally as handsome as he'd done the other night.

'Sit down,' said Mary, pressing a buzzer and asking Jinny if she'd bring in some tea. 'Oh, don't worry . . .' Dan muttered, but Mary just smiled.

'I want to hear all about it,' she said. 'What happened after we were so rudely interrupted.' Dan smiled awkwardly, not knowing how to reply.

'Don't worry,' Mary continued. 'You've no need to feel embarrassed. It was Paul who was at fault, not you or I.'

You're not kidding, thought Dan. Paul Mason had behaved

like a complete slob. The buzzer rang. It was Jinny asking if Dan took sugar. He began to relax.

The news he had to tell Mary was exciting, but he warned her that he had a favour to ask. 'My agent,' he said, 'in London, he wants to see me on Thursday. To talk about a film.'

Apparently, a rapturous review had lured one of the film industry's top producers to see Dan's performance. He'd liked what he'd seen. His agent had told him there was talk of a part in a forthcoming blockbuster movie and Dan was to audition for a significant role.

'It would mean taking a couple of days off,' he said. 'I'd need to go to London.' Mary paused. Dan could hear the clock ticking. 'May I come with you?' she said.

Paul Mason put his key in the lock and opened it to an unfamiliar smell of cooking. Putting his briefcase down he followed the source to find Alex at the kitchen sink, peeling potatoes.

There was something not right about her appearance and when she turned around, Paul felt a strange stab of anxiety. A confusion that he couldn't explain. Then he realised what it was.

Alex was wearing no make-up and her hair was scraped back. Her shoes were flat and, though the clothes she had on were familiar, they looked all wrong.

'They look like Mary's clothes,' he thought as she came towards him and kissed him demurely on the cheek. He was sure that Mary had a skirt exactly like the one Alex was wearing. On Alex, it looked terrible.

'I've cooked dinner,' said Alex, smiling happily. 'It's good to have you home.' Alex poured a glass of wine and handed it to him. 'Why?' he said. 'You never cook dinner. We always go out.'

Alex smiled at him as if indulging a wayward child. 'Don't be silly,' she said. 'But we do,' replied Paul.

'Go and sit down,' said Alex, 'and I'll bring it through.'

Alex had made Beef Wellington followed by a fresh fruit salad. The more she trotted happily in and out of the kitchen, the more uncomfortable Paul became. It was when she brought in a tray of coffee that he suddenly focused on what was really bothering him. Alex was wearing earrings identical to the ones he'd bought for Mary. Silver earrings. Entirely unique. Made by an Edinburgh silversmith who, so he'd been told, designed all his own pieces.

'Where did you get those earrings?' said Paul. Alex looked startled and put the coffee pot down.

'Where did I get them?' she said, sounding distressed. 'What do you mean? You know where I got them.'

'No I don't,' replied Paul coldly. 'Or I wouldn't be asking.' Alex looked at him, her eyes full of hurt. Then she burst into tears, got up and left the room.

He found her in the bedroom, sobbing her heart out. 'How could you have forgotten that?' she said. Paul was at his wits' end. 'Alex,' he said, 'just tell me where you got the earrings.'

'At least I know exactly how much I mean to you.' Paul grabbed her by the shoulders and shook her. He shouted at her, begging her to tell him.

'You bought them for me, for our anniversary last year,' she sobbed. 'Don't tell me you can't remember?'

'You're wrong,' he replied, slumping onto the bed. 'I didn't. I want to know where you got them.'

Alex looked at him, her tear-streaked face full of hurt and confusion. Then she came across to him and took his hand. 'I haven't wanted to say this,' she murmured quietly, 'I've been trying to avoid it . . .'

Paul was intensely irritated. 'Avoid what?' he snapped at her. Alex sighed and squeezed his hand tighter.

'For ages now,' she continued, 'you've been getting muddled about things. Little things, silly things that don't matter. But still, it's worried me.'

'What are you talking about?' said Paul, pulling his hand away from hers. 'Like the earrings,' she said. 'Like the way you came in tonight and asked me why I was cooking. Paul, I always cook for you when you're home. You know I do.'

Paul looked at her as though she was mad. She'd never cooked a proper meal in her life. 'I think you should see a doctor,' Alex continued. 'I'm sure it's not much. Probably just strain due to overwork.'

Mary put the phone down and danced around the room. Then, pulling herself up, she glanced at her watch. She had exactly an hour to get ready before the taxi came, taking her to the city's Excelsior Hotel and her hastily arranged meeting with Jason Hannard.

He'd phoned three hours before, telling her he had to be in Manchester for a couple of days and asking her if she could meet him for dinner. Tomorrow, she was going to London with Dan. And then there'd been the phone call from Alex . . .

Paul, Alex had said, was totally confused. It had taken all her acting skills, but it had worked. She'd convinced him that the earrings she'd been wearing when he arrived home were a gift that he'd given to her on the anniversary of their meeting. He'd left for work the following morning quiet and subdued. He hadn't even attempted to make love to her, said Alex. And next week, she was going for a job interview. She'd taken Mary's advice. She wanted to get back into the hotel business.

Mary bathed and dressed with the utmost care, wearing the underwear that Jason had bought her. She was longing to see him, longing to touch him. Would he ask her to stay the night? she wondered.

Jason was waiting for her in the bar of the Excelsior, looking more handsome than ever. Filming of the new series was going well, he told her. They had two scenes to film in Manchester the next day.

'How are you, my love?' he asked her, cupping her face in his hands. 'Now you're here I feel wonderful,' said Mary. 'You couldn't have come at a better time.'

They hadn't wanted to sit in the restaurant with Jason being gawped at. After a couple of drinks, Jason had suggested they order some champagne and a meal to be sent up to his room. 'If that's okay with you, Mary,' he said, leaning across and looking at her. Mary nodded. If he hadn't taken her to his room she thought she would have died of longing.

They stood side by side in the lift in total silence, listening to the gentle hum as it whirred between floors. When they alighted at the eighteenth, he took her hand and kissed the tips of her fingers. She wanted no food, no drink. Nothing but the familiar, half forgotten feeling of his skin against hers, his heart beating across her own.

Shutting the door behind them, he led her across the sitting room of his sumptuous suite and into the bedroom. There was a knock at the door and Jason went to answer it, returning a moment later pushing a trolley.

'I wouldn't let the waiter bring this in here,' he said. 'This is private. I think we have everything we need. I know I have.'

His arms were around her and his hand was stroking the back of her head. 'I've missed you so,' he murmured, his lips against her hair.

She wanted to sob with longing and with misery, to tell him how sad everything seemed without him but instead, she simply clung to him, breathing in the smell of his skin. 'I've missed you too,' she replied. The phrase seemed so inadequate.

Jason squeezed her tightly to him and then he pulled away. Sitting her on the bed, he knelt before her and slipped off her shoes. Mary was wearing a full skirt and Jason reached beneath it, moving his hands along her thighs to remove first one stocking and then the other.

He picked up one of her feet and began to kiss each toe in turn. Mary felt her body ache and the lips of her pussy moisten and swell. Holding her foot cupped in his hands he began to suck each of her toes, sliding each polished nail between his lips as Mary closed her eyes and gave herself up to the strange and delicious sensation. 'I'm going to make love to you all night,' said Jason, turning her foot over and kissing its sole. Jason got to his feet. Mary lay back on the bed and he stood over her. He lifted up her skirt and pressed his lips to her stomach, tracing the outline of her suspender belt with his finger tips. The nerve endings in her skin felt super-charged, his touch alone causing her body to melt, sending a rush of liquid desire into her warm chasm. Mary felt her body soften in preparation for the hardness she craved. She longed for nothing on earth but to feel his penis inside her, stretching her completely, filling her senses, soothing her soul as he slid into her body.

'Please,' she murmured. She felt his fingers brush the crotch of her panties and a dart of pleasure shot through her clitoris. He would be in no doubt she was ready for him. Mary spread her legs. She felt his fingers against her thighs. She throbbed as she felt him push the crotch of her now-sodden underwear to one side, spreading her fat and pulsing labia between the fingers of both his hands.

Open and vulnerable, Mary was aware that he was looking at her, holding her wide apart as he inspected her most intimate creases and crevices. Taking one hand away he pinned her labia back with the fingers of the other as he reached for the zip on his trousers and eased it over his rearing cock.

Mary felt the head of his penis riding the bumpy terrain of her inner lips as he dragged it backwards and forwards, trailing it through the folds of her open vulva.

The feeling was exquisite – her clitoris, exposed and unprotected by the folds in which it normally sheltered was pushed forward like a protruding tongue.

The smooth touch of his fleshy knob against her pleasure centre caused her to cry out, begging him to fill her, to stop teasing her with such delicious torment.

Mary was afraid that she would come without feeling the force of his penis inside her, that his meander through the pink border of her womanhood would lead her too quickly to the crisis that she longed to savour, holding him close.

She felt his fingers let go of the hairy bush which closed over her slippery labia, hiding her pleasure zone once again from view, wrapped in its furry coat.

She heard the familiar rip as Jason undid a condom packet. He rolled the rubber along his straining prick and got to his knees at the bottom of the bed.

The throbbing that had momentarily subsided began again, fiercer than the last time as Mary felt the brush of his soft hair against her belly and the tip of his tongue between her legs. Slowly and methodically, Jason lapped the juices which had poured into her chasm like a fragrant waterfall.

Mary felt the heat build up in her belly and knew that if he didn't enter her soon she would come in his mouth, pressed against his face, unable to contain her pleasure a moment longer.

With the perfect timing of a master of the dramatic, Jason took his face away from her at the very last moment, pulling himself on top of Mary and sliding his penis into a body that held him fiercely and with all the pent-up longing which he alone could satisfy.

Some hours later, Mary awoke from a deep and peaceful sleep. She was laying in the crook of Jason's arm, the slight aroma of masculine sweat drifting towards her as she sighed and stretched, luxuriating in the warmth and comfort of his body.

It was dark outside and she could hear traffic going by. It wasn't a steady stream of traffic as yet, just the occasional lorry, car or motorbike cutting through the silence. She reckoned it must be about six o'clock.

Jason was still soundly asleep. She thought back over their brief times together and how happy she had been. With Jason, she had experienced moments of pure joy. Like the day he'd taken her shopping, making love to her in the limousine on the way back to Tingles. This moment, too, was pure happiness. Just lying here in his arms, listening to his breathing.

Though she didn't know him well, she had no secrets from Jason. Last night she'd told him all about Paul and how the situation was still far from resolved. He'd seemed concerned and she'd told him not to worry. 'I'll work it out,' she'd said.

To change the subject and to cheer herself up, she'd then told Jason about Dan. About how he'd been right to praise his abilities as an actor, and how marvellous his performance as *Hamlet* had been.

She told Jason that she was travelling to London with Dan that week because he had an audition and she had business to attend to in the capital. 'I'm just going along for the ride,' she'd said. 'It seemed like a good idea.'

Jason had understood. 'It's exciting to be around someone

who's about to hit the big time,' he'd said. 'The boy's on his way up . . . there's no telling where he'll be this time next year.'

That was what she loved most of all about Jason. He'd accepted what she'd told him with no searching questions and no real comment. Mary herself didn't know why she'd asked the young actor if she could share his trip. She had no real business in London. She just wanted to be part of his excitement.

She and Dan were travelling by train to arrive in London by lunchtime. Dan's audition was at two o'clock and Mary had already decided that he would arrive as full of confidence as was possible. It was presumptuous of her, she knew, to believe that she could make any difference to his state of mind. After all, what could she contribute to the preparation of an actor, auditioning for what sounded like the most important role of his fledgling career?

Undeterred, she'd decided that as a surprise, she'd book them first class tickets. It would add gloss to an already exciting journey. But was she being pushy in inviting herself along? Supposing he just wanted to sit and think about his audition piece all the way to London? Was he just being polite in agreeing to travel with her?

Mary had decided to dismiss these fears. If he'd wanted to travel alone, he would have said so. And the tickets, she'd explain away as a going-away present. He'd get the part, of that she was convinced and that meant he'd be leaving Mason's employ sooner rather than later. Jason, too, would soon be leaving. He'd told her last night that once the last episode of *Heartbreak Hospital* was in the can, he'd be flying out to Africa to take part in a new movie due to start shooting in the early summer.

Jason was to play a British officer-turned-deserter, who fought alongside the Zulus during the Boer war. Driven by his tormented love for the wife of a fellow British officer, the man had rejected everything he stood for and turned his back on honour, dignity and his comrades.

'Of course, it all comes right in the end,' Jason had said, smiling at Mary as he recounted the unlikely tale. 'It all comes right, especially as I'm being paid half a million to make it.'

Mary had laughed at the improbable tale and at Jason's lighthearted attitude to his latest venture. But Africa! He'd be away for nearly a year. And the saddest thing of all was she had no right to object, even to herself.

They'd gone to sleep happy and she'd woken full of a joy and a peacefulness she found only in Jason's arms. Soon they would have breakfast and then he would leave her. She had the rest of her life to get on with.

Paul had lied to Alex. He hadn't left London as he'd said, but had booked himself into a hotel round the corner from their flat and decided to spy on her.

Her behaviour had been so peculiar that he felt sure there was something strange going on. Though what that might be, he had no idea. He felt unwell. Her suggestion that he should see a doctor had upset him greatly. There was nothing wrong with him. It was her.

He followed her to the supermarket. He trailed her around Harvey Nichols and Browns. He tailed her the length of New Bond Street and browsed with her as she strolled around the Tate Gallery. He watched her go to the cinema alone, buying a ticket and creeping into the darkness to see if she met up with anyone, once inside. He saw her, sitting alone eating ice cream. After two days, he got fed up.

He followed her one day and watched her go into the hairdressers. Then he turned back towards the flat, parking his car in a nearby street to avoid detection.

She must not know he had stayed in London. Must not know that he was concerned.

He rang the buzzer of flat twenty-two and Gina's voice answered. 'It's Paul,' he said. 'I need to talk to you. Can I come up?' Gina sounded surprised, but pushed the buzzer. What did he want? she wondered. Knowing how much he disliked her, she knew it wasn't a social call.

Gina felt quite sorry for him. He plonked himself on her sofa and poured out his tale of woe, telling Gina he felt sure that something was wrong with Alex and asking if she knew what it might be.

Gina hesitated, seeing the perfect opportunity for revenge and savouring the moment. Paul was sitting here, almost begging her to reveal her poisonous secret. She longed to tell him about Kurt. She could ruin Alex's life in the next five minutes and cause trouble for Kurt into the bargain. The feeling of power made her giddy. But she decided to hesitate. To bide her time.

'Would you like some coffee?' she said to Paul. He nodded, miserably. Gina walked through to the kitchen, her mind racing.

She could tell Paul all that she knew and that would be an end to it. But maybe there was a better way. A way of making sure she hurt both Paul and Alex as much as possible and that, once she had finished, there'd be no possibility of forgiveness between them, no hope of a reconciliation.

Gina carried the coffee through to the sitting room. She sat at Paul's feet.

'I don't think she's having an affair,' she said, 'if that's what you're worried about. But I agree with you. There is something strange about her. I've noticed it myself lately.'

Paul told Gina about the earrings. Though naturally he didn't mention Mary, he said that Alex had been wearing a pair of earrings that he'd never seen before, but Alex had claimed he'd bought for her as an anniversary present.

'I didn't,' said Paul, his head in his hands. 'I didn't buy them for her. I'd have remembered.' Gina looked at him, a sympathetic expression on her face. Served him right.

She leant forward and took his hand, giving a reassuring squeeze. 'I'm sure,' she said, 'it will all be okay. Maybe she's just under some kind of a strain.'

'So am I,' he replied. 'I've got problems in Manchester as well as here. This, I just don't need.'

He's a selfish bastard, thought Gina.

'Paul,' she said, 'Paul . . .' He looked up. She smiled. 'I'm so sorry,' she said, leaning across the hand she'd been squeezing and brushing it with her lips. Paul looked at her curiously. 'You don't deserve this,' said Gina, kissing his hand again.

Paul had always felt that Gina was somehow laughing at him, undermining him to Alex. Now he looked into her eyes and saw nothing but concern. They were pretty eyes, a soft brown, with thick lashes.

'I'd better be going,' he said, testing the water. 'Paul, please don't go,' Gina replied. 'Stay with me for a while.'

Her mouth tasted of coffee, her breasts of fresh soap. She hadn't long since showered and dressed. She was wearing a loose shirt and leggings and he didn't even bother to take them off. He stood her against the wall and pulled them down over her hips. Then he fumbled between her taut thighs and found the warm valley and the narrow little passage beneath it. She didn't seem to mind being fucked against a wall though she made him put on a condom. 'My husband,' she said. 'He might smell you . . .' Paul didn't mind. Just as long as she let him shaft her.

He held her buttocks, digging his nails into her flesh. She was making little grunting noises as she squeezed her body against him, pushing his prick as far inside her as it would reach.

He felt her breath against his face. He hadn't even wanted to kiss her. He didn't like her, never really had, but she'd offered herself to him on a plate. And she was tight inside. All that exercise, he thought, all that tennis.

He wished he hadn't told her a thing about his problems. But he'd needed someone to talk to. He wished now, though, that it hadn't been her. But it was. It was too late to turn back.

Paul felt his cock begin to throb as the familiar build-up to orgasm began. But he wanted more. He was here, he was fucking the silly bitch and he may as well make the most of it.

He pulled his prick out of Gina. 'What the fuck are you doing?' she said with all the elegance of a street walker.

Without a word he took hold of her wrist and forced her to the floor, making her kneel on the carpet.

He could smell her pussy. There was a film of sticky fluid around her arse. Hot bitch, he thought as he brought his hand down across her buttocks and gave her a slap.

'Ow,' she said, 'you're hurting me.'

'Keep still,' said Paul. She knelt with her hands flat on the ground, her arse sticking up in the air. It was a pretty arse. Paul leant forward and gave it a nip with his teeth.

'Don't bite me, you bastard,' she said. 'Fuck me, bugger me, do what you like but don't bite me. I don't want any bite marks.'

Gina's sheer matter-of-fact crudeness excited Paul as she knelt in front of him, waggling her rear end in the air. 'Okay,' he said, 'I won't bite you. I'm sorry. I forgot about Marcos.'

'The old bastard notices everything,' said Gina.

'Then I will treat you like a precious piece of porcelain,' Paul murmured, sliding his prick between the globes of her upturned bum and leaning forward to nibble her ear.

'Don't overdo the "precious porcelain" bit,' she replied with a dirty laugh. 'I can take whatever you want to dish out.'

Holding his prick in his hand, Paul guided it down towards her hairy pussy, the sticky pink skin between her buttocks giving way to a sudden torrent of wetness at the mouth of her womanhood. Dipping his rubber-covered prick in the entrance to her chasm, he spread the film of juice back up between her cheeks, coating her in a slippery film which spread the whole length of her arse to the entrance to her vagina.

'Which hole?' he said to her, as Gina began to rock back and forth against him, her body pressed against his prick as she lifted one hand from the floor and began to pinch and twist her own nipples.

'Just fuck me, I don't care where,' she groaned, and Paul knew she meant it. He could poke his prick wherever he liked and she'd cry out for more. She reminded him of one of those weird, blow-up rubber dolls. Not human at all, just a collection of orifices. But she excited him. Her demanding, greedy body turned him on though at the same time he found her strangely repugnant.

She was jolting herself against him harder now, pinching and twisting her tits as she thrust her body against his own, each thrust more frantic and desperate than the last.

'Get on with it,' she hissed, raising her hips and squashing her hot, open pussy against his groin. Paul felt his prick give a huge lurch and he grabbed her arse, ramming himself inside her pleading pussy, which tightened around him like a vice.

The inside of her passage felt even narrower now that she was in the kneeling position. Paul could reach deeper into her, feeling the exquisite sensation of being held and squeezed by a body that was as athletic and muscular as it was tight.

He knew that Gina worked out as well as playing tennis. She worked out pussy-wise too, he decided. She was swallowing his cock like a snake swallows its prey, her body contracting around him in rippling spasms while she moaned and swore, a torrent of filth and expletives pouring from her mouth as she crushed against him, spitting out her hunger and her need.

'You are one randy bitch,' said Paul as he pumped harder into her and Gina moaned and purred deep in the back of her throat.

He could feel her throbbing grow more intense and he knew that at any second she would come, squeezing her tight little body around him as her hungry womb gaped open, craving the caress of his thick and rampant organ.

The pressure around his engorged member was firm yet soft, her mounting orgasm bringing him to the edge of his own climax. Holding her by the hips and digging his fingers into her belly, he began to thrust viciously.

'Be careful,' she snapped. 'Don't dig your nails into me. I told you, no marks.'

Paul held her tighter still, hating her as much as he wanted her. Stupid bitch. Digging his nails into her belly just to spite her, he thrust harder till with one huge spurt, his orgasm relieved him of his frustration and anger.

He heard her cry out as he reached his own climax, her deep and primitive wail telling him that Gina, too, had reached the point of no return.

Sliding out of her, Paul stood up without a word and zipped up his fly. 'Thanks,' he said as he would to a whore. 'You're a great fuck. I hope you know it.'

She got up. She pulled up her leggings and walked behind

him to the front door. Her make-up was smudged and her hair dishevelled.

'Paul,' she said, 'one thing before you go. I hadn't wanted to tell you this. I felt . . . awkward.'

'What is it?' he said, now irritated by the sight of her. 'The earrings you mentioned,' she continued. 'I know the ones you were talking about. You *did* give them to Alex as an anniversary present. I remember her showing them to me.'

Gina opened the door. Paul glanced at her. He looked like a beaten dog and she felt glad. She'd destroy him and she'd destroy Alex. And if she destroyed her own marriage in the process, so be it. She needed sex and she could no longer pretend that the performance she enacted with Marcos could take its place. The fumblings of an old, fat man had begun to nauseate her till she could hardly bear him near her. She could no longer trust herself to maintain the fiction of a happy marriage. She could no longer rely on herself to be 'discreet'.

Chapter 14

Dan didn't know which he was looking forward to the most. His forthcoming audition or the thought of travelling to London with Mary, spending time in her company, lost in the depths of her hypnotic blue eyes.

He'd woken at five o'clock and, knowing that he would be unable to get back to sleep again he had got up and run himself a bath. He would lay in the bath and relax. He had all the time in the world.

Though he couldn't remember what he'd been dreaming about, he knew that Mary had been part of the picture. He knew, because he'd woken with a huge erection, his engorged penis making a pyramid of the sheets and blankets.

Easing himself into the hot bathwater, Dan lay back and thought about her. He wanted to kiss every inch of her from her eyelids to the tips of her toes. At least, that was the theory – though he knew that if he was travelling in a downward direction across her body, he might be in danger of encountering the occasional diversion. Like the little forest between her legs, for instance. He'd want to explore in the undergrowth down there for hours.

Dan's penis appeared to be floating, bobbing in and out of the bathwater which moved in little waves across his stomach. His erection had refused to go down and now pointed up along his belly, the rounded head of his penis reaching almost to his navel.

Soaping his fingers he wrapped them around his shaft, feeling the familiar tension and pleasure as he began to pull and rub his thick member. Laying back in the bath Dan pretended that instead of his soapy fingers, Mary was leaning over him, tongueing him. Her soft lips were wrapped around the throbbing head of his glans, the tip of her tongue sliding backwards and forwards through the valley at its head. He imagined her pretty little mouth, slipping and skidding in the white juice that even now was escaping from him.

Dan longed to see her lips glistening with his juice, ached to feel her sucking him till his balls tensed and he shot his load inside her throat. But maybe she wouldn't like that. Maybe Mary didn't give head. He knew nothing about her really. But he wanted to know everything.

He wanted her in the bath with him so that he could soap her breasts, cupping them in his hands and dragging her nipples through his soapy fingers, feeling them harden into firm little bullets of flesh beneath his touch.

He wanted to lift her on top of him, feeling their bodies meet beneath the warm water, pushing his penis inside her as the water lapped around them, rippling through their pubic hair which would sway like seaweed as he explored the mystery of her body.

She wouldn't weigh much, he felt sure. Her little buttocks would rest easily against his thighs, her open pussy gliding its slippery trail across his groin as she opened her furry lips and guided him inside. Dan moaned gently as his firm strokes tipped him over the edge and Mary's face floated before him on the clouds of steam that filled the bathroom. She was gorgeous. And just a few hours from now, they'd be together.

Mary had told Jason Hannard that she was accompanying Dan to London primarily for the pleasure of his company. She'd hinted at 'business' to attend to in the capital, though it was only the night before they were leaving that she decided exactly what form that 'business' should take. Once she'd thought things through, she'd packed a large suitcase with the utmost care. Though she had no intentions of staying in London, it was necessary to her plans. So was the long phone call she made to Alex just two hours before the time she was due to meet Dan at the station.

Paul had left Gina's flat and wandered aimlessly for hours. He didn't know where he was heading or what he was doing, simply that he needed to get away and think.

Gina's remark about the earrings had shaken him to the core. He couldn't imagine that she was telling the truth, not for one moment. He hadn't bought those earrings for Alex. Yet on the other hand why would Gina lie? Was he going mad, he wondered?

He went to his office in Holborn. He asked his latest secretary for the number of the temp agency they always used. 'Don't worry, Mr Mason,' she said. 'I can call them if there's something you want.'

'Just give me the number,' he replied. Even though she'd only worked for Mason's for a week, the girl knew better than to argue.

One hour later, Paul Mason was comfortably ensconced in his favourite armchair at the gentleman's club of which he was so proud to be a member. It would take the girl a while to get here from the East End, though he was quite prepared to wait.

The temp agency said she hadn't worked for them for a while and he was lucky that they still had her phone number. 'That's another fifty quid on my bill,' Paul had thought as he put the phone down.

He'd remembered her name this time. Suzie. He remembered how she'd turned to him in the sleazy drinking club and said that she was the one who made his coffee just the way he liked it.

She was simple and uncomplicated and pretty. Most of all, she was a stupendous fuck. Would she turn up? he wondered. Much to his surprise, he realised he was nervous.

Suzie Wesley knew that her life was spiralling out of control and that if she didn't get a grip very soon, she'd be in big trouble. Since her boyfriend had dumped her and gone off with her best friend six months ago, Suzie had started to go off the rails.

She was seventeen. She'd had only one serious boyfriend in her life. But when Pete left her, somehow it didn't seem to matter any more what she did. Though she'd stopped short at taking drugs, she'd gone out night after night and got drunk with her mates. Blindly, staggeringly drunk. So drunk that most of the time she hadn't known what she'd been doing. She had good mates, though. They'd known what she was going through and had made sure that no real harm came to her. But then there'd been that afternoon in the drinking club with Paul Mason. She'd hated herself afterwards. Hated him. Hated the world. She knew that to him, she'd been nothing but a convenient fuck. She'd been there and she'd been available. Nothing more, nothing less.

He'd bunged her in a cab and sent her home. She'd had a note from his office with some money in it and she'd been told that her services as a temp were no longer required. Maybe he thought he was being good to her to send her money. He'd made her feel like a tart. He'd made her bitter.

Suzie had stayed clear of working 'up west' after Paul Mason. But then she'd got the phone call, saying that he wanted to see her, to meet her at his posh club. The temp agency was gushing in its enthusiasm. 'Maybe he wants to offer you a permanent position,' they'd said, thinking of their commission if this were to be the case.

Why had she decided to go? To settle old scores? She couldn't explain. Why had he phoned the agency asking for her? She didn't understand anything any more. But she put on her smartest and most businesslike outfit and waited for the cab that she'd been told would come to collect her.

When he saw her walk through the door, Paul Mason felt an unaccustomed tremor of nervousness. He must be in a bad state to feel like this, he told himself. Normally, he wouldn't allow anything to make him feel uncomfortable. Least of all a woman. But things had been so strange of late that not even his own emotions could be relied upon.

She was prettier than he remembered. He gestured her to a nearby chair and asked her to sit down. Would she like some tea? Though it was four in the afternoon, Suzie said she'd prefer a drink. 'A vodka and tonic,' Paul said to the waiter. 'On second thoughts, make that two.'

The girl's blonde hair was tied up in a kind of a knot. Her cheap suit was a sober grey and she wore pearl studs in her ears. Paul wondered what she was thinking, what she thought she'd been brought here for.

He decided to start by apologising. He said that he knew he'd treated her very shabbily and that his only excuse had been a mixture of business and relationship pressures. He told her that his relationship problems were now over. He and his girlfriend had split up. And he hadn't been able to stop thinking about Suzie.

Paul hadn't known why he was doing this and what was prompting him to talk in this way to this girl. He simply knew that he was desperate for some uncomplicated affection. For someone who'd love him like Mary used to do. A girl who would care for him unconditionally and without reproach.

He'd set her up in a flat. That's what he'd do. Then, if both Alex and Mary continued to cause him grief, he'd have somewhere to run for comfort. He didn't want this girl, not really, but for a while . . .

She agreed to have dinner with him. She told him that she had been hurt, deeply hurt by the fact he'd never called her again after . . . well, after that day.

'But I did,' he said. 'I called you today. I didn't want to get in touch until I had more to offer than . . . well, you know.'

She was as daft and giggly as he remembered. After dinner at a nearby hotel he had booked a room and she had gone with him, willingly. In the silent darkness she had stood before him and slipped out of her jacket and skirt, placing them carefully over a chair so that they would not crease.

He'd lifted her on top of him on the bed and she had moved up so that her pussy was level with his face. She was wearing flesh coloured stockings with a white suspender belt, but no briefs. All the time she'd been sitting opposite him in the club she'd had no panties on. The thought excited him and Paul felt his cock give a lurch as he reached up to stroke the silk of her inner thigh.

Her skin was a rich golden colour and seemed to blend seamlessly into the glossy material of her stockings. Her thighs were taut and firm, athletic almost, and Paul raised his head to kiss her, savouring the smell and the warmth between her legs, touching her carefully, taking the trouble to make her feel she was about to be made love to and not simply fucked.

He was scared by how much he needed this empty-headed little creature, this fluffy little teenager whose affections, it seemed, could be bought for the price of a good dinner.

He'd enjoy setting her up in a flat and watching her get used to good food and having some money to spend. The fact that he intended her to be only a temporary diversion worried him not at all. Once he'd finished with her she'd go back to the East End again, like she did before. But this time at least she'd have a few good clothes and some insight into how life was lived by those who set their sights higher than the average.

Paul took his time. The smell of her was overpoweringly delicious and he had no desire to devour his treat all at once. He carried on kissing her between her legs till he heard her sigh and tentatively, he poked the tip of his tongue out and made contact with one of the outer curls of her pubic bush. The hair was wet. Slowly, Paul extended his tongue bit by bit, reaching deep into the mass of curls until he felt the touch of skin and his taste buds registered the familiar but always surprising taste of fresh young pussy.

Some men, he thought, went into raptures over the taste of caviar or *foie gras*. For Paul, the flavour of pussy was the greatest delicacy known to mankind. He felt his cock begin to swell as his balls throbbed and he reached up and took hold of her buttocks, pulling her down on his face, sucking the little pink clitoris that had lain hidden in wait, skulking inside her bush of soft curls.

He felt her wiggle and press herself down on his face. For a moment he couldn't breathe properly and with the edge of his teeth he gave her clitoris a tiny nip. He felt her jump, and seconds later, his face was bathed in a new torrent of pussy juice. She liked that, he thought as he began to run his tongue in ever-increasing circles around her clitoris, spreading his licks wider till he reached the outer folds of her labia. Then he moved inwards again, taking trouble to avoid the little pink bud at the centre of her till the anticipation of his tongue across her throbbing pleasure centre grew too much. 'Please,' she moaned, 'don't tease me,' and Paul set about tongueing her again, stopping to dip into the opening of her womanhood to drink at the source of her well.

With his tongue inside her, Paul stretched out his arm and groped around on the bedside table till he found what he was looking for. With one deft movement he unzipped his trousers and released his pulsing cock, rolling a rubber down its length.

Paul tensed his tongue, turning his action from soft licks and laps into firmer strokes, using his tongue as a hard piece of muscle with which to rasp against the inner walls of her flooded cavern.

She was hot, open and ready. Holding her around the waist he lifted her down his body, impaling her on the fleshy spike that stood waiting to drive into her eager softness.

She gave a deep groan, part pain, part pleasure. Paul knew from experience that he was plunging into a body that had known few such invasions; and the thought that the girl was as inexperienced as she'd seemed to be excited him still further.

Almost a virgin, he thought to himself as he lifted his hips off the bed and thrust inside her savagely. He liked hurting her. He liked driving himself into this silly little piece of female fluff and making her squeal. But whatever he was doing to her she appeared to be enjoying it. Her eyes were half closed and she was licking her lips, her tits straining against the lace of her bra which he reached up and ripped apart at its front fastening. Her tits sprung out of their confinement and he remembered the last time he'd seen them bouncing around inside a cheap cotton shirt in the back room of a dingy club. Now they were free and fleshy, springing against her ribs, their hard little nipples poking out of two rich circles of deep pink, like port-wine stains against her creamy skin.

Paul reached up and took hold of each nipple between his fingers, rubbing and caressing them as the girl pressed down harder against his prick, circling her hips and groaning as she strained to feel him in every part of her pussy.

How greedy women are, he thought to himself as he

watched her squeeze herself against him. She was now lost in a world of her own, abandoned to her own pleasure, pursuing her own orgasm with as much determination as a pack of dogs chasing a hare.

Paul pinched her tits harder and felt her body respond, closing around his prick in a luscious, sucking movement as the muscles in her passage contracted sharply. Her blonde hair cascaded over her bare shoulders, spreading in a silken curtain over his fingers as they kneaded her nipples, each strand of her soft, shiny hair stroking the back of his hands as they luxuriated in the touch of her tits, warm and firm beneath his grasp.

She began to pant. 'No,' she breathed. 'No . . .' but Paul could tell from the throbbing in her vulva that all the no's in the world could delay her climax no longer. As she poured her pleasure onto his body he began to gyrate deep inside her, pushing her climax further into her, spreading each wave of sensation wider with every thrust of his cock.

'Do you like that, little baby?' he murmured as his hips jolted against her and her circling around his cock grew faster and more frantic. Her groans told him all he needed to know and he held her waist, her slim, pretty waist as he pushed her down against him, harder still, and his climax exploded between her thighs.

Paul Mason slept soundly and woke to the glare of bright sunlight. His eyes flickered open and he closed them again, not quite ready to face the dazzling day. It had been a long night of love and he knew that his little companion would be as exhausted as he was. He lay still, enjoying the anticipation of opening his eyes to see her girlish body, golden and voluptuous, her hair spread out across the pillow next to him.

Today he'd take her out and find her a flat. Somewhere not too expensive. She'd be impressed with anything, he felt, so it really didn't matter. Paul felt his cock begin to stir and decided that a quick work out before breakfast was just what it needed. She'd enjoy it, too. He opened his eyes. The girl wasn't next to him. He slipped out of bed and followed his pointing penis to the bathroom. She wasn't there either. Paul

Mason was suddenly very wide awake. He moved across to the writing desk on the other side of the room. His wallet, which he'd left there last night, was empty. His Rolex watch was gone. Suzie had gone with his valuables. He walked to the wardrobe. Thank goodness, his jacket and shirt were still hanging up. But where were his trousers?

Gina had been reluctant to take Marcos along to the wedding reception. After all, he didn't know the girl who was getting married. He didn't know anyone from the Mottlesham Club and it was better for her image, she felt, that he didn't.

All the money in the world couldn't make Marcos look like a gentleman. He was a rich Greek peasant and even the most skilfully cut suits in the world made little impact on his less than pleasing silhouette.

But if Gina wanted to go to the wedding and the reception afterwards – in a marquee on the tennis club lawns, no less – she was stuck with her husband, for he wouldn't let her go without him. Something about her general demeanour had put Marcos on alert and made him jealous. He would come to the wedding. He had insisted and Gina had had no choice.

She would have been fine if she'd stuck to champagne, resisting the temptation to move onto champagne cocktails, but the brandy-based concoctions were just too delicious to say no to and by the third, she was feeling fine and dancing every dance with anyone who asked her. It was a warm afternoon and the marquee smelt of perfume and champagne. Gina was excited and obviously enjoying herself. Marcos watched her closely but he didn't seem to mind. After all, she looked good. He enjoyed the puzzled and envious looks of other men, relished their awareness of the fact that this pretty prize was his and his alone.

He was getting on her nerves, though, watching her like a hawk. She had looked up to see Steve and Kurt appear at the back of the marquee and, fuelled by alcohol, felt an overpowering urge to walk across to them. She felt the need to speak to them both as if they were simply acquaintances, to show them that what had occurred in the men's changing room meant as little to Gina as it had done to them.

Leading Marcos across to the particularly dull wife of a particularly dull stockbroker of her acquaintance, she dumped her husband and wandered idly to where Steve and Kurt were chatting.

'Hi,' she said, looking up at Kurt, her gaze steady if a little unfocused. 'Hello, Gina,' he said, holding her gaze. 'You're looking very well.'

Gina had expected Kurt to treat her with his customary indifference and his pleasant and affable tone threw her off balance. 'I'm here with my husband,' she said, nodding in the direction of Marcos. 'Poor you,' said Kurt and smiled at her. Gina found herself smiling back.

The music slowed and couples on the dance floor moved closer. Kurt looked at her and though not a word passed between them, she knew that he wished to lead her onto the floor. As he wrapped his arms around her she sank willingly into the warmth of his embrace. She could see Marcos dancing with the stockbroker's wife and she looked across at her husband and smiled. Marcos rarely danced. He must be getting on with the old bag. Gina sighed. At least he was off her case, for the moment at least.

She felt Kurt stroking the back of her neck very gently and a stab of lust shot into the pit of her belly. She could feel his taut thighs pressing against her legs and the outline of his penis, which even in its flaccid state felt firm and demanding.

Gina was very conscious of the power and strength of Kurt's body and she closed her eyes, her mind drifting back to the afternoon of sweat and heat and lust she'd spent with him and Steve. The afternoon of which she felt she should be ashamed, but was not.

She felt Kurt take her arm and without a word, guide her off the dance floor. Marcos was deep in conversation with the woman he was dancing with and much to Gina's relief, they passed through the other couples on the floor without being noticed.

Kurt took her hand, gently and surprisingly affectionately, and led her towards the club house. She knew that it was madness to disappear like this but she didn't care.

Kurt guided her up the steps and through the deserted bar. They walked towards the changing rooms and he pushed open the door to the men's room.

Gina walked in and he closed the door behind them. 'I didn't think you wanted me,' she said.

'Well, what do you think now?' he replied, stroking a strand of hair from her face.

Gina needed no coaxing. As Kurt unzipped his fly, she pulled her skirt up around her waist. She opened her handbag and handed him a rubber. 'Put it on for me,' he said.

'No,' said Gina, 'I can't. My hand is shaking.'

She watched in fascination as Kurt dressed his thick red prick in its opaque coating of rubber. He sat on the bench and she straddled him, sitting in his lap as he sank into her and his mouth came down over her own. He'd never kissed her before, not really, not like this, and she felt her body respond as his tongue pushed its way against hers and she opened her mouth.

Gina had kept perfectly still, knowing that even the slightest movement would make her come. She had been on the edge of orgasm since they were dancing, since she'd felt his body and the outline of his cock pressed against her leg as they moved around the floor. It was good to be so responsive, so easily aroused, she thought. She knew that her body was made for love and for the rich embrace of a man who was young and virile, not old and past it.

She didn't hear the door open. Steve had glanced inside the changing room to see if he'd won his bet and was amused to find that he'd lost. Kurt had said that he would get inside Gina within an hour of turning up at the wedding and he'd done so. Cocky bastard. Steve had ambled off, leaving the door ajar. He'd passed a swarthy-looking man in the corridor, stopping to wonder for a second who he was. He didn't look like a tennis player, so what was he doing heading for the men's changing rooms? Steve didn't bother to ponder the question for more than a split second. There were other, more pressing matters to demand his attention back in the marquee.

Gina knew what had happened when she saw that the tyres of her car had been slashed. With a sickening lurch in her stomach she walked back towards the marquee, hoping that her instincts were wrong, hoping to find Marcos still prancing around with the woman she'd left him with. One of the bridesmaids told her that he'd left in a cab ages ago. He'd left no message for her. In fact, he'd said nothing at all.

Gina had thought that if something like this happened, she really wouldn't care. But as she sat in the car park numb with shock and still drunk, she realised that she cared very much.

Chapter 15

Mary and Dan had caught a cab from Euston station and she'd dropped him off in Wardour Street. She had some time to kill before meeting Alex and she asked the driver to take her on to Liberty's where she intended to do a little shopping.

Two identical jars of face cream, two identical coffee mugs, some soap, two copies of the latest bestseller from one of the country's favourite authors . . . Mary bought everything she needed and piled them into the suitcase she'd brought with her from home.

Alex saw Mary the second she stepped out of her cab. She ran towards her, wrapped her arms around her and held her close. 'It's so good to see you,' said Alex and Mary knew she meant it. Alex looked wonderful, and within the first five minutes had blurted out her news, telling Mary all about her brand new job as a management trainee with one of the country's largest hotel groups.

'The old bastard at the place I worked before gave me a good reference,' she said. 'I was amazed, but very grateful.'

'He obviously thought you were good at what you did,' said Mary, 'whether he fancied you or not.'

Mary opened her suitcase and took out one of the copies of the book she'd just purchased, one jar of cream, one mug and one of the two bars of carnation soap she'd chosen. She kept them all in a bag and handed the suitcase to Alex. 'Yours are in there,' she said. 'It's all exactly the same . . .'

'I've got all the stuff you asked me for in the car,' said Alex. 'It's only round the corner. We can go and fetch it when we've had lunch.'

* * *

It was six o'clock and Mary was beginning to get anxious. She had arranged to meet Dan in a café near Euston station and had begun to wonder if she'd mistaken the venue and she'd have to travel home alone. She didn't want to. She wanted to be with Dan and to find out how the audition had gone. But whatever happened, she'd try not to be too disappointed. It had been a good day.

Seeing Alex again had been wonderful and Mary was relieved to find that Alex hadn't forgotten anything she'd been asked to bring with her. Everything Mary had requested was carefully packed into the holdall that now stood under the table next to her seat. Mary kept fingering it to make sure it was still there, for what it contained was essential to her plans.

Dan burst through the door at a quarter to seven, his eyes shining. He walked straight up to Mary and took her hand, lifting it to his lips. 'Let's go,' he said. 'There's a train in ten minutes.' Picking up her bags, Mary followed him out of the café.

He took the largest bag out of her hand. 'What on earth have you been buying?' he joked.

Mary blushed. 'Just a little shopping,' she said. 'Just a few essentials.'

The first class tickets had been a good idea and Dan had been delighted and very touched. But before he'd agree to let Mary pay, he had insisted that he buy her dinner on the way home. 'You can't afford it,' she'd said, smiling. 'Not on what we pay you at Mason's.'

'I'm trying to impress you,' he'd replied, brushing her hand lightly with his own. 'You make it very difficult.'

The dining car was crowded even as the train pulled out of Euston station. Dan and Mary took their seats, starting to relax as the waiter served their drinks and the train gathered speed, snaking through the twilight of suburbia as it ploughed on into the gathering darkness on its journey north.

Mary had known from the second she'd set eyes on Dan that the audition had gone well. By the time they'd ordered their second drink he'd told her all about it, and though his modesty prevented him from saying so it became clear that barring a major accident, he'd got the part he'd auditioned for. 'Hollywood,' he said. 'Tinseltown. Can you believe it?'

'I can believe it very easily,' she said.

Mary looked across the table and into his beautiful brown eyes, framed by their extravagant sweep of dark lashes. She'd always thought how handsome he was, but tonight she saw him as the film star that he was destined to become. She could picture his face on magazine covers. She knew that his exotic, almost Arabic features and his sculpted cheekbones would soon become familiar to every young woman who went to the cinema, whichever side of the Atlantic she lived on. Very soon, he would be on his way. But tonight he was here.

They had journeyed to London together only a few hours before but to both of them, the morning was a dim and distant memory. But though very little had been said, nothing of real significance, Mary had got off at Euston knowing that when they got back to Manchester that night she wanted to go home with Dan.

If the audition had gone badly she wanted to be there to comfort him. If it had gone well, she wanted to be the one he'd celebrate with. She hoped he felt the same. Sitting in the café waiting for him and worrying that he might not come, she'd realised just how much she wanted him.

Dan apologised for his scruffy digs, though his place was just as she had imagined. She asked him if she could take a shower. 'It's been a long day,' she said.

They'd left the train at Manchester Piccadilly and caught a cab. Dan had given the driver his address without hesitation. Dan hadn't asked Mary if she wanted to come home with him but somehow, on the train journey back it had become clear that this would happen. They understood each other. They needed each other. There was no more to be said.

Mary stood in Dan's shower and felt the water running down her body. She knew that he wouldn't come to her in the shower. She knew that he would wait for her to be comfortable. Wait for her to offer herself.

Mary thought of Dan in the next room. What was he

thinking? Was he touching himself as he waited for her, stroking his penis into wakefulness? Mary felt aroused knowing that he desired her, knowing that his bulging prick would soon be inside her, sliding backwards and forwards, probing the secrets of her eager body.

She felt aroused simply by standing in the shower cubicle, touching the things that belonged to him. There was a bar of plain soap. She picked it up and rubbed it between her palms. Dan has used this soap, she thought. She imagined the soap travelling across the black hairs on his chest, leaving a trail of lather. She imagined him rubbing it under his armpits, around his groin . . . she imagined his penis as foam and water ran down it, pouring off the tip. She saw herself on her knees in front of him, bathing her body in the stream of water that cascaded from his manhood . . .

She would like to be there when he showered. She would like to rub soap across his chest, moving her hands down to wash his hard belly then feeling him tense as her fingers strayed towards the thick black hair that circled his prick. Gently, she would begin to soap the dense curls, ignoring his upright prick as she spread lather around it. Then she would move her hands down to stroke the tops of his thighs, massaging slowly till he opened his legs a little and she could reach, ever so carefully, and take his scrotum in her hands. She wanted to feel it slip and slither as she soaped it. Then it would be the most natural thing in the world to reach up and hold his penis within her grasp, washing its length, easing the foreskin backwards and forwards as she soaped in every crease and crevice.

She longed to touch him, but now she was touching herself, rubbing foam across her nipples as she reached for Dan's loofah. She spread her legs and held the loofah between her thighs, easing it carefully backwards and forwards, enjoying the rough feel of its uneven surface against the tiny tip of her clitoris which poked from beneath the pale bush of hair between her legs.

When she emerged, wrapped in a towel, she found Dan laying on the bed. He'd made coffee. He poured her a cup. For a moment, they drank in silence. Then Mary asked the question she'd avoided all the way home. 'If you get the part in the film,' she said, 'which you will . . . then when do you leave?'

Dan took the cup away from her hands and placed it on the table by the bed. 'In about a week,' he replied softly. He leant across and kissed her. His skin was warm and she smelt the faintest trace of aftershave.

'My turn now,' he said. 'Quick shower. Won't be long.'

Mary lay back wrapped in her bath towel and listened to the water running. Her skin was still damp and the ends of her hair were wet. Strange how completely at ease she felt with this man. Her make-up had been washed off yet she felt not the slightest self-consciousness, no need at all to present him with anything but herself, clean and unadorned.

Mary looked at the ceiling. There was a long crack running from one side to the other. A real student's pad, this. Or a 'resting' actor's. The kind of place she'd almost forgotten about. The kind of place that Dan would never need to live in again.

Mary thought of Dan in the shower and her clitoris began to throb. The towel she had wrapped around her was rapidly beginning to dry and she rubbed it against her skin, wiping up any last traces of dampness. The rough towelling felt good. She dried herself carefully between her legs, enjoying the sensation. Laying on her back, Mary opened her legs beneath the towel and slid her fingers towards her parted bush. Dipping into herself, she coated one finger in her juices and, as if applying perfume, dabbed her scent behind her ears. Untying the front of the towel she sank her index finger into her body once again and spread a slick of her juices across each nipple, finishing by smearing her scent across her belly and between her inner thighs.

Dan emerged from the bathroom a moment later. He had one towel wrapped around his waist and was rubbing his hair with the other. Mary looked at his body, luxuriating in the sweet anticipation of what was to come.

He smells of soap, she thought, but I smell of me. All over. She wanted to get dirty with this calm, beautiful man. She wanted to watch him lose control.

Dan stood at the end of the bed and looked at her. 'Mary,' he said, 'I'm so glad you're here.' He hesitated. She knew what was coming next.

'Please don't ask me about Paul,' she whispered. 'Just love me.'

Dan smiled at her. A slow, beautiful smile revealing the tips of his perfect white teeth. Mary wanted to feel those teeth biting her nipples, wanted to feel the tongue that pronounced Shakespeare's immortal lines so eloquently, shoved up inside her pussy.

'I played with your loofah in the shower,' she said. He smiled at her again, rubbing his hair.

'I pulled it backwards and forwards against myself, like this,' said Mary, opening her legs and drawing her index finger the length of her clitoris, watching his reaction as she did so. Dan had stopped rubbing his hair and was watching her closely.

'That's good,' he said. 'I like to watch you do that.'

Mary could see the bulge rising beneath his bath towel. She spread her legs wider and slipped two fingers inside her body.

Dan came closer. 'Mmm,' he said. 'You smell wonderful.'

'Pussy juice,' said Mary, wondering, as she said it, what on earth had got into her. But she didn't care. This was fun.

'Will you . . .' he said, suddenly looking shy. 'Will you masturbate for me? Properly?'

'Don't you mean improperly?' said Mary, and laughed.

'I'd like to watch you . . . get excited,' he said and Mary nodded.

She pulled the bath towel from her body. Dan could see that her nipples were hard and fat. He sat and watched, fascinated, as Mary dipped her fingers deeper into her pussy and spread the slippery juice across the tips of each nipple, pinching them as she did so.

'You have a beautiful pussy,' he murmured as Mary held the lips of her womanhood back between her fingers so that her labia protruded, her crinkly pink folds and the cavern beneath, on full view.

She knew that he was aroused by watching her masturbate

and his arousal added to her excitement. Squashing her clitoris between two fingers she held it and began to pull and rub it, sending tremors of pleasure darting through her labia and up into the wet pool of her desire.

'Come closer,' she said, 'watch closely.' Dan brought his face to within inches of her pussy. He watched the little pink bud of her clitoris as Mary slicked it with fresh juice from the opening between her legs and began to stroke its tip, gently at first, then more forcefully as her pleasure mounted.

'That's so good,' she groaned, lifting her hips off the bed to press her body against her fingers which were now flicking furiously across the surface of her clitoris.

'I want you,' she said, opening her eyes to see Dan, his penis in his hand, as he gazed at her, transfixed.

'I'm so wet for you,' Mary murmured, circling her body beneath her fingers, spreading her legs even wider so that the entrance to her womanhood gaped open, inviting Dan to drive into its welcoming warmth.

'Hold on,' he said. 'Wait for me.' Getting to his feet, he began to search frantically around the mess that was his room till at last he found the little packet he was looking for.

Mary watched him as he searched for the condom packet. He was utterly beautiful. His waist was slim, his buttocks small and neat and though his prick wasn't over-long it was very thick with a huge, bulbous head. She imagined it inside her and she longed for him, slowing her strokes against her clitoris to delay her orgasm until his body was heaving and thrusting inside her own.

Dan slipped the rubber over his prick and climbed onto the bed, kneeling across Mary's open legs. She realised that she'd hardly touched him and leaning up, she kissed his chest. She felt a tremor go through him as he bent forward to taste her nipples, compressing each in turn between his lips, squashing them in a half kiss, half bite that Mary had to fight to prevent from tipping her over the top into orgasm.

Trailing the fat head of his prick across her inner folds, he entered her with one smooth thrust. She thought of Hamlet, rapier poised, as she felt Dan sink into her and she brought her legs up around his back, sucking him into her depths.

She came at his third thrust, her face buried in his shampoo-scented hair. Her orgasm was as rich and deep as she'd known it would be, extended by Dan's slow, firm thrusts within her as he felt her come.

He was a wonderful lover. As the throbbing in her subsided she lay limp and exhausted beneath him, enjoying the feel of his probing, holding his buttocks and pulling him into her until she felt his body tense and knew that his climax was upon him.

His excitement was infectious. Much to her surprise Mary felt the familiar pulsing begin again as Dan's orgasm flooded from him. With her nails digging into his buttocks and her tongue deep inside his mouth, a second wave of rich pleasure coursed through her, flooding her stretched pussy and drumming its delicious beat from the mouth of her womb down to the tip of her clitoris as Dan dragged the little bud back and forth beneath his thrusting body.

It had all been very embarrassing. Paul had had to phone the office and ask one of the girls to come to the hotel with a bundle of cash. When the girl eventually arrived he had made up some cock and bull story about being out with friends for a stag night which had got out of hand.

He told her that a group of 'the blokes' had come back to the hotel and that they'd all been pretty much 'out of it'.

'My trousers are missing,' he said to her. 'Someone must have stolen them as a joke.'

'I thought that only happened to the bridegroom,' she'd replied, suspiciously.

'Look,' he'd said. 'Just go and buy me a pair of trousers so I can go downstairs and pay the bill.'

The whole episode had shaken him up. For the first time ever, Paul Mason felt that the world was out to get him. He'd never have believed that the simple little girl he'd been with the night before was the type to have robbed him. He wondered what on earth could have happened to make her react in this way. He'd been kind to her and she'd repaid him by stealing from him.

Were all women bitches underneath? he wondered.

He decided to go home. Even though he hadn't left London, he'd try and look as though he'd just returned from a trip. But a shorter trip than usual. Alex would be pleased to see him, though he hoped he wouldn't run into Gina.

Paul had decided not to bother to report the loss of his wallet or his valuable watch. Then he'd remembered that he'd had two credit cards in the wallet and realised that he'd have to say something. But only to the credit card people. He'd tell them he must have dropped the cards. He didn't want to report the theft to the police who would only start asking awkward questions. Questions they might wish to ask in front of Alex.

He thought he would go home and report the missing cards. That wouldn't look too suspicious, even if Alex was there.

Paul got a cab and let himself into the flat. He walked into the sitting room. He flopped into a chair and sat staring at the object in front of him thinking that Gina was right. He must be going mad. On the table was a cigarette lighter. Not any old lighter, but a heavy brass lighter that he and Mary had bought together in a flea market in Manchester, many years ago. He'd stared at it, then he'd got up and walked into the bedroom. Mary's small hand mirror was on the dressing table, and some of her favourite face cream. Paul felt dizzy. Walking into the bathroom he went to wash his face and picked up a bar of Mary's favourite carnation soap. He dropped it as if it had burnt him. What was happening? What was going on?

Gina had managed to get to the bank before Marcos had put a stop on her account. She'd drawn out two thousand pounds in cash. The total balance. That would keep her going for a while.

She'd stayed away the night after the wedding and had gone to the flat the next day, hoping that she'd be able to at least collect some clothes. But she wasn't surprised to find that the old bastard had changed the locks. Still, she'd beaten him to the bank. At least she had enough money to buy herself a little breathing space.

It was Wednesday. The day that Marcos and a group of his oldest cronies always met up in *Zorba's* for one of their disgustingly long and over-indulgent lunches. They were all friends of his from childhood. Men who respected him because, like them, he'd 'made good'. He liked to talk to them of old times. They would drink and sing and occasionally cry with the grotesque sentimentality that only the entirely ruthless seem capable of. Gina thought of them all, gathered around a table stuffing themselves. Then the idea came to her. Brilliant.

The waiters all liked Gina. Probably, she'd decided, because they felt sorry for her, married to Marcos. She'd arrived at *Zorba's* half an hour before Marcos's usual time and had spoken quietly to Michael, the over-worked, underpaid head waiter who Marcos said he regarded as a son.

Michael had been horrified to hear that Marcos had thrown her out without a penny. Angered that his boss could treat his beautiful young wife in such a heartless manner, he agreed to stick his neck out and help her. Emboldened by the promise in Gina's eyes, he decided he didn't care if Marcos sacked him.

He would do what she wanted. He would hide her in a back room in the restaurant and, when the party arrived he would send Stavros through to speak to her so that she could plead with him to talk sense to her husband. That's what Gina had said she wanted to do. And if he, Michael, could help, then he would.

Stavros had gone to school with Marcos and was his oldest and dearest friend. When Michael came up to him and told him that there was a telephone call for him, he got to his feet reluctantly, unwilling to leave a party which after only ten minutes was into its third bottle of Retsina.

'Not that way,' said Michael as Stavros headed for the telephone. Guiding Stavros towards a back room, Michael knocked on the door and walked away. A female voice said, 'come in,' and Stavros opened the door. When he saw what was waiting for him he muttered an oath to himself in Greek and closed the door behind him.

Gina was sitting cross-legged on the floor. She was wearing a tight black rubber suit with a split at the crotch, from which her pussy was clearly visible in rich pink contrast to its matt black surroundings. She was covered in rubber up to the neck apart from the single slash between her legs and two small, round holes in the front of the suit from which her nipples protruded in fleshy contrast to their rubber surroundings.

'Marcos and I are finished,' she said to Stavros. 'I want you to fuck me.'

Friendship, conscience, the thought of his wife and his common sense of decency all prevented Stavros from accepting her offer. For at least a minute. Then, unzipping his fly and rolling the rubber that she had handed him in place with a sweating hand, he held his cock and got on his knees, pushing it into the gap in the rubber and sinking into the wetness of Gina's welcoming pussy. Stavros was even fatter and more disgusting than her husband, but at least his grunting and heaving needed no encouragement; he was inside her like a goat up a mountain. He looks like a goat, she thought.

'If I am to say nothing about this,' she said, 'you will find some excuse to send the next member of your happy little band in here to me. I intend to fuck you all. If the next one isn't here in five minutes, I will come into the restaurant and tell Marcos what has happened.'

The ridiculously named Sophocles was next. Wiry and rather handsome in a swarthy sort of way, he asked Gina to kneel, and while pinching her nipples as they poked out of her rubber suit, fucked her from behind, bringing her to orgasm with the gyrations of his enthusiastic prick. That's more like it, she thought, sad that he had to leave. 'Send in the next one,' said Gina. 'Or else.'

There were six of them in all. They used up two packets of condoms fucking Marcos's wife through her strange rubber suit. Towards the end she was really enjoying herself, sitting on their faces, sucking their dicks and behaving as outrageously as she'd wanted to behave from the first moment that she and Marcos had become man and wife.

The young waiter who she'd managed to collar when she'd first gone to the back room had needed little persuasion to hide in the corner with a camera. She'd promised him a fuck if he'd take pictures of her with all the other men, and she was more than happy to slide his young prick inside her as a reward.

He'd handed her the camera and unzipped his fly eagerly. She'd liked him best of all. Though ironically, he was the only one of the seven men who'd fucked her whose photograph would not end up in an envelope addressed to Marcos.

Mary had had a phone call from Paul saying that he was coming home. He sounded extremely upset, nervous almost, and she felt glad. Alex was obviously doing her stuff and all was going according to plan.

She phoned Alex on the new mobile phone she now carried. 'No,' said Alex, 'I haven't seen Paul today. I left home early. He must have gone back to the flat and then phoned you.'

Mary was glad she was in when Paul had called, though ten minutes earlier and she wouldn't have been. She'd stayed with Dan until nearly lunchtime, lying in his arms, taking his cock between her lips and between her legs and feeling happier than she'd felt since Jason had left. But now Paul was on his way home. She would be waiting for him. The house would be ready. It was all about to begin.

Chapter 16

Suzie Wesley wasn't a wicked or a vindictive girl. Not really. Only in bursts. She'd felt guilty about stealing Paul Mason's Rolex ever since she'd grabbed it and shoved it in her handbag along with his wallet and, as a parting gesture, his trousers – which she'd rolled up and carried off with all the nonchalance that a confused and angry seventeen-year-old could muster.

There had been no one about in the hotel foyer apart from the night porter. She'd managed to hail a cab and using Paul Mason's money, had got him to drive her all the way home. 'I don't usually go this far out of town, love,' the driver had said, implying that he was doing her a favour. Twenty pounds the cab had cost. It was a fortune to waste on a taxi. But then, she wasn't thinking clearly. And besides, it was so early all the tube stations had been closed.

As Paul Mason's secretary, albeit temporarily, Suzie had known that he had a haulage company in Manchester. She decided she'd send the watch back. And his wallet. Only the twenty pounds would be missing. Then she'd try and forget all about Paul Mason. It was time to get a grip on herself.

Kurt had hung around for hours, knowing that eventually Alex would show up. When he saw her car pass him and swing down the slope towards the underground car park he was relieved, for he'd needed to see her again before he left. Before he confronted whatever was waiting for him in Germany.

Kurt had had a phone call to say that his father had died. Though not altogether unexpected, it had still come as a shock and had meant not only that Kurt had to fly out for the funeral, but that he would be obliged to see his stepmother again. But all he could think of was Alex. Alex was the only one who could blot out the memories that now came flooding back, threatening to drown him. He had to see Alex. And then tomorrow . . .

Kurt pressed the entryphone to Paul Mason's flat and in a disguised voice told Alex that she had a delivery of flowers. She pressed the buzzer. She opened the front door. Much to his surprise she didn't try and slam it again when she saw who it was.

'What do you want, Kurt?' she asked and for a moment he wasn't sure how to reply. 'My father has died,' he said. 'I am returning home for the funeral. I fly to Germany tomorrow. I came to say goodbye.'

He looked at her. He could see immediately that something about her had changed. Her eyes met his and she held his gaze, steadily and without any trace of fear. 'I have just returned from work,' she said. 'I'm tired.'

'I may never see you again,' he said quietly. 'My stepmother will need help. My father had lands . . . property . . . I may not come back. She may need me to stay.'

'Good,' said Alex. 'Now please, will you go?'

Stunned and shaken, Kurt began to walk towards the door. Alex followed him and held it open. 'Goodbye, Alex,' said Kurt. 'If—'

'Yes, you did,' she interrupted. 'You hurt me very much. In all sorts of ways.' Kurt leant forward and kissed her on the cheek. It was a sad and gentle kiss. At the touch of his lips he heard a small sob break from the back of her throat and looking into her eyes he saw that they were filled with tears.

'Alex,' he said, 'I've been so crazy, so unhappy . . . but I always . . . you were always . . .' His words were stopped by the pressure of her lips against his. Pulling him back inside the door she closed it behind them and pushed him against the wall. She looked at him, a challenge in her glittering eyes.

She is taking control, thought Kurt. Like my stepmother . . . like Helena. The idea sent a wave of pleasure flooding into his belly, pumping into his groin.

Alex was kissing him. Then he felt her lips move down to

his neck, her fingers unbuttoning his shirt as her lips and tongue covered his skin, her kisses full of urgency, her auburn hair cascading about her shoulders as her long, pale fingers groped for the bulge between his legs.

She had pinned him against the wall and Kurt gave himself up to the sensations that were overpowering him, her touch blotting out the turmoil in his mind.

'I shall do what I want and then you will leave,' he heard her say as her beautiful head moved across his chest and she licked each of his nipples in turn.

His cock was bucking like a spring colt inside his underpants and then she was on her knees in front of him. Looking down he could see that she had unbuttoned her blouse and unclipped the front of her bra. Her tits spilled out of the jacket of her severe and businesslike suit and she was pinching them, rolling her nipples between thumb and forefinger as she began, at last, to unbuckle his belt and unzip his bulging, straining trousers.

'You're about to split the material,' she said, glancing up momentarily and laughing a rich and throaty laugh.

Alex pulled Kurt's trousers down over his hips and eased his penis out of the front of his underpants. His white juice had left a damp patch on his pants which she slid down over his thighs, ordering him to step out of them and throwing them to one side.

Kurt felt his prick give a sharp jolt as she took it between her hands and stroked it across her nipples. He could feel every detail of her tits through the ultra-sensitive tip of his prick, from the thick, hard buttons of her nipples to the tiny circle of little bumps on the areola which surrounded each pink protrusion.

His juice was leaking from him and Alex was rubbing it into her breasts, using it as lubrication with which to coat her nipples as she flicked and squeezed them, squirming with pleasure as she spread his sticky film with her fingers.

Kurt felt his balls throb as Alex's fingers reached beneath them, taking the weight of his hairy pouch in her palm, balancing the weight as she rolled his testes against her thrilling fingers.

He looked down. She was stroking his prick with her nose as if sniffing a good cigar, running her face along its length, the touch of her warm skin making him want to cry out with longing.

He felt the tip of her tongue then, exploring the cleft at the end of his penis. Running her tongue through the valley at the tip of his glans, she skated backwards and forwards across the tiny hole through which his juice leaked steadily. 'Alex,' groaned Kurt, 'please . . . I can't hold on . . .'

He heard the throaty laugh again. A confident, self-assured laugh, the like of which he hadn't heard since he was a boy.

Then he felt her smooth lips embrace his burning knob, her fingers sliding round to his buttocks as she held him and drew his penis deep, deep into her yielding throat.

Her tongue was stroking hard against his glans, now sunk into the magical depths of her throat while the muscles of her mouth sucked steadily. Kurt felt his life force being drawn from him, her fingers kneading his balls as her lips and tongue combined to coax him towards that sweet release which every woman thought was within her power to offer, and so few really knew how to provide. This, thought Kurt, had nothing to do with mere sex. This was incredible. This was Alex.

She was a beautiful, mesmerising witch. And he might never see her again. Another witch waited for him just a short flight away. A ghost, a memory, a woman whose grasp on his life must be broken before he could hope to be happy. Before he could ever again hope to feel Alex's lips wrapped around his cock, taking him to paradise.

Mary had sat in her car, far enough away from the house not to be seen, though with a clear view of the front door. She saw Paul's car pull up and watched as he let himself in. She decided to give him about half an hour before 'arriving' back from the office.

She had left the brightly coloured and distinctive coffee mug from Liberty's on the draining board in the kitchen. The one identical to Alex's. All the other items that she had bought that day in London were dotted about the house and Mary knew that Paul, with his sharp powers of observation, would notice everything. His flat in London and his home in Manchester now contained much that was identical. Added to which, Alex had many personal items from Mary and Paul's home and had taken great pains to leave them around the flat, and vice versa.

Alex's slippers, her alarm clock, even the paperback she was reading – she'd packed up so many things and handed them all over to Mary. But the watch had been the *pièce de résistance*. Mary had received it, addressed to Paul, along with his wallet and a little note saying 'I'm sorry. Suzie.' It hadn't taken much imagination to piece the story together. Poor, bitter Suzie, whoever she was.

Mary had been delighted to be able to leave the watch prominently displayed on the dressing table where Paul was bound to find it. Yes, she'd give him half an hour to look around.

It was a pleasant evening. From her car window, Mary could see the trees and shrubs in her neighbour's garden, waiting to burst into bloom. She felt a stab of something resembling homesickness and blotted it out by thinking about Alex. The crazy girl she'd met at the health farm was now the only person in the world she trusted completely. Though she cared for Dan very much and had, for a while, adored Jason, it was Alex who she'd trust with her life. 'Just as well,' she thought as she pulled the car key out of the lock and got out of the passenger seat. It was time to go home. Time to face the music.

She'd known that Paul would be upset but she hadn't expected to find him crying. But there he was, sitting on the sofa with tears running down his face. His Rolex was on the table in front of him, a look of bewilderment in his eyes.

'Mary,' he said, looking up as she walked in. He got to his feet and wrapped his arms around her. She looked at him. 'What on earth's the matter?' she asked, her eyes full of concern.

'I thought I'd lost my watch,' he said. 'In fact, I *know* I lost it. But it's here. All sorts of things are happening that I don't understand. Mary, I think I'm going mad.'

It took a lot to calm him down, but eventually she managed it. Pouring him a stiff drink she sat beside him on the sofa, stroking his hand.

'Paul,' she said, 'you're not going mad. You're just very tired, that's all. Years of travelling, years of working . . . no holidays, no real breaks. It's all . . . just too much.'

'But things have been happening lately,' he said. 'Things I can't explain. Even you seem different. But you're not, are you Mary? Please tell me you're not.'

Shooshing him like a baby, Mary told him to put his feet up and relax. She'd fetch him an aspirin. Dinner was all ready and simply had to be heated through. He was home. He was safe.

Paul did as he was told. Mary would take care of it all, like she'd always done. He closed his eyes, trying to control the pounding in his head as he waited for her to return with his pill.

He must have drifted off to sleep and was woken by cool, long fingers stroking his brow. He opened his eyes. Alex stood over him. 'Your headache tablet,' she said.

They hadn't reproached him and that was deeply unsettling. They'd simply sat, Mary on the floor in front of him and Alex on the chair opposite, and told him how he'd been discovered.

'We know about Suzie, too,' said Mary. 'And no doubt there have been others.'

Paul had been unable to stop shaking. But at least now he knew he wasn't crazy, that they'd joined forces to play a trick. To rattle him. The bitches.

It was the calmness of both the women that had frightened Paul most of all. The way they'd sat there and eaten their dinner, their air of perfect self-control.

Paul hadn't been able to eat a thing. They told him they didn't want him to explain. That they'd talk about it again in the morning.

Twelve o'clock, one o'clock . . . not a wink of sleep. Paul got up off the settee and crept up the stairs. His own stairs. His own house yet he felt like an intruder. Quietly, he pushed open the door of Mary's room. *Their* room. She was awake, as he knew she'd be. She hadn't changed so much that she didn't care. That much was a relief.

'Mary,' he said, sitting on the side of the bed, 'I just don't know how to explain or how to begin to beg for your forgiveness.'

'Was she the only one? The only one you've lived with?' said Mary.

'I swear to you,' said Paul. 'I only got the flat when I met her.' Mary smiled to herself in the darkness as the lie rolled off his tongue. She held out her arms. Paul's mouth came down over hers, his tongue moving between her lips with a desperate hunger that, despite everything, set her pulses racing. She felt the familiar melting between her legs that happened whenever he was near.

Paul lifted himself onto the bed and lay beside her. His hands moved over her body and down between her legs. His fingers parted her labia and began to tease the fleshy folds and she felt her body move in response, straining towards him.

Why was she so wet? She didn't know, didn't care any more. Her body had a mind of its own and, lifting her legs around his back she felt him slide into her, moving his body in long, slow circles so that his prick penetrated deep, stretching her smooth passage.

He was thrusting now, his movements slow and controlled. 'Is that good?' he whispered, sliding into his old routine. He knew it was good. Oh, he was a confident bastard, despite everything.

How could she climax in the arms of this man? she wondered. But she knew she would.

Mary felt the base of his penis pressed against her open labia as he rotated his body in slow, languid circles, rubbing and coaxing her into a frenzy of lust.

She felt his mouth on her tits as Paul moved one hand beneath her and slipped one finger into the puckered hole of her arse, circling his fingertip in time with the thrusts of his penis. Mary felt herself shiver as the throbbing between her legs intensified and Paul lifted his head from his licking and sucking and looked down at her. 'Mary, I love you,' he whispered hoarsely. 'You must know that. It's always been you.'

She pretended to be asleep as, about an hour later she felt the bed move and saw his shadow in the darkness. The door opened softly and then he was gone. Mary closed her eyes and drifted off to sleep. She must sleep. Tomorrow would be a long day.

Alex tiptoed through to the kitchen, carrying her suitcase. She saw Mary silhouetted in the darkness, her own case by her side. 'We'll go out the back way,' said Mary and Alex nodded. Paul was soundly asleep on the sofa. To open the front door would disturb him.

It was 4am and getting light. As they carried their cases towards Mary's car, they both breathed a sigh of relief.

'He came to you, of course?' said Mary and Alex nodded. 'Yes,' said Alex, 'about three o'clock. Told me I was the only one who mattered, the only one he truly loved.' Mary gave a hollow laugh as she unlocked the passenger door and Alex got into the car beside her.

'We've plenty of time,' said Mary as the car picked up speed and the sun began to rise over the horizon in a huge, red ball. She handed Alex an envelope. 'It's all there,' she said. 'Your new bank account is open and there's two thousand dollars in cash, just to get you over the next few days.'

'How much time have we got?' said Alex. 'We both need to check in by eleven,' Mary replied. They fell silent for a while, lost in thought. Then Mary turned off the road and pulled over, stopping the car. 'Come,' she said to Alex.

They left the car and climbed a fence into a nearby field. It was a warm morning and by now the sun had turned from a pink stain on the horizon to pale gold, hiding coyly behind a thin covering of white cloud in an otherwise blue sky.

The field was empty save for the occasional rabbit which popped its head up and then darted away when it saw them.

Mary sat on the grass beneath the shade of a hedge.

'It's okay,' she said to Alex, 'the grass is dry.'

'You look tired,' said Mary as Alex sat down beside her and she gazed into her eyes. 'I suppose we're both tired,' she sighed. 'But it's over. We're going to be all right.'

Mary took Alex's hand in hers and kissed it. Then she held it to her breast, rubbing it against the outside of her shirt so that Alex could feel her nipples as they hardened beneath her touch.

'I didn't think we'd be together again,' said Alex. 'Not like this.'

In reply, Mary lay on her back and pulled her blouse over her head, placing it on the grass beside her. The morning smelt fresh and clean and the grass felt good against her skin, like a soft blanket. As natural as the touch of Alex's beautiful body against her own.

Alex sat next to Mary and removed her own shirt and bra, reaching down to unhook Mary's bra and release her breasts into the sunlight.

'Will you take all your clothes off?' whispered Mary as Alex leant down to kiss her neck. 'I want you to lay on top of me. Will you?'

Alex smiled and began to suckle Mary's nipples like a baby.

'Please,' Mary moaned, 'lay on top of me. I want us to really be together.'

Mary liked the weight of Alex's body on top of hers. She liked the feeling of Alex covering her, their breasts squashed together. Mary spread her pussy lips between her fingers and whispered into Alex's ear to do the same. 'I want to feel your clitoris kissing mine,' she said. 'If we can . . . I want to . . .'

Alex leant down and pulled the lips of her vulva apart. Mary sighed as she felt the strange, wet embrace of Alex's womanhood as it stroked against her pussy lips, the bud of Alex's clitoris hardening as it slithered across her own, their juices mingling as Alex began to move her hips, pressing her open pussy down harder, rubbing her clit like a tiny penis against the folds of Mary's glistening pussy.

Mary lay on her back in the sunlight, savouring the delicious sensations that flooded through her. Alex's fingers were stroking her tits and she was licking her neck while between her legs the soft and urgent embrace of Alex's womanhood was delicious in its strangeness, her clitoris throbbing in thrilling response as Alex's hardening bud slicked over it like, she thought, two puppies rubbing their wet noses together.

Mary pictured them laying there. Imagined the dent they would leave in the grass once they'd gone. And they'd be gone very soon . . . Alex to her new hotel management trainee job in Houston and Mary to Hollywood with Dan.

'Who knows what's going to happen?' she thought. She had no illusions that Dan was to be the love of her life, but for now he seemed to need her and she wanted to be with him. 'I'll think no further than that,' she'd decided. 'Tomorrow is all that matters. I no longer believe in forever.'

Alex was biting her nipples and rubbing her clit faster and harder against Mary's and suddenly Mary felt the first deep, rich tremor of orgasm as Alex's clit began to throb against hers. Mary could feel its thrilling pulse, a throb which spread through both their bodies as they came together, their limbs entwined, their juices sticky and mingled as the soft cushions of their pussy lips squashed together, the blonde and red curls meeting and tangling as their bodies opened to each other in a last embrace.

As they dressed, they knew that by now Paul would be waking to find them gone. In a very short while he would discover that most of his capital had gone with them. His business empire would survive, but only just. And so would Paul. He was a survivor, if nothing else.

Alex and Mary knew that it would be a long time before they met again. They would part at the airport and fly away to new and uncertain lives.

As they got back in the car, Mary leant across and kissed Alex softly on the mouth.

'There's something I want to ask you,' said Alex. Mary adjusted the mirror over the dashboard and then looked at the beautiful girl sitting next to her. 'What is it?' she said.

'I want to know,' Alex continued, 'if you still love Paul.'

Mary sighed and clicked her seatbelt into place. 'Yes,' she said, 'I still love Paul.'

'Crazy,' said Alex. 'So do I.'